Francis Buhagiar was born in the Dick Whittington Hospital and has been seeking adventure ever since. After school at one of the oldest Benedictine Abbeys in England and gaining a degree in Economics and History at University College London, Francis travelled the world in pursuit of his passions of surfing and scuba diving. Some of the people he met along the way have inspired the cast of characters in this book. His most recent travels have included walking the South West Coastal Footpath with his children. Home is Somerset but with regular visits to the island of his forefathers – Malta.

For Agnes, Ambrose and Nurse Thomas.

Francis Buhagiar

THE UNOFFICIAL GOOD TURN SOCIETY

AUSTIN MACAULEY PUBLISHERS™

LONDON • CAMBRIDGE • NEW YORK • SHARJAH

A CIP catalogue record for this title is available from the British Library.

ISBN 9781398424500 (Paperback)
ISBN 9781398424517 (ePub e-book)

www.austinmacauley.com

First Published 2021
Austin Macauley Publishers Ltd®
1 Canada Square
Canary Wharf
London
E14 5AA

1

Swoosh!
Up they fly.
Down they swoop.
Banking to the left.
Banking to the right.
A game of dare?
Who can fly the lowest?
The fastest?
Undercarriages threaten
To skim the rough stone path.
Closer and closer.
Contact never made.
Wings threaten
To clip ancient hedgerows,
Made of stone
But smothered in grass.
Closer and closer.
Contact never made.
Eyes fixed
On the meandering run ahead.
Left.
Right.
Right.
Left.
One finishes.
Another begins.
Back and forth.
Forth and back.
Again and again.

Six of them
In all
Come from afar,
From another land,
Across an ocean,
Chasing the summer,
The endless summer.
Stakes raised.
Orders received:
"Squadron. New formation!"
A flap of the wings,
Then another,
And another.
Soaring
To the heavens.
Out of sight,
Not quite.
First the climb,
Then the dive.
Dive.
Dive.
Dive.
Wings tucked in.
Faster.
Faster.
Faster.
Head first,
Like an arrow
Loosed
By the invisible bowman of the sky.
Back down
Towards the track.
Faster.
Faster.
Faster.
Bullseye?

No.
Perfect timing?
Yes.
Head up.
Wings spread.
Loop the loop.
Over to the next,
Then the next,
And the next.
No hunt.
No ritual.
No predator.
A celebration.
Nothing more.
Of what?
Of life.
Of love.
Of companionship.
Of course.
Who knows?
The swallows.
A rest?
No chance,
Too much fun.

2

A schoolgirl wakes.
Bed linen a mess,
Covers on the floor,
Bad night.
No sleep.
Thoughts racing
In her mind
Round and round,
Over and over,
Again and again.
Pointless argument
Maybe,
Bitter contest
Certainly.
Felt it.
Puts on her uniform.
Enters the kitchen.
Opens the fridge.
No milk.
Of course.
Curses her luck,
Her bad luck,
Of course.
Off to the village shop.
Out of the house,
A glorious summer's morning revealed.
Blue sky
In every direction,
Not a cloud in sight.

Across a field.
Path sighted.
Path reached.
Foot hits rock.
A tumble to the ground,
A shriek of pain,
A curse of luck,
Always bad luck,
Always a dark grey cloud up above.
Always rain,
Nothing but rain.
But what is this?
Sunshine.
Rays of sunshine.
Who are they
Swooping
Down the track,
Soaring
Up into the sky,
One after the other?
Count.
1…2…3…4…5…6…
Six swallows
Dancing in the sky.
Passing the girl on the left,
Passing the girl on the right,
Passing the girl above,
An invitation to join:
"May I have this dance?"
Pain gone.
Pain forgotten.
Steps become lighter.
Walk becomes a hop.
Hop becomes a skip.
Scowl becomes a smile.
Cry becomes laughter.

"But why do we dance?"
"Look around you and behold."
Path ends.
Girl stops.
Girl turns.
Girl sees.
With a heart that is lighter,
And eyes that are wider,
The girl reaches the village.
Passes the stone house,
Where the old man lives,
And heads to the store.

3

Tick tock,
Tick tock.
Down the stairs
And into the storeroom.
Boxes on boxes.
Bags on bags.
Apron found.
Apron tied.
A glance at the mirror.
A tut,
A sigh.
A glance at the clock.
A tut,
A sigh.
Tick tock,
Tick tock
No time
To waste.
Races into the shop.
Much to be done,
Still.
Deliveries to be made.
Shelves to be stacked.
Customers to be served.
Glides over to the front door.
Pause.
Deep breath,
Before it all starts,
Before the rush.

Here goes.

Skirt flattened,

Blind up,

Latch off,

Sign turned.

"Open!"

To the counter.

Count:

1...2...3...4...5...6

"Good morning Mrs B!"

Like clockwork.

"Good morning Alice!"

"What a wonderful morning, Mrs B."

"You sound very chirpy, Alice."

"Saw swallows dancing up and down the lane. They put a big smile on my face, Mrs B."

"What a lovely way to start the day. How can I help you, Alice?"

"A bottle of milk please. How are you, Mrs B?"

"Bless you, dear, for asking. I'm in a bit of a muddle. Too much to do and too little time to do it all."

"I've got five minutes to spare. I can do a job for you if that helps," offers Alice.

"Oh, my dear, would you? Old Man Stevens needs his eggs. Gets grumpy if he doesn't get them before eight. But I have to wait here for the papers, which are late as the delivery man called to say he is stuck in traffic. Oh, and to top it all off, I've gone and lost my glasses," says the store owner.

"Tortoiseshell and round?"

"Yes, that's right. Can you see them?" asks Mrs B hopefully.

"Down there on your right," reveals Alice, pointing to a pair of spectacles half covered by sheets of paper on a table behind the counter.

"So they are. You star! Thank you, Alice."

"Now I'll take the eggs to Old Man Stevens."

"Oh, my dear, you are a godsend."

"Have a good day, Mrs B!" says Alice, as she picks up the eggs and the bottle of milk and heads to the door.

"You too, Alice."

Deep breath out.

A wipe of the brow
With the back of her right hand.
Glasses on.
Suddenly,
All seems clear now.

4

One minute
Cars jammed,
Bumper to bumper.
Next minute
Cars moving,
At speed.
No sense at all,
To the traffic.
No reason at all,
For the jam.
A man in a van
Stuck.
Same time.
Same place.
Same road.
Same load.
Same as yesterday,
Same as every day.
Stop start,
Start stop,
Inching his way
Towards a corner
For what seems like an eternity,
Until suddenly,
With no warning whatsoever,
For no reason whatsoever,
It's green on go,
As cars accelerate away.
Relief.

Autopilot on.
Knows the way
Like the back of his hand.
Takes the second left.
Passes the church with the steeple
Just a short drive from here.
And yet,
And yet,
Even though,
He knows exactly where he is,
Even though,
He knows exactly where he is going,
Man in the van
Feels lost,
Man in the van
Feels down.
Store in sight.
Right!
Snap out of it.
Time to deliver.
The man parks
The van.
Opens the door
Of the van.
Hops out
Of the van.
Scuttles off
To the back
Of the van.
Grabs a bundle
Of papers
Out of the van.
Reads today's headlines
For the first time.
The trade dispute,
All about the trade dispute

In some far-flung land.

Enters the store,

"Sorry for being late, Mrs B. Traffic was bad," says the delivery man.

"Forget about being late. Why do you look so sad? Where's that wonderful smile of yours?" asks Mrs B.

"Oh, don't mind me. Just feeling sorry for myself."

"Oh, that won't do, do you want to talk about it?"

"I won't bore you, Mrs B, but basically deep inside of me, there's a writer bursting to get out. I'm not a delivery man, you see."

"What do you mean?"

"I love to write, but I need to earn a living."

"So you drive around delivering papers to me?"

"You and plenty of others. Don't get me wrong, Mrs B, I like coming here and making deliveries, but I like writing more," admits the man.

"Come sit down, have a cup of tea and let's talk about it."

"No time, I'm afraid. I am already running late."

"Five minutes that's all. Be good to get it off your chest."

Man in a van pauses,

Briefly.

Pops out of the shop,

Fleetingly.

Shuts the door of the van,

Firmly,

And returns to the shop,

Promptly.

"Right, where's that cuppa, Mrs B?"

He talks,

He listens,

He hears his voice,

He hears his thoughts

Out loud

For a change,

Not in his head

For a change.

Fog lifts.

It all makes sense.

No more sitting on the fence
For him.
No more feeling sorry
For himself.
Going to write
In his spare time,
For now at least.
Stories about love,
Stories about crime.
Deliveries,
A means to an end,
That's all,
Not the end,
At all.
"Thank you, Mrs B, for being such a good friend."

5

School run.
No fun.
Dropping off
Her two children
At school,
On time,
Always equals
One mad,
Crazy dash.
Then there is the traffic,
Always bad.
Then there is the right turn,
The dreaded right turn,
Always dreadful.
Cars and trucks
Whizzing by
This way and that,
Racing down the road.
The road
She needs to join,
Of course.
Everyone in a rush,
No quarter given,
Not even to a mother
On her daily mission.
Queue
To the junction,
The dreaded junction,
Looms up ahead.

Yesterday's struggle
Enters her head:
Waited for an age,
Before she made it to the front.
Edged the car forward,
Just an inch,
Maybe two,
At most,
But enough
To trigger
A chorus of horns,
A volley of abuse,
A show of angry hands.
Finally,
Eventually,
A gap emerged,
The junction cleared
And she was on her way,
But at what cost?
A few years of her life?
A few more grey hairs,
That's for sure.
More of the same today?
Will soon find out,
As slowly,
But surely,
The front of the queue approaches,
Ominously.
Knows it will be her turn
To run the gauntlet,
Soon.
Nothing to be done.
No magic trick
To magic away the fear,
To magic away the stress.
Just three cars ahead now,

Then it is her turn.
Fred and Lucy,
In the back,
Twiddling their thumbs,
Quietly
Hoping
Today's journey won't take so long,
Quietly
Hoping
Today their mother won't get it so wrong.
Only one car in front now.
Any moment now
And it will be all eyes on her.
Car in front
Zips off
To the right.
"Close call that one,"
Thinks the mother,
Out loud
To herself.
"Please may it not be so terrifying today."
Says a quick prayer
Out loud
To herself
And whoever else cares to listen.
Right, here goes.
But what's this?
Prayer answered?
Already?
A man in a van,
Could he be slowing down?
Don't jump the gun now.
But a flash
Of lights
From the van,
And a big broad smile

From the man
Driving the newspaper delivery van,
Signals to the mother
She is free to cross.
Riding a wave
Of relief
She drives forward,
Halfway.
Job,
Half done.
No horns,
No abuse,
Not today.
Spots a gap.
Turns right.
Speeds away.
"That was fine,"
She thinks to herself.
And all thanks
To the kind delivery man.

6

Boy
Sitting
Next to his father
In the front of a car
On his way to school.
No sign of a smile,
No sound of laughter.
"What's wrong, young man? You seem troubled," asks the father.
"After school club," replies the son.
"I thought you liked being there with your friends?"
"I'd rather be with you."
"Not today, I'm afraid, I have an important appointment."
"Take me with you. Please Dad. I won't be a nuisance. I promise," pleads his
son.
"I know you would be as good as gold. It's just I can't bring a child with me.
Besides, you would be bored out of your skin."
"Please Dad, I beg you, please."
"I'm sorry, son, I just can't."
"How about I go to a friend's house instead?"
"Where could you go? Fred's?" asks his father.
"That would be great. Please, could I? Would you ask his mother?"
"Let's see if we can find her at the school first."
"Oh Dad, that would be so great."
"It's such short notice so don't get your hopes up," warns his father.
School in sight.
Car parked.
Son jumps out.
Son runs off
To find Fred,

His friend,
And more importantly,
To find Fred's mother,
As quickly as he can.
Father follows behind,
Slowly.
Not just because
He can't keep up,
But to buy himself time
To remember
The name of Fred's mother.
Was it Amy or Anna,
Or something longer,
Like Amanda?
Too late,
Here she comes,
Along with her son, Fred,
And his sister.
"We'd love to have Oliver over for tea," says Fred's mother, as he approaches.
Oliver already worked his magic,
It seems.
"Only if it is not too much bother."
"Not at all, it will be our pleasure."
"Now Oliver, what do you say?" says his father.
"Thank you so much. You've just made my day!"

7

Early morning,
Middle-aged man
Arrives at the school
Where he teaches.
Anxious.
Three boxes
Full of paper
Cradled
In his arms.
Two bags
Full of paper
Slung
Over each of his shoulders.
Like this
At the start
Of everyday
At school
For the teacher.
A juggling act,
A struggle,
A fight
To hold on
To the awkward load,
As he makes his way to the classroom.
A high stakes game.
Dropping the boxes
In front of an audience of children would,
Quite simply,
Be too embarrassing

To mention.
Wishes someone would help him,
For once.
But a big taboo,
A pupil seen talking to a teacher
Outside class,
A big no-no,
The biggest no-no.
Would be mocked
For being a teacher's pet,
Forever more.
Teacher makes his way
Towards the school's entrance.
Pupils walk on by
Without even a glance.
No "Can I help you, Mr Brown?"
Or "You look like you need a hand, Mr Brown."
No chance.
Here come the steps.
Up one, two, three.
Clear these,
And he is home free,
Not quite.
Four, five, six.
Remember
Watch out for number six,
The top one,
The loose one.
Oh no,
Brick gives way,
On step number six.
Teacher wobbles.
Boxes wobble.
Time stands still.
Then moves in
For the kill.

Teacher falls backwards.
Boxes fly upwards.
Teacher lands on his back.
Smack!
Boxes empty their load,
Papers fly out,
In every direction,
Onto the steps
Onto the road.
Picks himself up,
Red-faced.
Only a graze
Or two,
As far as he can see.
Waits though,
For the laughter
From the children
To begin.
Will hurt
Much more
Than a silly old scratch.
Prepares for the worst.
But who is this?
A boy,
Picking up the loose papers.
Can't be a pupil,
For pupils do not do teachers favours.
This one does.
Oliver Metcalfe from year six does.
Come to the teacher's aid,
He has,
Like an angel sent from heaven,
He is.
"Thank you, Oliver, you are most kind," says the teacher.
"That's alright, Mr Brown, I really don't mind."

8

Teacher
Walking,
Slowly,
Tip toeing,
Slowly.
Reluctant to find out,
Maybe,
But needs to find out,
Certainly.
The lunchtime rota
Pinned onto the notice board
In the staff common room,
Sentence,
Or salvation?
Fears the worst.
Has had a feeling,
All morning,
His name will be on it.
Reaches the board.
Spots his name
Immediately,
Spelled out
In black and white
For all to see.
Worst fears realised.
Today of all days.
His wife won't be happy.
Only this morning,
Mrs Butterworth had pleaded:

"Please darling, don't leave me stranded".

An appointment

With the local bank manager,

To buy a home,

Their first together.

But what can the schoolmaster do?

The duty roster

Never lies.

Worst still,

The duty roster

Rarely changes.

Set in stone

Once up there,

On the common room notice board.

"Morning Mr Butterworth, how are you today?"

"In a spot of bother, Mr Brown."

"Oh dear, is everything alright?" asks Mr Brown.

"Turns out I'm on duty during lunch," reveals Mr Butterworth.

"What's the problem, do you need to be somewhere else? Catch up on marking?" asks Mr Brown.

"I was hoping to accompany my wife to the bank today."

"Is this to do with buying that house?" asks Mr Brown.

"Yes, the small one, barely big enough to swing a cat."

"Well why don't I just swap with you?"

"Is that something you'd be happy to do?"

"Yes, of course, I'll clear it with the Head. Can't let anything stand in the way of you getting a roof over your head!"

"I would be so grateful, but only if you don't mind? It would be such a help!"

"Don't mention it at all. I'll go and speak with the Head now."

"Thank you so much," says Mr Butterworth.

A wave of the hand

And Mr Brown is off,

Leaving Mr Butterworth

Standing

All alone,

Happy in the knowledge,

His wife won't be going to the bank
On her own.

9

A long-haired man
Wanders along the street.
A long-haired man
Wonders what he will find to eat.
Hungry,
Always hungry.
Doubly so,
After yesterday.
A bad day,
Yesterday.
What today will bring,
He does not know.
Never knows.
A half-eaten sandwich
Tossed
Into a bin?
A few beans
Stuck
In the bottom of a tin?
A bunch of bananas,
All soft and black?
Won't bother him.
And what about a drink?
A half-finished carton of milk,
A can of cola?
But more than food
What he yearns for most,
A conversation
With anyone

About anything.
Yesterday,
A young woman
Stopped by
For a chat
At the station.
The highlight
Of the day.
But that was it
For the day,
As far as speaking was concerned.
Five minutes,
That's all.
Would take that today though,
If he gets the chance.
As for money,
A handful of coppers
And two silver coins,
All there is
In his old cardboard cup.
No way near enough
To buy a hot drink.
Another three or four days
And who knows maybe.
Spots a half empty bag
Of sweets
On the street.
He'll have those
Thank you very much.
A good omen
For the rest of the day.
All about good omens,
Life on the streets.
Takes it as a sign
To stop
Where he is,

Outside a bank
And set up camp
Outside the bank
For the rest of the day.
A routine,
Well-rehearsed,
Takes over.
First things first,
An old piece of folded cardboard
Retrieved from one of his bags.
The long-haired man unfolds the cardboard
Piece by piece,
Before he lays it out flat
Onto the ground.
His seat.
His mattress.
Takes the edge off
The cold
Hard
Unforgiving
Stone
Of the pavement.
Places his bags down
Onto the ground,
Strategically,
So an eye,
Or two,
Can be kept
On each and every one of them
At all times.
Sitting down
At ground level,
Beneath the forest
Of passing legs
And the cocktail
Of fancy footwear,

He puts out his sign.
"Donations gratefully received"
Scrawled on a piece of cardboard
With a black pen
He once found
But soon lost.
All in order,
He crosses his legs.
He crosses his arms.
He retreats
Behind a line,
The line
Of invisibility.
Must be invisible,
He thinks to himself.
For countless pairs
Of trainers,
Of high heels,
Of brogues,
Of boots
All come and go,
Without the slightest hint
Of a break
In stride.
Right to left,
Left to right.
A blur of shoes
Just walk on by,
As if he is out of sight,
Out of mind.
Wonders to himself
If it is possible
He will lose his voice one day,
If he doesn't use it.
Use it or lose it.
But he has no choice.

A pair of brown shoes
Worn laces,
Cracked leather,
Walks on by.
About-turn,
Brown shoes start walking
Towards the long-haired man.
Brown shoes stop
In front of the long-haired man.
Brown shoes turn
To face the long-haired man.
Brown shoe man bends down
In front of the long-haired man.
Brown shoe man starts to talk
To the long-haired man.
A conversation!
A schoolmaster on his break
Meeting his wife
For an appointment
At the bank.
Question
For the long-haired man.
How did he end up
Here,
On the streets?
Slowly,
Slowly,
The long-haired man
Explains how he was once sold a pup
And ended up
Sleeping rough
These three years past.
Worst thing about his life?
The lack of talking,
And the endless walking.
"I'll look out for you from now on." A promise made by the schoolmaster

To the long-haired man.

"In the meantime, please take this money and buy yourself a hot drink and something to eat. I'll be back."

10

Woman
On her lunch break
Out and about.
Hoping
A spot of fresh air
Will do the trick
And clear her mind.
Full of thoughts
About all and nothing.
Work,
Family,
Outstanding chores,
Broken resolutions.
First things first,
What to eat
For lunch?
A tuna salad,
Perhaps,
And a drink,
One that packs
A punch.
Perhaps not,
But would be just the ticket,
Especially,
After the morning she's had.
First stop,
The bank
To withdraw some money.
Weaves in between

All those in a hurry.
Cash machine reached,
The one outside the bank.
Queue joined,
Fourth or fifth
From the front.
Mind begins to wonder,
Again.
How will she get through
The rest of the day?
The queue at least
Keeps her away
From the office,
From her boss
For a few seconds
More.
Every second counts
Today.
A shuffle forward,
Now three from the front.
Join the other queue?
Too late.
Two people arrive
Just as she was about
To make her move,
As if they had read her mind.
Makes up her mind
For her
To stay
Where she is.
One away
From the front now
Anyway.
Won't be long now
Anyway.
Hey presto!

Her turn.
Don't take too much out.
No money to burn,
After all.
Every little counts,
After all.
Card
Swallowed slowly
By the machine.
Pin
Punched in quickly
By the woman.
Dot, dot, dot, dot.
Decision to make.
How much to take?
Decision made.
Card removed.
Money collected.
But not all.
Missed the rogue note
That slipped
From her fingers,
And fluttered
All the way down
To a long-haired man
Sitting on the ground.
She starts to walk off,
Oblivious to the note,
The one that got away.
Without a moment's hesitation,
The long-haired man leaps
To his feet.
He knocks his cardboard cup over.
Coins spill out
In every direction.
But,

He does not stop
To retrieve his lost treasure.
Instead,
He hurries
To catch up with the woman.
"Excuse me, Miss, but you dropped this note."
The woman turns
Puts her hands in her coat.
Grabs her purse.
Counts the notes.
The long-haired man is right.
Wonders to herself
Why he did not take the money,
And run?
After all,
Could do with the money,
Judging by the way he looks.
"Thank you very much for this. How very kind of you."
"No trouble at all."
Thanks the man again.
Offers him some loose change.
Thinks again.
"On second thoughts, please keep the note you found."
"Oh, I couldn't do that," replies the long-haired man.
"Think of it as a reward for being so honest."
"I'll be happy with just the change, Miss."
Before she can argue,
The man walks off
Back to his spot
Outside the bank.
One by one,
He starts picking up
All the coins
That had spilled out
Of his cardboard cup
And onto the pavement

Just moments before.
Not a big job,
Before he knows it
He is back sitting
On a piece of cardboard
On the pavement
Outside the bank
With his legs crossed.

11

Woman
Wearing glasses.
Just finished her classes.
Not convinced
That they are right,
For her.
Worries
She is wasting
Her time,
Her money.
It will all be worth it,
If she gets a full-time job,
She keeps telling herself.
A big if.
Been looking,
Constantly,
These past few weeks,
Ever since
She was summoned
To the grubby little office
Of her grubby little manager,
Only to be told
That she was no better
Than a novice.
It was only a small mistake,
She had protested.
One that anyone could make,
She had suggested.
Not good enough,

No second chance,
Marched off the premises
There and then
And all before
The clock had struck ten.
A demoralising search,
Any old job taken
Just to pay the bills,
Just to put food on the table.
Works the late shift
On the check-out
Of a local supermarket store.
Needs must
And all that.
Then a suggestion
From a friend
To take a course,
To learn a new skill.
Nothing to lose,
She had thought,
At the time.
Retraining,
Not as easy as
She had thought,
At the time.
Like being back at school.
And for what?
How will she cope
When she finds herself
Back in an office,
Back answering to a new boss?
Full of doubt,
She leaves the college.
Full of doubt,
She walks to town,
Face contorted

Into one big frown.

"Hey Sarah! Surprise!"

"Janet! You're a sight for sore eyes."

"Oh no what is the matter?"

"I wonder if I am wasting my time with this course I am taking."

"Oh dear. Sounds like you could do with a chat."

"Oh yes, I could do with that."

The two friends sit

At a table

In a café.

A waiter approaches

Carrying two bottles

And two glasses

On a round wooden tray

With one hand.

Removes the caps

Of the bottles

Effortlessly.

Pours sparkling water,

From the bottles

Expertly.

Places the two glasses

Filled with ice

And a slice of lemon

Onto the table,

Discreetly.

Sarah thanks the waiter,

Then waits

For the waiter to go,

Before she pours

Her heart out

To Janet,

Who listens,

Intently,

Quietly.

"Oh, how can people be so mean," wails Sarah.

"I know, Sarah, but you mustn't think everyone is bad! Just before I met you, a long-haired man came up to me. At first, I thought he was up to no good. But he held out a note in his hand. He said he saw me drop it. A homeless man finding money and, instead of pocketing it, returns it to the owner. That's heart-lifting, isn't it?"

"It truly is," replies Sarah.

12

No
Time
To
Lose.
Just enough time
For a quick stop
At the supermarket
On his way home.
A man with a trolley,
A man in a hurry.
A glance at the trolley.
An assortment
Of vegetables,
Of fruits,
Of special treats,
Of everyday consumables.
But something is not right.
A glance at his list
For anything missed.
A bottle of wine!
How could he miss that?
Scrawled down in pencil
On the other side
Of the crumpled piece of paper
That serves as his list,
That is how.
To the drinks aisle,
Off he speeds.
Man and trolley

In perfect harmony.
Skims round a corner,
Just a little bit further.
Before bottles,
Endless rows of bottles,
Come in to view.
How many?
One?
Perhaps two?
A red and a white.
That way he'll be alright.
The race is on
To get to the check-out.
Hurtles along,
No fear shown,
No quarter given.
Check-out spotted
One without a queue.
Commits
But,
Oh no!
The assistant is off.
The man fakes
A gentle cough.
"Any chance, madam, you could squeeze me in. I'm in a terrible rush, you see."
The woman peers,
Over her glasses.
Then gets out
One of her passes.
Sits back down
Onto her stool.
"Tough day?" she asks.
"You wouldn't believe what a crazy day I've had."
"Well, let's help it end on a high," says the check-out lady.
"It's my wedding anniversary, you see, so I just can't be late," reveals the man.
"Don't worry, sir, I'll be as quick as can be."

Name tag spotted.

Name tag read.

"Thank you, Sarah," replies the man in a hurry.

13

Baskets.
Always use baskets.
Pick one up,
And just walk around.
The simplest operating manual there is.
No need to mind the gap,
No need to play
At fairground bumper cars,
No need to join
The never-ending procession,
Of trolley
After trolley
After trolley,
Each taking it in turns
To manoeuvre into position.
Baskets.
Always use baskets.
Free to move,
Whenever
And wherever
The carrier likes.
Nip into one aisle,
Then nip out of another.
No need
To hover,
No need
To wait for the right moment.
Pick up and go,
That's all.

Woman wearing a blue scarf

Curses.

"So why did you have to take a trolley?" she asks herself.

She knows why.

Tired

Of having to lug around a heavy basket

Full to the brim.

Tired

Of having to put a heavy basket onto the floor

To rest her arms.

Tired

Of having to push a heavy basket

Around with her feet.

That's why.

Regret,

Full of regret.

Why?

Not because getting around the supermarket with a trolley was a struggle,

Not at all.

She moved with ease,

Glided

From shelf to shelf,

From aisle to aisle.

'Pile 'em high, sell 'em cheap' offers lurking randomly?

All successfully navigated.

Time it took to check-out?

A channel magically opened up before her.

All done most satisfactorily.

Until that is,

It was time

To return the empty trolley.

Trolley taken to trolley park.

No problem.

Shopping removed from trolley.

No problem.

Deposit coin successfully retrieved.

Problem.

"How on earth does it work?" she asks herself.

Tug of war

With the key.

Pushes and pulls

The key

This way and that.

First the key

Then the chain,

Again and again.

But the coin

Refuses to budge.

She asks a woman for help.

"Sorry, never use a trolley."

Neither will she

From now on.

Woman wearing a blue scarf asks another.

Too busy

To stop.

Mad rush.

Have to get on.

So does she

Have to get on.

Maddening.

Leave the coin?

Not much,

Not in the grand scheme of things.

But she knows

How it will gnaw away,

The one that got away.

A man appears with a trolley laden with shopping.

A handful of bags

And two bottles of wine.

One red and one white.

"Excuse me, sir, do you know how to retrieve the coin from the trolley?"

"Of course," says the bottle man.

"This is all you need to do," he says.
A wiggle here.
A wiggle there.
Coin pops out
From the slot.
"Thank you so much!"
Coin safely rehoused
Inside her purse.
Back where it belongs.

14

Short.
Agonisingly short.
Annoying.
Shouldn't have bought that drink.
Labelled 'Taste the summer'
Didn't taste of summer,
At least not to him.
What to do now?
Need to buy a ticket
To get on the bus
To get home in time.
Driver not budging,
Not one inch.
Only the full fare
Will do
On his double-decker bus.
Boy scratches his head.
Runs his hands
Through his scruffy blond hair.
Checks his pockets
For the umpteenth time.
Still no coin
Magically appears.
Now what?
Buy more time,
That's what.
Boy shuffles
To the back
Of the queue.

A temporary fix only though
Before the final reckoning.
Now what?
Ask the person in front for a coin?
One coin,
One pound.
All he needs.
"Excuse me, sir, I'm a pound short for a single. Do you have any change you
could spare?"
"Sorry, I don't, I'm afraid."
Convenient for the man.
Inconvenient for the boy.
Queue gets shorter.
Driver's eye caught.
Final reckoning approaching,
Fast,
They both know it.
Might have to walk it.
Be at the expense of watching the movie
And spending time
With his family.
Promised he would be back
In time.
Won't be popular,
For a time,
But the lesser
Of two evils.
The only evil now available to him anyway.
Nothing left to do
But to hop off the bus.
Boy turns around.
A woman,
Wearing a blue scarf,
Blocks his path.
Where did she come from?
One last chance,

Perhaps.

Yes means bus.

No means walk.

"Excuse me. But do you have any change you could spare. I'm a tad short, you see."

"As a matter of fact, I do."

Woman with the blue scarf puts down her shopping.

Purse out.

Hand in.

Hand out.

Hand opened.

Coin revealed.

Coin offered.

Coin taken.

"Thank you so much. You've saved the day!"

"Not at all."

Boy turns around.

Places the money,

The exact amount of money needed

To buy the fare,

Onto the small counter

By the driver.

Ticket printed.

Ticket handed over

By the driver,

Who smiles

At the boy,

Who smiles back

At the driver.

He won't be late

For the family date.

15

Proud old soldier
Standing to attention.
Blue blazer
Buttoned-up,
Just.
Threatens to burst free
Any minute,
Any second.
Green beret,
Well worn,
Flattened perfectly
On his head.
Regimental tie
Tied neatly
Around his neck.
Regimental badge
Stitched securely
Onto the breast pocket
Of his blazer.
Shoulders
Curved,
Not straight.
Back
Bent,
Not straight.
Not like
The old days.
Didn't have a stick,
In the old days.

Never leaves home without one
These days.
Still waiting,
Just like the old days.
Not for a truck
To transport him to the front,
But for a bus
To transport him back home.
Should have been here by now.
Hardly ever on time,
These days.
The old days!
Buses were on time
In the old days.
Seniors like him
Were seen
In the old days.
Never had to ask for a seat
In the old days.
Was better
In the old days.
Seniors like him
Invisible
These days.
The young don't care.
The young don't know,
The sacrifices he made.
They don't know what hell is.
They may soon.
Hopes they won't,
Of course.
But seen it all before.
"It's different this time."
Said that in the old days.
A bus appears.
But is it the right one?

Eyes take the strain.
No good.
Will have to wait
A little longer
For the bus to get
A little closer.
Stands to attention,
As the bus approaches,
Waits anxiously
For the number
To reveal itself
To his tired old eyes.
Hussar!
That's the ticket!
Bus stops.
Doors open.
Left hand on rail
Right hand on stick,
The old soldier clambers on board,
Not like the old days.
At least seniors go free,
These days.
Where to sit?
Nowhere to sit.
Old soldier looks around,
Tries to catch an eye,
Or two.
But no eyes catch him.
Beware, the gorgon Medusa
Approaches!
Eyes on papers.
Eyes looking out of windows.
Eyes closed.
Eyes down.
Eyes on anything,
Anything but on him.

Doors close.
Old soldier braces himself.
Hang on time.
Not like the old days.
"Excuse me, sir. Would you like my seat?"
Old soldier looks up.
A boy with scruffy blond hair
And a smile on his face.
A turn up for the books.
"Thank you, dear boy. That is very kind."
A bit like the old days.

16

A glance
At the clock,
Another one.
One hour
Before her shift starts.
Three hours
Before the cavalry,
Her husband,
Arrives back from work.
A two-hour deficit to navigate.
Doesn't sound like much,
But it is.
She can't be late.
Not ever.
But especially,
Not today.
Children
All fed,
All settled.
All that's needed
Is someone,
Anyone,
To watch over them.
Until at least,
Her husband returns
From work.
Babysitter bailed.
Telephone calls made.
No one free.

Uniform on.

Ready to go.

Just waiting

For a miracle

To set her free.

Her husband arriving back early?

Babysitter turning up unexpectedly?

She steps out of her front door.

Looks around

For anyone,

In hope.

A forlorn hope?

Miracles.

Time to see

If they really exist.

Theory tested.

Theory failed.

No one.

Apart from the grumpy old major,

Who lives two doors down,

Walking back to his home.

Eyes meet.

He touches his brow

With the top of his stick,

An informal salute.

"Evening Major," she says, but distracted.

"Good evening, Mrs Smith. Is everything alright?"

"Need to go to the hospital, but I can't until Mr Smith comes home to watch the children."

"Oh dear. No babysitter?"

"Cancelled. And there's no time to find a replacement."

"Oh dear. Perhaps I could watch over them."

"Would you be happy to? You have never offered before."

"Happy to help in time of need."

"Well, if you could, you would be getting me out of a jam. I'll pay you the going rate."

"You will not."

"Well, let's discuss another time. But thank you ever so much, Major."

"Not at all, Mrs Smith."

17

Father-to-be
Sits
In a waiting room.
In a hurry
To ditch the 'to-be'
And become
A fully fledged
Fully signed up
Father,
Finally.
Fifteen hours
And counting
Of labour,
Of pushing,
Of pain.
Tick tock.
Tick tock.
Still no sign of the baby.
"Time to help mummy, little one," he mutters to himself.
Poor darling wife.
All a far cry
From the swoon
Of courting,
Of falling head over heels in love at first sight,
Of two lives being pledged together forever,
Of pure, uncompromised joy.
Only cries of pain now
From his wife,
His darling wife.

Nothing he can do for her,
Nothing.
Words of encouragement?
Words of love?
Useless.
Wiping the sweat
From her contorted face
With a towel?
Pathetic.
Thank goodness for the midwife,
Mary,
Mary Smith,
What a hero.
What would he,
What would his wife,
Have done
Without her?
For fifteen hours
She has been here,
A constant.
Soothing,
Monitoring,
Encouraging,
Soothing,
Monitoring,
Encouraging,
Again and again.
For fifteen hours.
Shift ended
Hours ago.
And yet here she remains.
Has her own children,
Her own family,
But insists on staying,
At least until
His darling wife and baby come back

From the theatre
All safe and sound.
Only then
Will she go home.
How would they have coped
Without Mary Smith?

18

Man
Sits
All alone
In a bus shelter.
Leg in plaster.
Fell off a ladder.
Should have been more careful.
Took a short cut.
To what?
Six weeks of regret.
Six weeks on crutches.
Stupid.
Had plans for those six weeks.
Good plans.
All lying in tatters now.
What will he do,
What can he do
While his bones mend?
Everything will be a trial.
Going to work.
Cooking.
Shopping.
Washing.
All things he takes for granted.
Not anymore.
From independent to dependent
In the blink of an eye.
Who can he turn to?
Family and friends.

They'll help.
Won't they?
Hates asking for favours though.
Beggars can't be choosers though.
First trial,
Making his way home
From the hospital.
Where's that bus?
There's that bus!
Magically,
A bus,
His bus,
Appears at the top of the road.
Action stations.
The man scrambles
For the crutches.
But oh dear,
The man drops the crutches.
The crutches clatter
Onto the ground.
Hopping,
Bending,
Wobbling,
The man tries to pick them up,
Only for the bus
To drive on by.
"Hey stop!" he yells,
But in vain.
The bus ignores him.
"Stop!"
Crutches clatter to the ground,
Once again.
"Stop please!"
A flash of movement.
A man running
In the middle of the road

Chasing the bus,
Waving his arms.
The bus stops.
Could it be?
Doors open.
Could it be?
The runner returns,
Breathing heavily.
Could it be?
"I saw you were in a spot of bother. And thought I'd see if I could help. The driver said he didn't see you."
"Yes, I dropped my crutches. Had to bend down to pick them up."
"All sorted now. Here, let me help you onto the bus."
"Thank you so much but I'll be okay. You've done enough already."
"No trouble at all," says the man.
"Are you sure?"
"Absolutely. It's the least I can do."
"Least you can do? I am sorry, I don't follow."
"Today has been the greatest day of my life. I have become a father for the very first time to a baby girl called Mary and I feel on top of the world," says the man.

19

Autopilot on.
Everyone walking
With their autopilot on.
Rushing around
In every direction,
Seeking out
The path
Of least resistance,
Trying their best
Not to collide with each other.
One great mass of bodies.
Individual minds,
Maybe,
But all share a common goal,
Probably,
To get to work
On time.
A daily ritual
Performed twice a day.
Morning
To the office,
Afternoon
Back to home,
As quickly as possible.
Woman in a red dress
Standing at the exit
Of the train station,
Watching the daily mass migration
Unfold before her very eyes.

Was the same yesterday.
Will be the same tomorrow.
One mass melee,
One unseemly scramble.
And for what?
To get to work.
Takes a deep breath.
Steps out
From the shelter
Of the station.
Autopilot
Automatically
Switches on.
Thinks of nothing else
Save get to her office,
As quickly as she can.
A gap appears.
Take it
Before it disappears.
A channel opens up briefly
But all too briefly.
Soon enough
It is blocked.
Quick,
Slam on the breaks.
Stuck,
Behind a slow coach,
Walking no faster than a snail.
"How can anyone walk so slowly?" she asks herself,
Almost loud enough
For the snail to hear.
"Do snails have ears?"
Struggles to match
The painful crawl
Of the man in front.
Must find a way

Round the man in front.
Thinks she spots a chance.
But no.
Blink and you miss it.
Still stuck.
Still going slow.
"Going to be tough to get past this one, Julia," the woman mutters to herself.
Divine intervention.
Without warning,
Slow coach peels off.
Without warning,
Her legs quicken.
Not long now.
Destination in sight.
Double doors appear,
The heavy double doors
Of her office block.
Why so heavy?
Herculean effort required
Just to move them a fraction.
Only a slight girl.
Fit and strong
For her size,
But slight nevertheless.
Hates those doors.
Man with leg in plaster
And a pair of crutches
Appears
On her left.
Sneaks
In front of her.
Gets
To the doors
Before her.
Just her luck,
She thinks to herself.

Man on crutches
Will slow her down,
She thinks to herself.
Too hasty
In her judgement.
Man deftly juggles both crutches in one hand
And with one mighty shove
With his shoulder
And one big hop
Off his good leg,
The resistance
Of the heavy double doors
Is broken.
"Watch out for the doors slamming back,"
She thinks to herself.
But the man doesn't walk through the doors.
Instead he stops,
He waits,
And he holds
The doors open
For the woman
To breeze through.
"Thank you so much!" she says.
"No trouble at all," says the man with his leg in plaster.

20

Workload
Piling up.
Two reports,
Three meetings,
One external,
All before lunch,
Why before lunch?
Who decides
Reports have to be done before lunch?
End of the world
If they are done after lunch?
Of course not.
But who is he
To question the great and the good?
A lowly junior,
Is all he is.
Should be grateful he has this chance
To prove himself,
To climb up the ladder.
"To where?" he asks himself.
To more reports,
To more meetings,
To more deadlines.
"Focus!" young man wearing glasses admonishes himself.
Got to keep working,
Otherwise he will fall behind.
Will be alright,
As long as no last-minute jobs fall onto his desk.
Two months since he started.

And always

There are last-minute jobs falling onto his desk.

"Focus."

Movement

To his right.

Don't look up.

Avoid eye contact,

At all costs.

Head down.

"Focus."

Look busy.

Shouldn't be too difficult.

"Morning, Robert. Could you read this file and put together a report for me?"

Heart sinks,

Like a stone.

Robert raises his head,

Slowly.

His line manager, Julia,

Looms large above him.

"Of course, Julia, when do you need it by?"

"Any time before lunch will do. Thanks."

She turns to walk away.

Job done,

Buck passed,

"Thank you very much."

Now he is in trouble.

"How can everyone want everything done by lunch?"

Head down.

Not working.

Not working one bit.

Tempted to call it a day

There and then.

Up sticks.

Walk out.

No looking back.

"Everything alright, Robert?"

Julia is back.

Another report?

Can't possibly be,

Can it?

"Yes thanks. Got quite a lot on, that's all."

"Why didn't you say?"

"Didn't think it was my place to."

"Robert, you must not be afraid to say if you have too much on. How else will I know if you're struggling with your workload? Hand me back the file I just gave you. I'll deal with it."

"Thank you, Julia."

"That's alright, Robert, but promise you will talk to me from now on."

"Promise."

21

Woman,
Sitting at her desk
In an open plan office,
Thirsty.
Very thirsty.
Glass empty.
Been empty for a while.
Water cooler empty.
Been empty for a while.
Refill needed.
Too big,
Too heavy,
Too awkward.
Always a struggle,
Always trouble,
Always embarrassing
Lugging around a full bottle,
Let alone
Heaving one up
Onto the top
Of the water cooler.
Sore back to boot.
Options weighed.
Fetch a refill bottle herself
And risk the back?
Or stay thirsty
Until someone
Comes along
With a refill?

Scans the office,
Trying to work out,
Who will blink first?
Spies out
The glasses
On the desks
Around her.
More full
Than empty.
Could be a long wait.
Working,
That will help
Pass the time.
Not working.
Aching head.
Dehydrated.
Overheating.
Needs water.
Eyes
Fixed on the report
Laid out on her desk.
Blinks once.
Blinks twice.
Words dancing.
Can't focus.
Head sinks
Into her hands.
"You feeling alright, Sally?"
Raises her head
From her hands.
It's Robert.
Recently joined.
"Little headache, that's all."
"Let me fill your glass with water."
"Water cooler needs a refill."
"No problem, I'll get a new bottle now."

"Would you? That would be so nice of you."

"Happy to. They're rather heavy and awkward to carry, aren't they?"

"Yes, I hate having to pick them up."

"Next time it runs out, let me know, and I'll be happy to fetch a new one."

22

The clock
Ticking,
All he can hear.
The sound of time
Running out
Fast.
The sound of pressure
Building up
Fast.
Needs to finish up for the day.
Needs to get away early.
Not that early,
Not in the grand scheme of things.
Daughter has an important match,
And he can't be late.
Big trouble otherwise.
Missing one game was rotten luck
When bad weather
And train delays
Conspired against him.
Missing a second.
That would be inexcusable.
No second chances.
Always knew
It would be a close call.
Contract day.
Match day.
Why did they have to be on the same day?
Always going to be tight.

Always going to be a mad scramble,

Another one to look forward to.

Not good for the heart.

Doctor wouldn't be impressed.

Client signature

All he requires.

Then he is free to go.

Client due in at 1600.

Clock says 1627.

Of course

Client had to be late.

How long does he give it?

1700?

The very latest.

And then making the match

Would be very tight.

"Haven't you got to get away early for your daughter's match, John?" asks a colleague.

"Well remembered. Yes, I do," replies John, as he takes off his big black round glasses and rubs his eyes.

"What time are you leaving the office?"

"I was hoping to have been on my way by now, but I'm still waiting for Mr Hendry to come in and sign the papers."

"Oh dear, that's bad form. Leave the papers with me and I will wait for Mr Hendry. You need to get going. Can't miss the match."

"Are you sure? You would be doing me such a huge favour, Sally."

"Quite sure, John. Now show me where he needs to sign and off you go."

23

Five minutes
Before the train arrives.
One minute,
Two minutes at the most,
For passengers to disembark
And embark.
Six maybe seven minutes then
To get to the platform in time.
Man in a suit
Carrying a briefcase
Approaches the station
In a hurry,
Trying to work out
If he will make the train.
Easy as pie.
If it wasn't rush hour.
But rush hour it is.
So close it will be.
Walk becomes a trot
Whenever he spots a gap.
Trot becomes a walk
Whenever he meets a wall
Of slow-moving bodies
All trying to get home,
At the same time.
Ticket barrier approaches.
Ticket held in his free hand
Ready to flash
In front of the inspector.

Every second helps.

Inspector passed.

Ticket stashed away

In his jacket pocket,

Inside right.

"Excuse me, sir, can I see your ticket please?"

Inspector not passed.

Man in suit stops.

Ticket retrieved.

Ticket inspected.

"Thank you, sir."

If it was close before.

It is even closer now.

Man weaves in and out of the crowds.

Glances at his watch.

Two minutes to go.

Stairs not even reached yet.

Train could be late.

Driver's watch could be slow.

Stairs reached.

Train enters the station.

Train not late.

Driver's watch not slow.

Two steps taken at a time.

Platform reached.

Platform full

Of people.

Whistle blows.

But the path

To the nearest doors

Of the train

Blocked

By a never-ending stream

Of people,

A stream he cannot seem to cross.

"Arrghh!" the man winces to himself.

So close yet so far.

No chance of getting through.

No chance of boarding the train.

Until that is,

A man

Wearing big black round glasses

Stops and clears a path

So that the man in the suit carrying a briefcase

Can hop through the closing doors

And board the train.

Made it.

Just.

All thanks to the man wearing big black round glasses.

24

Baby
In a pram
On a train
During rush hour,
Not ideal.
Not the mother's fault.
Appointments overran.
Trains were cancelled.
Baby needed changing,
Three times.
A conspiracy.
Result?
Mother in blue dungarees
With a tattoo
Of the sun
On her arm
Finds herself
On a train
With a baby
In a pram
During rush hour.
Battle royale to board
The train.
Battle royale to park
The pram
In a safe spot
Away from the doors,
Away from the passengers.
Impossible.

Another battle royale to get off?
Soon find out.
Train stops,
At her stop.
"Excuse me. Can I get through please?"
No one hears.
Edges pram towards the door.
A gentle nudge here.
A forceful budge there,
No one moves,
Until,
Mother and baby find themselves
Swept up
In an irresistible tide
Of passengers,
All looking to disembark the train.
Mother and baby find themselves
On the platform,
Doesn't know how they managed it,
But terra firma reached
And that is all that matters.
Moment taken.
Composure regained.
Time to go home.
But,
A sting in the tail.
Lift out of order.
Stairs only.
Winding stairs.
155 steps,
According to the sign.
What to do?
People
Jostle past.
Everyone,
In too much of a hurry

To see the mother
With the baby
In the pram.
Except,
For a man
Dressed in a suit and carrying a briefcase.
"Need a hand with the pram?"
"Oh, if you wouldn't mind? That would be fantastic, thanks."
"My pleasure. I remember the days of carrying prams up and down steps all too well!"

25

42 seconds.
Small improvement.
Two more lengths,
100 metres,
Then drink,
Two or three sips,
Then rest,
For two minutes,
Then kickboard
For 200 metres
For four lengths.
For now though,
Focus
On every stroke,
On every breath,
On every third stroke.
Kick from the thighs.
Kick hard.
Reach.
Stretch.
Glide.
42 seconds
Again.
Last length.
Push hard.
One, two, three.
Breathe.
One, two, three.
Breathe.

Slow swimmer ahead.
Gap spotted.
Kick.
Kick.
Kick.
Another swimmer approaches,
In the opposite direction.
Will she make it?
Kick.
Kick.
Kick.
Woman in blue and red swimsuit,
Orange cap,
Black goggles
Races
To pass the slow swimmer
Ahead of her,
Without colliding
With the slow swimmer
Coming towards her.
Makes it,
Just.
Wall fast approaching.
Touch.
39 seconds.
That's more like it.
Swig of water.
Breather
Well-earned.
Not long though.
Goggles on her forehead,
Kickboard in her hands,
Head above water,
She kicks
Hard
With her thighs,

Not her knees,
For 200 hundred metres.
Time
To look around.
To see
Who else is in the pool,
To see
Who else is in her lane,
To see
How fast they are,
Will they slow her down?
Slow swimmer still in.
One other,
A man,
Swimming freestyle,
Fighting against the water
Rather than working with the water,
Like she does.
200 metres completed.
Another break.
Before another 200 metres
Of freestyle.
All out.
38 seconds.
First length.
39 seconds.
Second length.
Come on.
Third length.
Feels faster.
Looking good.
But what's this?
Slow swimmer ahead.
A woman.
Going to meet
At the end of the length.

Going to mess up

The final length.

Prays the woman will let her pass.

Touches the wall.

"After you," says the woman who, she notices, has a tattoo of the sun on her arm.

"Thanks!" she gasps back.

Right kick on.

36 seconds!

Best time yet.

26

Man eases himself
Out of the water,
Carefully.
Enough for today.
Slowly, slowly.
That's what he was told
By Diane,
The physiotherapist.
One step at a time.
Don't overdo it
Or risk further injury
That's what he was told
By Diane.
Pleased.
10 lengths today.
500 metres.
Five more lengths
Than last week.
He'll get there.
Slowly, slowly.
Limps into the shower block.
Warm water
And strong jet
Combine
To massage
His aching muscles.
Quick soap and shampoo
Before he hobbles to the locker.
Towel,

Clothes,
Shoes
All still there.
Knew they would be.
Still,
Good to see them.
A recurring nightmare of his:
Having to take the bus
With a pair of wet trunks on,
And nothing else.
Towel and clothes retrieved.
Shoes left behind
To stand guard
Over the locker.
Changing room,
Small.
Barely enough room
To turn
Or to fall
Come to think of it,
One positive at least.
Dry and clothed.
Back to the locker.
Socks on.
Shoes on.
Job done.
Limps to the exit.
"Sorry. I think you forgot this?"
Wobbly about turn.
Woman in blue and red swimsuit,
Orange cap,
Dripping wet,
A pair of black goggles in one hand.

A coin in her other hand.

His locker deposit.

"Oh, thank you very much."

"Not at all."

27

Five bags.
There were five bags.
Only four now.
Where could it be,
The fifth bag?
Woman wearing fingerless gloves counts,
Again.
Four.
Definitely four.
Tatty old blanket,
Tatty old scarf,
The occupants of the fifth bag.
They'll be missed,
Especially,
When it gets colder.
Must have left it behind
At the bus shelter.
Stupid!
Be long gone by now.
Stupid!
Looks up
And down
The street,
As good a spot as any.
Bags down,
All four of them,
Should have been five.
She curses herself.
Stupid!

She sits down
On the pavement
Outside a supermarket
Underneath an overhang.
Shelter
From the rain.
Hunkers down
For a long stay.
Body covered
By her oversized coat.
Arms wrapped
Around her knees
Tightly.
Head bowed
Between her arms.
Eyes closed
Tightly.
Ears opened
Wide.
Footsteps.
She hears footsteps
From all directions
All moving
To different beats.
Fast.
Slow.
Light.
Heavy.
One-two.
All even one-twos.
Except now a one,
Followed by a long drawn out two.
More of a slow shuffle.
Curious,
She looks up.
Man carrying a bag on his shoulder.

Limping heavily
Towards her.
He stops
In front of the woman.
"Cool evening. Do you have enough warm clothes?" asks the man.
"Yes, but I lost my blanket and a scarf."
"Oh, I'm sorry. Here, let me give you this. Hopefully, this will help."
Brings out a wallet.
Brings out a note.
Hands note to woman.
Hand in pocket.
Finds a coin,
A coin he would have lost anyway
At the swimming pool
If it had not been
For the swimmer
In the orange hat
And blue and red swimsuit.
Hands coin to woman.
"Bless you, Sir."

28

Hungry.
Lonely.
Weak.
Lost.
Wasn't always like this.
Well fed.
A loving family.
Strong.
Safe.
That's how it always was.
Until it all changed,
In an instant.
A flash of movement
And that was it.
A new world,
A new life.
A worse world,
A worse life.
A life of scrambling around
To find scraps of food to eat,
A life of struggling
To find a warm, dry place to sleep.
A life of searching
For loving companions.
Where are they,
The others?
What happened to them?
Did they just vanish?
Did they give up on him?

Almost time,
To give up on himself.
Too weak to run far.
Pain
In his stomach,
In his guts,
In his legs.
Time,
Time to curl up
And sleep
And dream
Of his old life,
Of long walks,
Of abundant food,
Of family love,
Of tender strokes.
He squirms
As he remembers
The strokes
Around his tummy,
Under his chin,
Behind his ears.
So real.
Too real.
He opens his eyes.
A woman wearing fingerless gloves,
Kneeling beside him,
Stroking him
Gently,
Talking to him
Softly,
Soothing him,
Calmly.
After a time,
She picks him up.
Puts him in one of her four bags.

Full of softness.
Full of memories.
Happy memories.
Woman stops
In front of a building.
Gently places her bags
On the ground.
Knocks on the door.
Door opens.
Light.
Warmth.
Safety?

29

Woman
Dressed in a nurse's uniform
On her way to work
On a Saturday evening.
Frustrated.
Missing a party.
Friends will be there.
All of them.
Missing out.
For what?
No animals in-house overnight,
At least there weren't any,
Last night.
Likely be
Another night
Of sitting behind a desk,
Waiting
For something
To happen
When she could be
At the party.
Arrives at the surgery.
No sooner does she get through the front door,
Nurse Williams approaches.
"Lucy, praise the Lord you're here."
"Is there something wrong, Hyacinth?" she asks.
"We have a new patient. Needs plenty of care."
"Oh dear. Just one moment and I'll be right there."
Jacket off.

Jacket hung
On peg,
Her peg.
Bag off.
Bag shoved
Into locker,
Her locker.
Uncomfortable shoes off.
Uncomfortable shoes placed
Under locker,
Her locker.
Comfortable shoes on.
A well-rehearsed routine
Executed
In a matter of seconds.
Following behind Nurse Williams,
Nurse Thomas enters the ward.
"He was brought in this afternoon by a homeless woman."
Nurse Williams steps away
To reveal a cage.
Empty?
Not quite.
A bag of bones
Covered with a coat
Of white fur
With large black patches
Curled up
Tightly
In a corner.
Drip attached
To front right paw.
Then,
As if struck
By a bolt
Of lightning,
It happens,

Unexpectedly,

It happens

There and then,

It happens

With no hint of a warning,

It happens,

The moment the dog's eyes open,

Lucy's heart is lost,

Forever.

Gently,

She strokes his back,

"He's adorable," says Lucy.

"He was in a bad way when he came to us."

"Don't worry, Hyacinth. I'll keep an eagle eye over him tonight."

"I have no doubt about that, my dear," says Hyacinth with a smile.

30

Empty bottle,
Fifth one today.
Found
Next to a paper bag
Half squashed
And lying on the pavement,
Just metres away
From a bin.
Disappointing.
Upsetting.
"Not the first time and won't be the last," mutters the road cleaner on his early morning shift.
Will be his last time, though.
Back home soon.
Back where he belongs.
Back with his family.
His wife,
His children,
His mother,
His aunt.
Three years
Since he was with them last.
Since he was at home last,
Before he travelled to London
To stay with a distant cousin
He had never met before.
And all to earn
The equivalent
Of a monthly wage back home,

Each day!

How?

By picking up other people's rubbish.

Still has to pinch himself

To check

It has not all been one big dream.

Time

To go home now though.

Time

For the English to pick up their own rubbish.

Turns his cart

Into the next street.

Neat line of houses

On either side.

Always liked this street.

No one in sight.

All quiet.

A few lights on

Here and there,

As some residents stir

For the day

Inside their homes.

Clean street this one,

Always is.

Usually means he rattles through it,

Except,

When he sees Nurse Thomas

Just before she sets off for,

Or comes back from,

Her shift.

"Good morning, Mr M. How are you today?"

True to form,

The nurse does not disappoint.

"Oh, I am fine, thank you, Miss. I see the little one is getting stronger."

He points to the black and white dog,

Scuttling beside the nurse's feet.

Never leaves her side,

Not since she took him in.

"Oh, he is doing fine, thank you. Is this your last shift?"

"Yes Nurse. Flying back home in two days."

"Bet you can't wait to see your family."

"That's right, Miss. Been a long time."

"Would you mind staying there for just a moment. I have something for you inside."

"Okay. I will stay here."

The nurse

Disappears into her home,

Black and white dog,

Trotting by her heels,

Disappears into his home.

Moments later

The nurse,

Holding a bag,

Reappears from her home,

Black and white dog,

Trotting by her heels,

Reappears from his home.

"Here's a little gift to take back with you. To remind you of us and to give your family a taste of Britain."

The road cleaner looks inside.

Jar of Marmite,

Box of English tea,

Box of biscuits,

Packet of humbugs

And lots more.

"Miss, you are very, very kind! Thank you."

"Have a safe flight home, Mr M, and send our best wishes to your family. We'll all miss you."

31

Another hot afternoon.
Hot
And humid.
Every day is hot and humid.
Fine in the morning,
When the young boy walks
For two hours
To his school
In the next village.
Not so good in the afternoon,
When the young boy walks back
For another two hours
From school
To his village.
He knows how long the walk takes
Because his father's old watch tells him.
He used to try and set a new record every day,
Once made it to school in one hour 52 minutes,
But that meant
He had to spend more time at school,
On his own
Until his friends and teacher arrived.
He likes school.
He likes to learn,
About words,
About numbers,
About the world.
He wants to see the world,
And to see the world,

He needs to know
About words,
About numbers.
The walk is a good time to learn
His times tables,
His spellings.
Recites numbers and words
To himself
On the dusty road.
More like a track of dry red clay
Hammered into shape
By thousands of feet,
By thousands of wheels,
Over thousands of years.
Beep-beep.
The boy turns.
Man on a scooter
Heading towards him.
Scooter stops.
Man stretches out a leg
Onto the track.
Removes his helmet.
It's Mr Mbabazi,
Recently returned from England.
The boy has his heart set on going to England.
One day.
"Morning Peter. On your way back from school?"
"Yes, Mr Mbabazi. That is right."
"Would you like a lift? I have a spare helmet in the box if you like."
"Oh yes please, Mr Mbabazi. I can't believe it!"
"I tell you what. If your mother says it is okay, I am happy to take you back from school every day."
"Would you really, Mr Mbabazi?"
"Yes, no problem, Peter. It's on my way and it will be good to have a little company."

32

Two jobs.
At least,
That is what it feels like.
First job,
Teaching a class of 62 pupils
Maths,
English,
Science,
History,
Geography,
Music.
Second job,
Tidying up the classroom
At the end of the school day.
Ensuring chairs are all in place
Underneath the tables,
Ensuring books are all
In the correct shelves,
In the correct order.
The children do their best,
But the chairs and tables never end up in a straight line,
Until she comes along,
That is.
The books never end up in the right place,
Until she sorts them out,
That is.
She could be harder on the children
But most of them have a long walk
Ahead of them

To get back home.
Wouldn't be fair
To keep them back.
So she does the job herself,
Her second job.

"Miss Eriyo?"

"Peter, why are you still here? Shouldn't you be on your way home?"

"Mr Mbabazi from my village is picking me up, Miss. He said from now on, he will take me home from school on the back of his scooter. It takes me less than an hour to get home now."

"Well, that is very nice of him."

"It is, Miss. It means I have a little time before he picks me up."

"That's nice, Peter. What will you do with your extra time?"

"Well, Miss, I was wondering if I could use that time to help you tidy up after class."

"Oh Peter. How thoughtful of you. You do not have to."

"I know, Miss. But Mr Mbabazi doesn't have to take me home from school every day."

33

Back home.
Late,
As always.
Lift
From the coffee plantation
To Mbale
Followed by a 45-minute wait
For the bus.
Two-hour journey time,
Equals late.
Equals tired.
Equals dirty.
But home
At last.
For a rest?
For a tasty meal?
How he wishes that was so.
Steps through the door
And Akiki,
The plantation worker,
Becomes Akiki,
The head chef
Of the family.
Knows they'll all be hungry,
His poorly grandmother,
His three younger sisters,
Lots of mouths to feed.
With what?
Yams?

Sweet potatoes?

Another vegetable dish,

No meat.

Again.

Will have to make do,

Somehow.

"Where are my little people?"

"Over here, Akiki," replies his little sister Dembe.

Cue giggling

From behind the curtain.

Akiki pounces.

Draws the curtain

To reveal his three little sisters.

Smiles all around.

"What's happened?" asks Akiki after seeing the smiles on all their faces.

"Miss Eriyo from next door has happened," answers his sister Beatrice.

"I don't follow, Bea."

"Miss Eriyo came earlier and brought us a feast."

"A feast?" asks Akiki.

"A bowl of meat stew. Enough for everyone," answers Beatrice.

"That is very kind of her but why did she do that?"

"She knew that you'll be tired after a long day at the plantation so she wanted to help out."

34

Sore feet,
Not from working
On the plantation
All day
But from football.
Barefoot football
To be precise.
No boots.
Can't afford them.
Bruises,
Lots of them.
Bloody toenails,
Cracked toenails,
Lots of them.
All worth it,
For his love
Of the beautiful game.
Dreams
Of playing for his country,
One day.
No.9
Centre forward,
Solomon Alupo,
Uganda's all-time record scorer.
Has a ring to it.
One day.
Needs boots first,
Then he will be able to kick on
To the big league.

Maybe he can get a second job

And save up

For boots.

Difficult.

45 hours a week

At the plantation:

7 am to 3 pm

Monday to Friday;

7 am to 12 pm

Saturdays.

Overtime?

Possibly.

Football training:

On Monday

And Wednesday afternoons;

Saturday match day.

Perhaps Tuesdays and Fridays?

"Good morning, Solomon."

It's Akiki, his friend,

Standing at the entrance

To the plantation

With a bag.

"Morning Akiki. How are you?"

"Not as good as you."

"What do you mean, Akiki?"

"I've got you something."

Hand disappears into bag.

Hand reappears from the bag,

Holding a pair of boots.

Football boots.

"For me?"

"For you!"

"But where did you get them from?"

"My father gave them to me a few years ago. But I never grew into them. They might not fit you perfectly. But I hope they help."

"They're perfect, Akiki. Thank you very much, my friend."

35

One on top of the head,
One in each hand,
Three jerry cans,
Each full
Of water.
Too heavy.
Much too heavy.
Used to be able to manage it,
The daily water run,
With no trouble at all.
A struggle these days.
Hurts these days,
Especially,
Hard on the arms.
Might have to become
A twice daily water run.
Not enough time in the day though.
Will have to find time.
First things first.
Needs to get back home
Before her arms fall off.
Needs to get back home
Before she catches the bus to Mbale,
For her appointment.
Put the load down
And have a rest?
Or carry on
And put an end to the pain
Sooner rather than later?

Options weighed
By the woman in the long pink flowery dress,
As she walks on.
Soldier on,
That's what she'll do.
The sooner
She gets home
The better.
Decision made.
But oh how her arms ache,
More and more.
The pull,
The lure
Of having a break
Grows stronger,
And stronger.
"Mrs Ako! Let me help you with those."
An angel.
"Solomon, my dear. That would be wonderful. I feel my arms are going to fall off."
"Here, let me take the ones from both your hands."
"But don't you have to go to the plantation?"
"I've got a little time."
"Well, thank you, dear, for coming to my rescue."
"As long as you keep carrying the can on your head. I prefer balancing a football up there."
"That's fine by me!"
"I'll look out for you tomorrow morning."
"Bless you, Solomon."

36

Another ticket sold.
How many today?
Too many to count.
And yet,
Not a word exchanged
Between her
And the customers,
Other than
The standard
"Can I have a ticket to…"
Followed by
Wherever they are going to.
Every day it is like this
For the ticket lady
At the ticket office
At Mbale bus station.
How many people does she serve every day?
Too many to count.
How many people have a conversation with her every day?
Too few to count.
Some are in a rush.
Some say a polite thank you,
As they leave with their ticket.
Fair enough.
But a conversation,
That is what the ticket lady yearns for.
Doesn't have to be long.
She is working,
After all.

Would just like someone to speak to her,

For a change.

To ask her how her day is going,

For a change.

To ask her how she is doing,

For a change.

To smile at her,

For a change.

To say hello to her,

For a change.

"Hello. Can I have a ticket please to Kampala?" asks another customer.

Followed by a "Thank you",

As she passes the man the ticket.

A thank you,

Better than nothing,

She supposes.

"Good morning! How are you today?"

Ticket lady looks up.

A beautiful lady,

Dressed in a pink flowery dress,

Standing on the other side of the counter.

Beautifully upright.

Perfectly poised.

Ticket lady clears her throat.

Suddenly shy.

"Fine, thank you, Madam," she replies quietly.

"It looks like you are having a busy day," says the elegant woman, as she points to the queue behind her.

"Yes, we are. I do not know why, but it seems a lot of people are going places today."

"They are getting ready for the weekend perhaps," says the woman in the pink flowery dress.

"Maybe. What about you? Are you going anywhere nice?"

"Oh no, not me. Just back home. Only came to the city for an appointment. Looking forward to going home."

"I don't blame you."

"What about you? When do you get to go home?"

"Oh, not long now till my shift ends."

"Do you catch a bus home too?"

"Yes, I do."

"I hope you don't have to pay for a ticket."

"One of the perks of the job," says the ticket lady, with a broad smile on her face.

"Well, I'd better get my ticket as I expect everyone in the queue behind me wants to get home too!"

"Yes, I suppose you are right," chuckles the ticket lady.

First time today.

She looks at the clock.

Last hour of her shift,

Usually the longest hour of the day.

But not today,

Flies by today.

Takes a bus home

To her village

And then,

With a spring in her step,

She walks the short journey home.

But what's this?

Something soft and furry,

Lying on the edge of the road.

Thinks it is an animal at first,

Until a close inspection reveals,

A teddy bear,

Covered in mud,

Feeling sorry for itself.

Ticket lady picks teddy up,

Carefully,

And carries teddy home,

Carefully.

37

Baby crying,
Again.
Need George,
Now!
Desperate mother
Pleading
To no one,
To everyone.
Where could he be?
Sure he was
In the last store
They visited
When little one had held George,
By one of his ears.
Remembers thinking
At the time
"Don't drop him little one."
Sure he was
In the bag,
When the mother and her child walked back
From the village.
Should have kept an eye on George,
A closer eye.
Did George even make it back
To the house?
Not sure.
If only she knew,
For sure.
She would turn the house

Upside down,
In search of George.
If only she knew,
For sure.
Most likely,
George lost in the street.
Little one not going to be happy.
Little one already not happy.
Too late to check now.
No George tonight.
Not for the little one.
Tomorrow,
Mother will retrace her steps
With the little one too,
Maybe he will be able to help,
In some small way.
He lost George,
After all.
Tomorrow arrives,
Eventually,
After a long, tough night.
Little one cried himself to sleep,
Eventually.
Mother exhausted.
Managed to snatch a few hours' sleep,
Eventually.
Need to find George,
As soon as possible.
Child back in scarf,
Slung up snugly
On the mother's back.
Back
On the street,
Mother takes the route,
She took yesterday.
Eyes fixed

On the ground,
Looking for George.
No sign of George,
Until,
A scream,
Not a bad scream,
A happy, excited scream
From the little one,
Makes mother look up
And follow the little arm
That is pointing to a wall
To George,
A clean George!
Sitting on top of the wall,
Sitting on top of a note.
"I am back from a big adventure, but oh, how I missed you…"
Reads the note.

38

Walls too thin.
Noise too loud.
Old man with white beard
Hears everything.
All the laughing,
All the talking,
All the bickering,
That comes from the hut next door,
The one on his right,
If facing the front door,
From the outside.
Last night it was the lamp.
Endless arguing about the kerosene lamp.
Too dark to read.
Too light to sleep.
The girl wanted to read her book.
Didn't get her way,
By the sound of it.
Peace and quiet,
All he yearns for.
Night before was toys.
Fighting over toys.
Children.
He never had any.
Too noisy.
Always kept his distance,
From children.
Until the family built their hut next door.
The irony.

The old man walks to the village.
Fresh air
To clear his head
Of the noise.
Sees a woman sitting.
Woman holding a baby.
Baby holding a teddy.
Giggling,
Laughing,
Smiling.
The old man stops.
Eyes transfixed
On the baby with the teddy.
The mother looks at him,
Curiously.
"Would you like to hold the baby and George, his teddy?" she asks him.
"Oh, I don't think so, Madam. I have never held a baby before."
"First time for everything. Here, let me show you."
Before he can say no,
Before he can make his excuses,
He finds himself holding the baby.
Baby smiles and giggles
At the old man.
The old man smiles and giggles
At the baby.

39

Words.
Numbers.
She loves them both,
In equal measure.
Some people love sports,
Some people love music.
She loves
Words
And numbers.
Can't get enough of them.
Always studying,
Always reading.
Wants to go to university.
Will go to university,
If her little brothers and sisters would just let her read.
Never enough light,
Especially,
After the sun goes down.
Fighting over the kerosene lamp,
Fighting over everything,
As only brothers and sisters do.
"Joyce, do this. Joyce, do that."
"Joyce, I want this. Joyce, I want that."
All Joyce wants,
Is to read
And study.
"Good evening."
A man standing in the doorway,
Bellows over the din

In the house.

"Just one second."

Answers Joyce,

As she marks the page

Of her book,

Before putting her book down

Onto the table.

At the entrance,

Stands the old man with the white beard

Who lives next door,

The hut on the left,

If facing the front door

From the outside.

Usually keeps himself to himself.

"Hello. I'm afraid my mother and father are not in."

"Oh, it is you who I want a word with."

"Me?" asks Joyce.

"Yes, forgive me, but the walls are so thin and I couldn't help but overhear that you like to read in the evenings?"

"Sorry if we made too much noise for you last night. I promise we will try to lower our voices."

"Oh, don't worry about that. I came to give you this."

What is that in his outstretched hand?

A torch

With a red handle

And a black strap

To go around the wrist.

"For me?"

"Yes, it sounds like you need your own light. So I thought you could do with this."

"Oh sir. You don't know how much this means to me. Thank you from the bottom of my heart."

40

4 am.
Early start.
Long day ahead.
Load up at Mbale.
Short drive to the border.
Long wait at the border,
No doubt.
Rest,
At least.
Once through the border
Drive to Nairobi.
Halfway point.
Stay overnight
In the cabin
Of the truck.
Uncomfortable.
Up first thing,
To beat the traffic.
Onto Mombasa
To a warehouse,
Near the docks.
Unload coffee
For export
To markets
All over the world.
Then load up truck.
Hides,
Clothing,
Footwear,

All sorts of goods
For transport
Back into Uganda.
Turn around.
Drive back.
Stop at Nairobi
For a rest.
Back to the border.
Long wait.
Rest,
At least.
Back to Mbale.
Unload.
Head home.
Three days away.
If he's lucky.
Could be more.
Depends on the border,
Depends on the traffic,
Depends on the queues at Mombasa,
To unload
And load.
Likely to be
More than three days.
Hopes it is
Just three days.
Will miss his family.
A noise,
Somewhere
In the house.
Someone
Is awake
In the house.
At this hour?
No one is ever awake,
At this hour.

"Morning Father."

"Morning Joyce. What are you doing up this early?"

"I didn't want to miss you before you went off."

"Come here, my beautiful daughter. Come and give me a hug."

41

Going to be late.
Going to be very late.
Didn't see the pothole
Until it was too late.
Thought he got away with it,
At first.
Carried on driving
For a while
On the A104 Road,
The road that connects Malaba with Nairobi.
Noticed something wasn't right.
Stopped to check.
A puncture.
No problem.
Change the tyre.
Problem.
Nuts too rusty.
Won't budge.
Tried with both arms.
Tried stamping on the spanner
With one leg.
Tried jumping on the spanner
With both legs.
No movement,
None whatsoever.
Stranded
On a remote section
Of the highway.
Going to be late.

Going to be very late.
Sergeant Major Kimani of the Kenya Wildlife Service
Is never late.
Sergeant Major Kimani of the Kenya Wildlife Service
Never lets the team down.
Sergeant Major Kimani of the Kenya Wildlife Service
Needs to lead the team
On an important mission.
Dangerous mission
To track down poachers
Can't miss it.
But what to do?
He looks around.
A truck approaches.
Slowing down?
Definitely slowing down.
Truck stops.
Driver gets out.
Driver jumps down.
Driver walks over.
"Everything okay?" asks the driver.
"Puncture. Need to change the tyre but the nuts and bolts are too rusty."
"Let me have a go," says the driver.
The driver tries.
Nuts won't budge.
"I think I have a better spanner in the truck. Never failed me before."
"Oh, I hope so. I have a long trip ahead. And I can't be late."
The two men walk together
To the back of the truck.
"What are you transporting?" asks the Ranger.
"Coffee to Mombasa," replies the driver, as he picks up a large spanner.
"Now let's see if this works," he continues.
Like a dream.
Nuts off.
New tyre on.
Job done.

All in a matter of minutes.

"Well, I hope you can still make it in time. Where are you off to?" asks the driver.

"Maasai Mara National Park. And thanks to your kindness, sir, I think I will make it in time."

42

"Duma. The boss wants to see you."
"Me?"
"Yes, you, Duma."
"Did he say why?"
"Afraid not."
"Is he in his office?"
"Yes. He's waiting for you there."
If the boss calls,
The boss calls.
No time
To put tools away.
Just time
For a quick wipe of the hands,
Before Duma is on his way
To the boss' office,
Wondering
If he is in trouble.
Has he forgotten to do something?
Has he done anything wrong?
He always tries his best.
He always tries to be helpful.
He always works hard.
Why does the boss want to see him then?
Soon find out.
Outside the boss' office,
Duma stops.
Deep breath.
Get it over and done with.
Quick tap on the door.

"Come in."

Duma enters.

"You asked to see me, Sergeant Major Kimani."

"Yes Ranger."

Duma stands to attention.

Eyes fixed straight ahead.

Arms straight by his side.

"I just wanted to have a word with you, Ranger."

Duma remains still

On the outside.

Duma is a bundle of nerves

On the inside.

"Your attitude and your work ethic, Ranger...are first class. I've been very impressed by you and I think you could go far in the service. Keep it up."

"Thank you, Sergeant Major Kimani."

Duma speaks calmly

On the outside.

Duma leaps for joy

On the inside.

"Now, you know we have an important mission at the Maasai Mara. Reports of poachers chasing rhinos. Go get some rest, could be a long night tonight. That is all."

"Yes, Sergeant Major Kimani. Thank you, Sergeant Major Kimani."

Door closes.

Duma jumps for joy.

43

Dawn.
Time for a bite to eat.
A black rhino,
With a scar
On his left thigh,
Wanders
Among the bushes.
Plucks a leaf
From a tree
And chews.
Picks a fruit
From a bush
And chews
With his pointed,
Rubbery
Lips.
Tasty cluster spotted.
The rhino charges forward
Head first.
The rhino forces his way
Through reluctant branches
That try to cling on,
Desperately,
To his two horns,
Wrapping themselves
Around the larger one first,
Before slipping off,
And trying their luck
With the smaller one.

Prize reached,
The rhino munches away,
Satisfied,
Contented.
But watched,
By men,
With rifles.
The horns.
They want the horns,
To sell
In far off lands
For a fortune.
Oblivious
To the danger,
The rhino bundles on.
More leaves.
More fruit.
But now in the sights
Of rifles.
One more fruit.
One more leaf.
One last leaf.
Whispers.
Hand signals.
Shouts.
Not from the men
With the rifles.
But from men in uniform,
Rangers.
The rangers charge
The men with rifles.
The rhino charges
The men with rifles,
Before turning around
And scurrying away
Out of sight

Out of harm's way.
Men surprised.
Men captured
By Duma
And the rangers.

44

Five.
The Big Five.
Lions.
Clicked.
Leopards.
Clicked.
African elephants.
Clicked.
Cape buffalo.
Clicked.
Rhinoceros.
White
Or Black.
Not clicked.
Safari-goer from Austin, Texas
Needs the rhino
To complete the set.
The Big Five.
Buffalo,
Elephant,
Lions,
All snapped
These three days past.
Leopard
Captured
On camera
Today,
Her last day.
Crammed tight

With four other hopefuls
In the back
Of a Land Rover.
Guide
In the front
Of the Land Rover,
Sitting next to the birthday boy,
Jabali,
The driver.
Lived up to his Swahili name.
Strong as a rock.
Long drive,
Long day,
But still Jabali smiles.
One last attempt
To find the elusive rhino.
The Land Rover stops
In front of a cluster
Of thirsty-looking bushes.
Jabali whispers to the guide.
The guide whispers to everyone
To be quiet,
To be still,
To look around.
Camera at the ready,
The Texan safari-goer waits.
The Texan safari-goer hopes.
Movement in the Land Rover.
The Texan turns.
Jabali pointing
To a bush,
The big round one
In the centre.
The party follows the driver's arm
To the bush.
A black rhino

With a scar
On its left thigh,
In all its magnificence,
Feasting
On leaves
On fruit.
The Texan's heart leaps.
The Texan's camera bleeps.
Set complete.

45

A good day.
A rhino.
They all wanted to see a rhino.
So happy
That he found one,
A black rhino,
For the party,
Especially,
For Mrs Hamilton,
The Texan.
So excited she was,
When they set off.
So excited she was,
When she finally saw the rhino
To complete the set,
The Big Five.
Made his birthday,
That he found the rhino
For the Texan
And for the others.
He can hear the party
All celebrating
Back at the camp,
While he works on the Land Rover
Checking the oil,
Checking the engine,
Checking the brakes,
Ensuring the Land Rover
Is ready and clean

For the next trip.

Job done,

He walks to his hut,

For a rest,

Before he sets off for the village.

Passes the canteen tent.

For guests only,

The canteen tent.

"Jabali!" yells Mrs Hamilton.

"Do you have a moment to come into the canteen, Jabali?" asks the Texan.

Jabali enters the tent.

"Happy Birthday!"

The whole camp

In the tent,

It seems,

Erupt into song.

Guests,

Staff,

Managers,

All there.

All singing

To him,

To Jabali,

To the driver,

All wishing him,

Jabali,

A happy birthday.

"We thought we'd throw you a birthday party, Jabali. Please would you sit and have dinner with us this evening?" asks Mrs Hamilton.

"Thank you, Bibi. I do not think I should. It is not my place."

"Don't worry! I've cleared it with your bosses."

"But I need to see my cousin in the village," says Jabali.

"It'll just be an hour. Could you spare an hour? You can go to the village after."

"Okay, Bibi. I will stay for an hour. Thank you very much, Bibi."

"No Jabali. Thank you for everything you have done for us these past few days. You have made them the most memorable days of our lives," declares the Texan. "Thank you, Bibi."

46

A lion cub cries
For his mother,
For his brothers,
For his sisters.
Lost.
Scared.
Hungry.
Vulnerable.
With darkness
Comes danger.
The young one does not know
Why there is danger
Or why he is scared.
Instinct tells him
There is danger.
Instinct tells him
To be scared.
All alone,
He curls up
Into a ball,
A tight ball.
Feels safer
That way,
Somehow.
More cries,
Hoping
His mother will hear,
Hoping
His mother will come.

Noises,
Smells,
Shadows
Loom larger
And larger
In the darkness.
But none
Are those of his mother
Or of his brothers
Or of his sisters.
Noises become louder.
Smells become stronger.
Shadows become larger.
The lion cub cowers.
"I found it," whispers a voice.
"There you see. Curled up in the long grass."
Jabali squints,
Until he sees the cub.
"Ah little Simba, don't be afraid. We'll look after you. You are safe now," he
says.
Slowly,
The two men approach
The frightened cub.
Softly,
The two men reassure
The frightened cub.
Gently,
The two men pick up
The frightened cub.
"I'll take little Simba back to camp. They'll know what to do," says Jabali.
"You were right to call me," he continues.
"Even on your birthday?" asks his cousin.
"Even on my birthday," replies Jabali.

47

"This cub was brought to us two weeks ago. Must have gotten separated from his mother. We've been caring for him ever since. We call him Little Simba," explains the guide.

"What will happen to him?" asks one of the group,

A Mr James

From Sydney,

Australia.

"We'll keep him here for a while, but the hope is we can return him back to the wild," answers the guide.

"What happened to his mother?" asks Mr James.

"We don't know. We searched the area where the cub was found. But no sign of her."

"Does he bite?" asks another member of the group.

"Little nips but only playful ones. You'd know if he meant it. He doesn't bite the hand that feeds him, so to speak."

Laughter.

"Are we able to hold him?" asks Mr James.

"You're welcome to go in the pen. One at a time though. We'd advise you wait for him to come to you. Who'd like to go first?"

Cue

An arms race.

Cue

Mr James,

The victor.

Just when he thought his trip could not get any better,

It does.

Trip of a lifetime,

Claimed the travel agent.

Never a truer word uttered,

By a travel agent.
Lions,
Elephants,
Giraffe,
Zebra,
Cheetah,
Ostrich.
All seen with his own eyes.
All snapped by his own camera.
Now Mr James gets to enter
The lion's den.
Little Simba scampers
Up to him.
No fear
In his young heart,
Not anymore.
Mr James kneels.
The lion cub paws
At an arm
In mock battle,
In play.
The lion cub rolls
Onto his back.
"He's asking you to stroke his tummy," explains the guide.
Mr James obliges,
Gladly.
Little Simba squirms,
Joyfully.
All four paws
On Mr James' outstretched arm,
Pushing and pulling
At the fabric of his shirt
With pure delight.
Mr James squirms,
Smiling and laughing
With pure delight.

48

Two children,
One,
Four years old,
One,
Two years old.
One parent,
Three bags.
Eight hours
On an aeroplane.
The mother always knew
It was going to be tough,
Flying with children.
At least in the plane,
The little ones will be strapped
In seats,
Unable to wander.
But in the taxi?
In the airport?
Screams,
Tantrums,
Crying,
The full set.
Exhausted.
How on earth
Will she get through the flight?
Youngest still screaming.
Nappy changed.
More screams.
Feeds given.

More screams.
New toy bought,
A cuddly lion cub
From the airport shop,
More screams.
Screams
In the departure lounge,
Screams
On the stairs up to the aeroplane,
Screams
In the cabin,
Crying,
Non-stop crying.
Helpful air stewardess
Directs mother and children
To their seats.
Two seats,
One for her eldest,
The other for her,
And her youngest,
The screamer.
Man sitting on the end of the row stands up.
Poor man,
Thinks the mother.
Poor mother,
Thinks the man,
Who offers to hold the upset child,
While mother and the four-year-old settle down
In their seats.
Mother grateful.
Two-year-old grateful.
Silence.
Young eyes lock onto the man's eyes.
Young finger plays with the man's face.
Man pulls a funny face.
Child laughs.

Peace reigns.

"You have the Midas touch," says the baby's mother.

"Oh, I have two of my own. Lots of practice," says the man,

In an Australian accent.

Baby back now

In mother's arms.

Baby screaming

Again.

"I'm happy to hold the little one if you like," offers the man.

"Are you sure?"

"Yes, of course."

Baby back now

Sitting on the man's lap.

Peace reigns

Again.

The man brings out a picture

Of a lion cub,

Sitting on the man's lap

Taken just two days before.

Shows the picture to the baby.

Baby squeals.

Baby laughs.

Baby points

To his own cuddly lion cub.

49

Abu Dhabi International Airport
Transit lounge,
Packed
With passengers
Going nowhere,
Fast.
All stuck
In no-man's land,
All waiting
For a connecting flight
To take them
To their final destinations.
Bodies slumped
On seats.
Bodies stretched out
On the floor.
Heads resting
On bags
Or on shoulders.
Feet propped up
On luggage
Or on seats.
All trying to get some sleep
Or to while away the hours
Before they get the call,
The magic call,
To board.
A young child cries.
Peace disturbed.

Parents do their best
To settle the little one down,
While waiting for their flight
To Hong Kong.
Walking up and down the lounge
Again and again.
Playing peekaboo
Again and again.
Humming lullabies
Again and again.
Rocking the young one backwards and forwards
Again and again.
All in vain.
Another child approaches.
Drawn to the crying,
Stares
At the upset little one.
Runs back
To his mother and older sister,
Returns
To the upset little one
Holding a toy.
Presents the cuddly lion cub
To the upset little one.
And as if by magic,
And in an instant,
The cries give way
To smiles,
To laughter,
To peace.

50

Man,
Wearing a Panama hat,
Looks around.
Feet tapping
To a beat,
A beat
Only he knows.
People sleeping,
People reading,
People waiting,
Waiting for the call
To board.
Bored
Of the wait.
Two hours to go,
Still,
Before it is time.
That is,
If the flight is on time,
Of course.
Taps the case
On his lap.
Wonders if he should.
Looks around again.
A couple chatting.
A woman brushing her hair.
A young child humming,
While playing
With a toy,

A cuddly lion cub.
The inspiration,
The sign,
He was looking for.
Man wearing the Panama hat opens the case,
Brings out a red ukulele.
Plucks the strings,
Twists the knobs,
Only slightly,
A quick practice strum
Eyes turn on him.
The man starts to play a tune.
The man starts to sing a tune.
"Twinkle, twinkle, little star
How I wonder what you are
Up above the world so high…"
A whisper
Grows into a chorus,
As fellow passengers join in,
Singing,
"Like a diamond in the sky
Twinkle, twinkle, little star
How I wonder what you are."
Soon enough,
The whole lounge,
It seems,
Is singing.
Loud applause,
Loud cheers
Greet the end of the song,
But,
The man wearing the Panama hat is not finished.
The man wearing the Panama hat sings another tune
And another.
All the time
Accompanied by his fellow passengers.

The long wait,
Quickly forgotten.

51

Shift over.
Long day.
Feet throbbing
From wearing high heels
All day.
Back sore
From standing
For hours
On end.
Face aching
From smiling
To all those passengers
Waiting for their flights.
All looking forward
To going home.
Her turn now
To go home.
Home,
To have a soak in the bath,
To put her feet up,
To have a nice meal.
But first,
She has to navigate
Through the crowds
In the airport.
Easier said than done.
Passes through
Departure lounge
After departure lounge.

Weaves in and out
Of passengers,
Of luggage,
Of rows of seats.
Approaches the transit zone.
Hears music.
Hears singing.
Not blasting out from a speaker.
But live music.
Buskers?
Can't be.
Concert?
Would have been informed.
Would have seen the memo.
Singing grows louder
And louder.
Must be coming from the transit zone.
Voices,
Lots of them,
And a guitar,
Or a banjo,
Or a ukulele.
Singing stops.
Music stops.
Loud applause.
She turns into the lounge.
A man wearing a Panama hat
Holding a ukulele.
Passengers surrounding him,
Shouting out requests.
A request granted.
Man with the ukulele
Strums a new tune.
One she doesn't recognise,
At first.
But the passengers do,

Clearly,
As they join in the singing.
The airline worker stands
At the entrance,
And watches.
Until she too
Finds herself
Singing.

52

One month.
Only been one month
Since she saw her sweetheart.
One month
Too long.
One week
Would have been too long.
One day
Would have been too long.
All she wants
Is to be with her sweetheart.
Not long now.
Her luggage,
That's all that keeps her away
From her sweetheart.
Woman waits by the carousel,
Holding a book in her hand.
Finished it on the flight.
A good read,
A really good read,
Made the long flight
Fly by.
Woman waits for the merry go round to start.
Spots the opening,
Where the bags will appear,
First.
Positions herself,
Strategically.
Ready to pounce,

As soon as she sees her case.
Not alone.
Not anymore.
Other passengers hover,
All have the same idea
No doubt.
Beep-beep-beep-beep.
A warning light flashes,
Above the opening.
The carousel begins to move,
Slowly.
Everyone waits,
In anticipation,
Willing their bag to be the first.
But it's a phoney war,
For now.
No bag,
No case,
Nothing in sight,
Not yet.
Until finally,
A winner emerges.
A blue suitcase
Plops down
Onto the belt.
A man in a suit
Scoops it up,
With ease.
Lucky man.
He's on his way
To his loved one,
Thinks the woman
To herself.
A black case,
Comes second.
Looks like hers.

Could be hers.

Checks the label.

It is hers!

Picks it up

With two hands.

Grabs a trolley

With two hands.

Sights the exit.

Skips through customs.

Glides through the sliding doors.

Scans the crowd

Of hopeful faces.

There he is.

Abandons the trolley.

Ducks under the barrier.

Jumps into his arms.

Squeezes him tight,

Decides she is never going to let him go again,

Ever.

"Excuse me. Sorry to disturb you."

Reluctantly,

The woman lifts her head

And opens her eyes.

An airline worker.

"So sorry. But I happened to be passing by and I saw your beautiful embrace. I thought you need to see it for yourselves. So I took a picture with my phone. Would you like to see it?"

"Oh yes please," says the woman in an English accent.

"Yes, we'd love to," says her sweetheart.

"Here you go."

"Oh, that is lovely. Thank you so much. Would you be able to send it to me?"

"Yes, of course," replies the airline worker.

Numbers exchanged.

Picture forwarded.

Airline worker leaves

The lovebirds to it,

Humming a song,
A song she was singing
Just moments before
In the transit zone,
Along with a room full
Of waiting passengers.

53

Not looking forward to the flight.
18 hours
On a plane
To Sydney,
Australia.
Other side of the world,
Almost.
Needs a good book,
Been struggling with the same tome
For a month now.
Hard to read.
Finds it boring.
Sends her to sleep.
Needs another.
The bookstore
At the airport.
That's the answer.
Get a good book,
A page turner.
One that can't be put down.
That's how to make the 18-hour flight
From Abu Dhabi
To Sydney
Fly by.
Arrives at the airport.
Navigates the revolving doors
At the entrance.
Stops.
Suitcase

By her side,
She looks for a sign
To the bookstore.
There has to be a bookstore.
There is always a bookstore.
No sign of a bookstore.
What if there is no bookstore?
Standing
At the airport entrance
She places one hand on her right hip,
While the other runs through her short black hair.
"Are you lost?"
A woman with an English accent,
Clutching a tall man's arm
With both her hands.
While he holds a black suitcase.
"Er no. Sorry. Just trying to find a bookstore," she replies.
"Oh, I think there is one through passport control."
"Ah, thank you."
"But please would you take this? I just finished it on my flight. It is a real page-turner."
The woman,
Holding the man
With one arm now,
Retrieves a book
From her bag.
Hands over the book
To the woman with short black hair.
Reads the back,
"It sounds like a great read," she says, "here, let me give you some money for it."
"No need. Just give it to someone else in need of a good book when you are done with it."
"Well, that is so very thoughtful of you. Thank you very much!" says the woman with short black hair.

54

Plane boarded.
Easy part done.
Worst part
Yet to come
For the middle-aged man
In beige trousers
And green shirt.
Taking off.
Flying for 18 hours.
And then the landing,
The dreaded landing,
Will all be much harder,
Will all be a much higher level
Of stress,
Of fear,
Of anxiety.
Always hated flying
Ever since he can remember.
Not natural
To fly
Among the clouds.
Unless you are a bird.
No choice,
If he wants to get home
To Sydney,
Australia.
The alternative
By sea
And by land

Would take an age.
No choice
But to fly.
Never wanted to go on the trip
In the first place.
No choice.
Business.
Never again!
Until
The next time
He is told to
By his bosses.
Seat located,
By the window
This time.
Tried the aisle
On the way out.
Buffeted constantly
By people walking by.
Hopes he will be left alone
By the window.
Plans to shut his eyes
And sleep
For the entire trip,
All 18 hours of it.
Young woman with short black hair
In the seat next to his,
Reading a book.
She looks engrossed.
She looks up.
She stands up
To let the man through,
While still reading her book.
He thanks her.
He sits next to her.
He fastens his seatbelt.

He shuts his eyes.
He tries to go
To his special place.
But he can't.
The engines start revving.
The captain starts speaking.
The cabin crew start demonstrating
The procedures to follow
In case of an emergency.
The last thing
He wants to hear.
The plane taxis
Towards the runway.
Patches of sweat form,
Beads of moisture form
On his brow,
On his back,
On his palms.
Grips armrests
With his fingers,
Tightly.
Whole face crumples
Into one big deep frown.
Wants to scream.
"Stop!"
But can't.
Can't speak.
"Would you like to hold my hand?" asks the young woman with short black hair
in the seat next to his.
He opens his eyes.
Turns towards her.
Still no words.
"It's alright," says the woman.
She takes his hand in hers.

He grips her hand
Tight.
The plane takes off.

55

A whole day,
Travelling
From Athens to Sydney,
And still they wait
To see their son
And his family.
Two grandparents
Standing outside Sydney International Airport
In a queue,
A long queue,
Waiting for a taxi.
Lots of taxis.
Lots more people
Than taxis,
Unfortunately.
Seems like all are ahead
Of the couple from Greece.
Should have taken up the offer
From their son
To pick them up.
But they did not want to bother him.
He is a busy man.
He insisted.
They insisted more.
They won.
To the victor the spoils do not go.
Regret.
Want to see their son.
Want to take their shoes off.

Want to have a relaxing shower.

Eight away from the front now.

They spot a man

On his own

At the head of the queue.

How they wish they could be in his shoes.

A taxi pulls up.

The driver gets out,

Talks to the man.

The man turns around.

Looks along the queue.

Points to the couple from Greece.

Walks over.

"Excuse me. But would you like to take my place in the queue? It's been a terribly long wait, hasn't it?" says the man in an Australian accent.

"Thank you for the kind offer. But it's alright, we're happy to wait," lies the woman in a strong Greek accent.

"I insist. I'll swap places with you so that no one loses out."

"Except for you," says the man from Greece.

"It's okay. I'm just happy to have my feet back on terra firma. I hate flying, you see, and I've been stuck on a plane for 18 hours!"

"How did you manage for so long?" asks the grandmother.

"A kind stranger sitting next to me held my hand for take-off and landing. That's how. So please take my place. If I can survive that long a flight, I can manage waiting a little longer for a taxi."

"Well, we would love to get to our son's house," says the grandfather. "Thank you very much."

He shakes the hand

Of the middle-aged man

Wearing beige trousers

And a green shirt,

Before following his wife

Into the taxi.

56

Traffic bad.
Always is.
Too many cars
These days.
He can't talk.
After all,
He drives all day,
Every day,
For a living
As a taxi driver.
At least he keeps other cars off the road
By ferrying people
All over the city.
Nice people,
Generally.
Like the couple in the back.
Just flown in from Greece
To visit their son
And his family.
"How long are you here for?" asks the taxi driver.
"We're staying for two months," replies the man.
"We haven't seen our son's family for almost two years," adds his wife.
"And we've never even seen his youngest child," says her husband.
"Must be tough not seeing your son much."
Half asking a question,
Half thinking out loud.
Everything,
That is what his son is to him.
Maybe only 11 years old

But already his best friend.

Taking him to watch a rugby match tomorrow,

New South Wales Waratahs

Versus the British Lions.

Should be a great match.

"Do you have children?" asks the wife.

"Yes, I do. A son."

"Oh lovely. How old is he?"

"11 years old."

"Beautiful age," says her husband.

"What is his name?" asks the woman.

"Theo, short for Theodore."

"Beautiful name," says the woman.

"Greek origins. Is your family from Greece?" asks the man.

"No, afraid not, we just like the name," says the taxi driver.

"Means gift from God," adds the wife.

"That he is. Great kid. We're off to a big rugby match tomorrow. First time I am taking him."

"Does he like rugby?" asks the man.

"Yes, plays in his school team. But I have never had the chance to take him to a big game."

"Is rugby popular in Australia?" asks the man.

"Massive," answers the taxi driver.

"It's not played much in Greece. We love our football," adds the man.

"You don't know what you are missing out on. What number did you say is your son's house?" asks the taxi driver.

"119, why, is this his street?" asks the woman,

Excitedly.

"Yes, it is. And this is his house," says the taxi driver.

The taxi pulls up

In front of a two-storey

Red brick house

But before the car comes

To a standstill,

The front door

Of number 119

Swings open,
Wildly.
Out runs a man with dark hair
And a dark beard.
Heads straight for the taxi.
Opens the back door.
"Mama! Papa!" he yells.
Helps his parents
Out of the car,
One by one.
Hugs them both
At the same time.
Tears all around.
The father,
The mother,
The son,
Even the taxi driver
Has something
In his eye.
Leaves them to it.
Retrieves the luggage
From the boot
Of his car.
Carries the bags
To the front door
Of the house.
"Thank you so much. How much do we owe you?" asks the older man.
"30 dollars," answers the taxi driver.
"Here's 50. Keep the change."
"That's way too generous," says the shocked taxi driver.
"Take it please and buy your son a souvenir at the game tomorrow."
"That is so generous of you. Thanks very much."

57

Played three.
Won three.
Can they make it
Four out of four?
The British Lions
Need to keep winning.
Need to keep the momentum going.
Tougher challenges lie ahead.
Three tests against the Australians
Loom large.
Always hard
Against Australia.
Two friends
From Wales
Travelling around Australia
In a light blue camper van,
Following their heroes,
The British Lions,
On tour.
Friends
On tour
For the third time.
Four years ago
It was South Africa.
Four years earlier
It was New Zealand.
Now Australia.
Completes the set
For the two friends,

Former teammates
At their local rugby club
Back in Wales.
Friends
Of the road now.
Flew into Australia
10 days ago.
First thing they did,
Was to pick up the van,
Next thing they did
Was to roar on the Lions
As they beat the Combined Country XV
In Newcastle.
Easy.
Next up.
The New South Wales Waratahs
At the Sydney Football Stadium.
And right on cue,
The cathedral for sport
Comes into view,
Guarded
By its army
Of stewards
Who shepherd the cars
Into free parking spaces,
The few that are left.
Relief all round
As one is found.
Tight squeeze
But van parked.
Match programme bought.
Stadium entered.
The blue of the home team,
Swamped
By a sea of red,
The colours of the British & Irish Lions.

Far more red
Than the blue of the Waratahs
Agree the two friends.
Seats found.
Decent view.
Next to a father and son,
Presumably.
Both wearing Australia shirts,
Fresh out of the packet,
It seems.
Atmosphere building.
"Great stadium," says one of the Welshmen to the man with the boy.
"Yes, it is."
And they're off.
The three men and the boy
Share their love of rugby.
This match.
That match.
This player.
That player.
Did you see this game?
Do you remember that try?
Who's going to win?
Why are they not going to win?
Before they know it,
The two teams appear.
Kick off.
Half time.
Final whistle.
New South Wales Waratahs 17
British Lions 47.
Four out of four.
"Where are you staying tonight?" asks the boy, as the four make their way out
of the stadium,
Slowly.

"We don't know yet. We'll try and find somewhere quiet and park for the night. Then head up north to Brisbane for the first test against Australia next week," answers one of the two Welshmen.

"Would you like to have a look at our van?" asks the other.

Back at the van,

The boy clambers

Into the driver's seat.

"If you guys fancy a bed and a warm shower, you're both welcome to stay at ours for the night," offers his father.

The Welshmen look at each other.

No words needed.

Each knows

What the other is thinking.

"That would be amazing. But only if we won't be any bother."

"Of course not. Anyway, we've got lots more rugby to talk about. We'll go and get our car and you can then follow us."

58

12kms covered
In three hours.
156 hours.
Or six and a half days.
That's how long
It will take
To get to Byron Bay, New South Wales
From Newcastle,
If he carries on
At this rate.
At least he has made it
Out of Newcastle.
Not very far though,
Only to the spot
On the Pacific Highway
Where he has been standing
Underneath a road sign
For the last two hours
With his rucksack
And board,
His five-foot, six inch
Firewire Dominator.
Best board he has ever had.
Worked nights
To save up for it.
Used his travel money
To help buy it.
Having to hitch lifts
To Byron Bay,

Because of it.
The price
He has to pay
If he wants to make it
To the promised land.
A month
Of waves,
Waves,
And more waves.
All the 16-year-old boy
With sun-bleached hair,
Thinks about is waves,
Big waves,
Small waves.
So much so,
In his sleep,
His arms twitch
As he dreams of paddling out
Into the waves.
Just needs to get there now.
His mum thinks he's going with friends.
A lie.
A white one.
She'd worry
If she knew
He was travelling
On his own.
He'll make new friends
While he is there,
When he is not surfing,
That is.
Just needs to get there.
Needs a lift
For the six- or seven-hour drive.
More cars buzz by.
Still no luck.

Doesn't bother sticking his arm out
Anymore.
Hot and tired,
The schoolboy sits
On his rucksack
And waits.
More cars buzz by.
Still no luck.
Sees a van in the distance
Coming towards him.
A light blue camper van,
A surf mobile
If ever there was one.
Maybe they are surfers
Going to Byron Bay.
That would be too good to be true,
Wouldn't it?
Van slows down.
Van stops by the surfer.
Two men
Sitting in the front.
British Lions rugby team scarves
Hanging on the top
Of the windscreen.
"Need a lift, fella?" asks one of the men.
Sounds Welsh.
Or Scottish.
"Ah ye. That would be great."
"Where are you heading to?" asks the other man.
"Byron Bay."
"That's on our way. We're off to Brisbane for the rugby," says one of the men.
"Jump on board," says the other.
"Great, thanks. The name is Scott, by the way."
"Welcome on board, Scott."

59

Wax.
Forgot the wax.
Too much of a rush
To get into the water
To get some waves.
No one's fault
But her own.
Checked the board
At the beach.
Just a thin layer,
Covering just the critical sections
Of her board
And then,
Only in patches.
Knew it wouldn't be enough.
Too bad.
Took the risk.
Waves
Too good
To miss.
Went into the water.
An hour
In the sea,
That's all it took
For the slipping to begin.
Front foot sliding off,
Again and again,
Causing her to fall off the board
Again and again.

Frustrating,
Would be putting it mildly.
Young woman with short brown hair.
Angry,
Angry with herself,
For not bringing wax.
Rookie error.
Should know better.
Paddles out
To catch another wave.
Gets in position.
Sits on the board.
Waits for a set.
Doesn't have to wait long
For a nice set.
First wave taken
By Robbie,
Of course.
Great surfer,
Robbie
Always in the right spot
At the right time.
Catches wave
After wave.
Catches her eye,
As he zooms past.
"Hey Jules!" he yells.
"Whoo-hoo!" cheers on Jules.
She sights the next wave.
This one
Has her name
Written all over it.
Lies on the board.
Turns towards the beach
And in one,
Fluid,

Effortless,
Motion,
She paddles.
Faster,
Faster,
Faster,
Until the point
When the wave catches her board.
With perfect timing
She snaps up to her feet.
With perfect timing
She catches the wave,
For one brief moment
Until that is
She slips off.
"Arrggghh!" screams Jules.
Wax!
Need wax!
Enough!
Heads back to shore
To see if the good folk
Of Byron Bay
Have any wax
They can spare.
Board under her arm,
Her right arm.
Always the right arm,
No particular reason,
She scans the beach.
Sees a boy
With sun-bleached hair,
Waxing his board.
"Hey there. Any chance I could use your wax?" asks Jules.
"Sure. Help yourself," he replies,
As he tosses the bar over
Towards her.

She catches it with one hand.

"Thanks. You new here?"

"Ye, hitched a ride from Newcastle. Arrived yesterday. Here for a few weeks."

"Well, you've come to the right place for a surf fest. My name is Jules, by the way."

"I'm Scott."

"Nice to meet you, Scott. See you in the water!"

Hands the wax back.

Picks up her board.

Runs back

Into the water

To ride

Waves.

60

Paddle-paddle-paddle.
Feel the wave
Catch the board.
Jump.
Feet on board.
Yes!
Down the face.
Yes!
Turn.
Yes!
Down the line.
Yes!
Feel the power
Of the wave.
No!
What happened to the power?
Wave peels away
To the right.
While both he
And the board
Sink into the water,
Slowly,
Until,
Eventually,
He falls off the board
And into the water,
Again.
Can't get it right.
Catches waves,

Easily enough.

But can't ride them

Long enough.

Not like the good surfers.

They ride waves

All the way to the beach.

He,

On the other hand,

Gets down the face,

And that's all.

Man with blue stripe of sun block plastered over his nose,

Frustrated,

Very frustrated.

Slaps his hand into the water.

"You having trouble?"

Man turns around.

Young woman with short dark hair,

Paddling towards him.

"Just don't know what I am doing wrong. I catch the wave but then I lose power."

"Catching the wave is the hard part. Riding the wave is the easy part," she says.

"Not for me it isn't," says the man.

"Just watch the surfers around you. Here, watch Scott. See how he moves his body while on the wave? He is shifting his body weight. De-weighting himself so that he builds up speed to make it through the section. See how he uses his knees to pump the board. If you want to ride the wave, you've got to work for it. But it's so worth it, so you mustn't give up," she says.

"I think I get it. Thanks very much for the tip. And for taking the time to explain it to me."

"Any time. My name is Jules."

"Thanks Jules. My name is Johnno."

But Jules is off

To catch another wave.

Johnno follows her

To the line-up.

Waits his turn.

Spots a wave.

Turns around.
Paddle-paddle-paddle.
Feel the wave
Catch the board.
Jump.
Feet on board.
Yes!
Down the face.
Yes!
Turn.
Yes!
Down the line.
Yes!
Feel the power
Of the wave.
Yes!
Oh yes!
Legs bending at the knees one moment,
Legs extending at the knees the next
To a rhythm,
A rhythm he has never felt before
But one that feels so natural now.
Faster and faster.
He feels the energy of the wave
Coursing through his legs
Up into his body,
Up into his mind.
A feeling of pure exhilaration.
A wall of water lines up
Ahead of him.
Somehow he knows
What he has to do.
Or maybe
It is the board that knows
What it has to do.
Right-hand rail of the board

Slots into the wall of water,
As he speeds along the wave,
The longest,
The best,
The most thrilling wave
He has ever caught.
Rides it into shallow water,
Until he finally jumps off into the water,
Knee deep water.
What a ride.
Gathers his board.
Lies on it.
Paddles back
For more.
A good day.
Even the dolphins are out.
Surfing the waves out back.

61

Last day
At Byron Bay.
Came for a week.
Stayed a month.
Trip of a lifetime.
All the sacrifices
Finally paying off
For the middle-aged woman
From Geneva, Switzerland.
Struck a bargain
With herself
Years ago.
Work hard
For 20 years.
Make a fortune.
Retire young
And travel.
Paid off.
First up Australia.
Started in Sydney,
Blue Mountains,
Opera House,
The Harbour Bridge,
Melbourne,
Canberra,
Cuddling a koala,
Jet skiing,
Kayaking,
All ticked off.

And now surfing.
Or body boarding
To be precise
At Byron Bay.
Never tried it before.
Bought a board
And a pair of fins.
Hooked
As soon as she hit the water.
A rush
Words can't describe.
A drug,
A healthy drug.
Needs waves,
Waves,
And more waves.
Lies on her board
In the water.
Fins on her feet,
Waiting for the next set to come.
Just had a long ride,
Easily her longest ever,
All thanks to a surfer
With a thick blue stripe of sun block across his face.
Gave up a wave
So that she could ride it.
Would love to thank him
For being so generous,
If she sees him again.
Surfing conquered,
Now she looks ahead
To the next leg
Of her adventure.
Cairns.
The rainforests,
The Great Barrier Reef.

One last surf,
For now,
At least.
Knows it won't be long
Before she is back
Among the waves.
A splash,
Close by.
She turns.
Nothing.
She feels something.
An energy
Of some kind.
A fin
Breaks out of the water.
So close to her
She could touch it,
If she wanted to.
Her heartbeat quickens.
Concern.
A shark?
Relief.
A dolphin
Circles her,
Dives underneath
Her board.
Surfaces next to
Her board.
Rolls
Onto its back
And smiles.
At least she thinks it is a smile.
At least she is smiling.

62

A young man
Standing on the street,
Armed
With a guitar,
An acoustic guitar,
Hanging from his shoulder.
Case wide open
On the ground.
A miscellany
Of coins and notes
Scattered inside,
Randomly.
A collection
Of CDs
Stacked,
Neatly,
Next to a sign,
"CDs for sale.
Jake Simmons: Moments with a guitar."
Three hours,
Since he started playing.
Four CDs sold.
Plus the generous handful of notes
And smattering of coins
Tossed into the open guitar case,
A$40?
Maybe A$50?
At a push.
Hard to tell.

All gratefully received though.
Three or four more CDs
Should do it.
Would have enough then
To book
A week long liveaboard cruise
On the Great Barrier Reef,
An all-in scuba diving trip.
Four or five dives a day.
Heaven.
Arrived at Cairns
Three weeks ago.
Busking on the streets
Ever since
To earn enough
To go to the Coral Sea.
Finishes playing
Rodriguez's Guitar Concerto.
Opens his eyes.
A middle-aged woman approaches him.
"Hullo," she says.
An accent.
German?
"Gdday," says Jake.
"What an amazing sound," says the woman.
"Thank you."
"Are you classically trained?"
"Yes, I am. Went to music college in Melbourne. Came up here to feed my other passion. Scuba diving. Busking to book myself a trip on a liveaboard boat to the Coral Sea."
"Me too. Although I cannot call it a passion yet as I have never done it before. I'm booked on a taster dive tomorrow to see if I like it."
"You will. It's the most fantastic experience. Where are you from?"
"Switzerland."
"You been travelling a while?" asks Jake.

"Yes, a few months now. Trip of a lifetime. So how much do you still need to go on your boat trip."

"Another 40 bucks."

"Well, I'll take four CDs then. That's 40 bucks, right?"

"It is but I can't take that."

"Why not? Your music is beautiful and I want to give your CDs to some friends of mine. Now take the money and have a great trip."

63

"Gdday. Let me give you a hand with your bags."
An American woman,
Tightly braided blonde hair,
Turns towards the voice.
Sees a tall man
With deeply weathered skin,
Wearing a pair of green shorts,
A pair of sunglasses,
Attached to a black string around his neck,
And a faded blue sailor's cap,
Too small
To keep a sprawling mass of sun-kissed brown hair
Completely under wraps.
Standing on the deck of the boat,
One arm stretched out
In readiness
To receive the bags,
The man waits
For the woman
To hand over her kit.
After a pause
The woman hands over
A big blue bag,
The one packed with her diving gear.
She steps on to the boat,
Home for the next week.
"Welcome aboard. My name's Rod. I'm your guide for the week."
"Hello. My name is Stacey," says the woman.

"Nice to meet you, Stacey. This is Carlos. He will show you to your cabin. We'll set sail shortly. Travel all night. Dive first thing in the morning. We'll be serving grub in an hour on the main deck."

"Thank you," replies Stacey.

Feels very shy,

As she knew she would.

Was a battle of wills

To go on the trip.

Her love

For diving

Versus

Her yearning

To be alone.

Diving won.

But only just.

Follows Carlos

To her cabin.

Thanks him.

Closes the door.

Lies on her bed.

"What has she done?" she asks herself.

She can't survive on a boat

With 12 strangers

For a whole week.

No chance.

Best get off

While she still has

A chance.

Engine stirs.

Shouts heard

From the deck above.

Boat moves off.

Too late,

Now.

Plan B

Stay in her cabin

For as long as she can
That way she will be left alone,
Until it's time
For dinner.
Until it's time
To meet the other guests and crew.
Until it's time
For her idea of hell.
Before she knows it,
It is time.
Reluctantly,
She clambers onto the main deck.
Noise.
Lots of noise,
Lots of laughter,
Lots of chit chat,
Lots of people standing,
Lots of people sitting.
Couples,
Singles,
All ages,
From twenty somethings
All the way up
To seventy somethings.
Spots a buffet
Spread out
On a number of tables.
Grabs a plate
Of salad.
Sits down
In a corner
And eats,
Alone.
Rod appears on deck,

"Now that I have you all here, I thought it would be a good idea if we all introduced ourselves to each other. After all, we are going to be living on top of each other for the next seven days."

Laughter,

From a couple sitting opposite Stacey.

"I'll start things off. I'm Rod, your guide," declares Rod then turns to his right.

One by one,

Everyone stands up.

One by one,

Everyone says their name.

A tight knot forms

In the pit of Stacey's stomach,

As her turn approaches.

"My name is Jake Simmons. I'm from Melbourne," reveals the young man sitting next to her with a guitar by his side.

Finally,

It is her turn.

No escaping now.

Stands up from her seat.

"My name is Stacey Shapiro. I'm from New York."

Sits down

Straight away.

Resumes eating

Straight away,

Despite not being hungry.

Rod resumes speaking.

Talks about the trip.

The spots they will be visiting,

Boat admin,

The schedule,

The itinerary,

The safety procedures.

Stacey listens,

But all the time

She wonders

How she can get back

To her cabin,
As quickly as possible
So that she can be alone.
Just wants to be alone.
Rod finishes.
Stacey stands up
To leave.
A couple
From Germany,
Jan and Jana,
She remembers their names,
How could she not?
Jan and Jana!
Small talk.
Can't escape.
Fake yawn.
Hint not taken.
Desperate
To find a way out
Of the conversation,
Not to be
Rude,
But to be
Left alone.
More and more desperate
But Jan and Jana
In full flow,
No stopping them.
Then music.
Beautiful music.
Guitar.
Jan and Jana stop.
Relief.
All three turn around.
It's Jake Simmons
Playing

A fast, classical piece.
He catches Stacey's eye.
He smiles.
She smiles.
Stacey mouths,
"Thank you."
Stacey escapes.

64

First dive
On the Great Barrier Reef.
The pinnacle for every diver,
Or at least for him.
Will be remembered for what?
Breath-taking coral
Weaved into mesmerising patterns
By the hand of mother nature?
No.
Fish
Of all shapes,
Of all sizes,
Of all colours?
No.
The blue,
Like no other blue
He has ever seen before,
Even in the waters off his beloved Italy?
No.
None of the above.
A leaky mask.
His overriding memory
Of his first dive
On the Great Barrier Reef,
A leaky mask.
Not a small leak,
He could cope with a small leak.
A flood.
A torrent.

Having to clear his mask.
Every few seconds.
And when he is not clearing his mask,
It is filling up with water.
Fast.
15 minutes underwater
And clearing his mask
Is all he has done.
The beautiful fish,
The beautiful coral,
The beautiful water.
All passing him by,
As he struggles
With his mask
And his stinging eyes.
A tap
On his shoulder.
He turns.
He squints.
Stacey,
The American with tightly braided blonde hair.
She points to her eyes
Then she points at him.
Lost in translation,
He shrugs his shoulders.
Stacey opens the left side pocket
Of her jacket.
Pulls out a mask,
A spare mask.
Brilliant woman,
Thinks Giovanni.
What a brilliant woman
To dive with a spare mask.
Takes the mask off her.
Adjusts the straps.
Removes the leaky mask.

Replaces it with her spare one.
Clears the water
And sees,
The unique underwater world
Of the Great Barrier Reef
Clearly,
And uninterrupted,
For the first time.

65

All back on deck
After the dive,
All safe and sound
After the dive,
The second of the day.
Completed without incident.
The way he likes it,
Muses Carlos,
The divemaster,
Assistant to Rod.
Equipment stowed away.
Tanks refilled.
Boat on the move
To the next spot
For the afternoon dive,
And the night dive,
For those game enough.
Quick mop of the deck.
A bite to eat.
A refreshing drink,
Or two,
Before settling down
In a quiet corner
Of the boat
With his sketch book
And pencils
To draw
What he saw
During the dive.

Always draws

What he sees

During a dive

In his book,

His chronicle,

Of fish,

Of coral,

Of seascapes,

But never people.

"Mamma mia. That looks great. You've captured everything so perfectly."

Carlos looks up.

Giovanni, the Italian, looking down.

"Thank you," says Carlos.

"You have a real talent there."

"Oh, they are just scribbles really."

"Trust me, I am Italian. From the land that gave the world Leonardo, Michelangelo, Raphael. So I know what I am talking about."

"I would love to go to Italy one day and see their work for myself," admits Carlos.

"And you should, Carlos. If ever you are in Italy. Be sure to look me up. My wife and I have a flat in Rome and a spare room. You could base yourself there."

"What an offer. Thank you, Mr Bianchi."

"Well, I mean it, Carlos. You have been so kind looking after us today, it's the least I can do. What's more, you do have a great talent and you should take yourself more seriously."

"I will, Mr Bianchi. I promise. Thank you again. My dream is to become an artist one day."

"You are an artist already, Carlos. Believe."

66

Night dives.
Never been brave enough
To do one before.
Scared of the dark
On land,
Let alone
Deep underwater.
And yet,
Intrigued.
Plenty more life
Out at night
Underwater.
Or so he has been told
By Rod the guide,
By Carlos his assistant,
By practically all the other divers
On the boat,
All more seasoned than he.
No pressure to dive
From Rod,
Or from anyone else.
Minded to sit this one out.
No one would mind.
Still,
Fear of missing out
On a once in a lifetime opportunity
Niggles away at him.
"You okay about the night dive, Mr Johnson?"
It's Carlos.

"Think I will give it a miss, Carlos."

"Have you ever dived at night before, Mr Johnson?"

"No, I'm afraid not. Truth be told. I'm scared of the dark."

"Oh, that is a problem," admits Carlos.

"Half of me says stay on the boat. The other says go on, give it a go," reveals Mr Johnson.

"Well, night dives are spectacular, Mr Johnson. Only difference from diving during the day is that it is dark but you will have a powerful torch with you."

"I know, Carlos, but what if the torch stops working during the dive?"

"Rod and I always carry spares. You will be alright, Mr Johnson."

"But what about all the nasty creatures that come out at night, not to mention sharks?"

"As I said, no different to diving during daylight," Carlos says reassuringly.

"Oh, I don't know, Carlos."

"Tell you what. Why don't you and me dive with a buddy line tied around our wrists. That way, you will never be alone."

"That might work, Carlos. Reckon I could give it a go with a buddy line."

"You won't regret it, Mr Johnson," promises Carlos.

Black,

The blackest black,

Interrupted

Every now and then

By flashes

Of phosphorus

Stirred up by movement

On the surface.

And fish.

Fish everywhere.

Parrot fish,

Barracuda,

Sharks.

So many different types of fish.

They were all right.

Night dives are spectacular.

Mr Johnson surfaces,

Already thinking about,

Already planning for,
The next night dive.

67

Out of the blue,
Like a swarm of locusts,
They came.
No warning.
One minute
Crystal clear
Blue waters.
The next
Fish,
Thousands
And thousands of fish.
So many,
That the blue of the sea
Had no choice
But to give way
To a shimmering wave
Of silver.
All in a single heartbeat.
Rod,
Instinctively,
Freezes.
Motionless,
He hovers
In the water,
As the sardines
Zoom by
In a hurry,
On a mission
To get to where they need to be,

Wherever that is,

As fast as they can.

The guide swivels around.

Sardines

Everywhere.

And yet,

Not one sardine

Touches him.

And yet,

No sooner had they arrived

They are gone.

The blue returns,

As quickly as it had disappeared,

As if it had never gone away

In the first place.

Still,

Rod does not move.

Thousands of dives

He has clocked up

Over the years,

But never before

Has he experienced

Such a marvel

Of nature.

If only he had a picture

To banish the suspicions

That it was all a dream.

He looks around

For his group.

Wonders if any of them

Saw the sardines?

It was all over in a flash,

Could easily have been missed.

"Rod!"

Back on deck, Mr Johnson calls out.

"How was that for you, Mr Johnson? Did you see all those sardines?"

"I certainly did, Rod. And guess what, I think I got a great photo of you right in the thick of it."

"Oh wow, I'd love to see it. I don't think anyone has ever taken a picture of me diving before."

"Well, they have now," says Mr Johnson, as he shows the guide the picture.

"Hey, that's great. So many fish! Would you be able to send it to me? I'd love to have a copy."

"Of course, I will, Rod."

68

Six days.
24 dives in total.
Two night dives.
Every fish
They wanted to see,
They saw.
The Great Barrier Reef
Was everything they thought it would be,
And more.
A couple from Melbourne, Victoria
Looking forward to a week
Of relaxation
In Bali
After a week
Of diving,
Before they head back home
To work.
Sail back to Cairns.
Short flight To Darwin.
Longer flight to Bali.
Seven days of bliss.
But before then
There is still time
For the next instalment
Of their long-running,
Never-ending,
Saga.
How to tilt the work life balance
Heavily in favour

Of life?

Both not happy with the status quo

Back home.

Both not happy with their jobs

In the city.

Both not happy with the hours

They work.

Both not happy with the people

They work with.

Both not happy with their commutes

To work.

Both happiest in the great outdoors,

Especially,

In the water.

But how would they live?

What would they do?

Where would they go?

Always the same questions.

Always left unanswered,

At least up until now.

"Sorry, Mr and Mrs Kelly. I couldn't help but overhear your conversation," reveals Rod, standing tall above them.

"Oh, don't worry, Rod, we are continually going round and round in circles. Did you need us?"

"I just thought I might be able to help you."

"How, by offering us jobs on this lovely boat?" answers Mrs Kelly.

"Who knows? Maybe one day. But do you know what I did for a living before I became a diving instructor and guide?"

"No," answers Mr Kelly. "I assumed you were born and raised by the sea destined for a life on and under the water."

"Far from it. I spent seven years selling houses in Sydney," reveals Rod.

"No! I don't believe it. I never had you down for an estate agent," gasps Mrs Kelly.

"Neither do I when I look at myself now. But I was and I hated it. Never wanted to do it. I fell into the job and couldn't extricate myself out of the rat race."

"So how did you get out?" asks Mr Kelly.

"Took a leap of faith. Was a while before I plucked up the courage. But I quit my job and moved up here. I already had my diving qualifications and loved boats. So I thought Cairns would be the place for me. And I was right."

"Any regrets?" asks Mr Kelly.

"None whatsoever."

"But didn't you worry about money?" Mr Kelly asks,

Sheepishly.

"I did and that did hold me back for a while. Then I told myself to be brave, that I would be okay, that I'd find a job. And I was right."

The Kellys look at each other.

The Kellys look at Rod.

A diving guide

On a boat

In the middle of the Coral Sea

Might just have given them

The nudge

To be brave

That they needed.

69

Weeks,
Months
Of planning,
Of preparation,
Of hard work,
For one big day.
Friends,
Family
All gathered
In the same place
At the same time
For the first time
Either can remember.
All gathered
To celebrate
Their wedding,
The wedding of Mr Paul O'Connor and Miss Trudy Butler.
And,
Just as they had been told,
On countless occasions,
Before they knew it,
It was all over.
Worse still,
There was no chance
To have a proper debrief
About their big day
With their loved ones.
There was no chance
To catch up properly

With their loved ones.
There was no chance
To spend time
With their loved ones.
Next day,
Honeymoon.
Two weeks
On the beautiful island
Of Bali.
Picture book weather,
First class hotel,
Warm and friendly people,
Paradise.
And yet,
Both feel
So very low
After the high
Of the wedding day.
They were warned,
One minute
The centre of attention,
The next,
Just another couple on holiday.
Need to snap out of it.
Fast.
The new Mrs O'Connor,
Sitting down
At a table
In the open air
In the luxury
Of the hotel's renowned brasserie,
Looks around.
Sees a couple arrive
At the table next to hers.
Tanned.
Been here a while,

She presumes.

Avoids eye contact.

Doesn't know why.

Wishes her new husband,

Her husband,

Would return

To the table,

Fast.

"Are you on your own? Would you like to join us?" asks the woman.

"Oh no, thank you though, just waiting for my husband to join me," replies Mrs O'Connor.

"Not to worry. I'm Jean. Jean Kelly. And this is my husband, Gerry."

Gerry waves.

"Nice to meet you. I'm Trudy Butler. Sorry, O'Connor. Keep forgetting. Only got married on Saturday."

"Oh congratulations. You must be on honeymoon then."

"Yes, that's right."

"Is everything okay? You seem a little down for a newlywed. Post wedding blues?"

"I guess that's what you could call it. Both of us are feeling a little low after the big day."

"We felt the same on our honeymoon. Didn't we, Gerry?"

"Yes, we did. A few years ago now," answers Gerry.

"Any tips for snapping out of it?" asks Trudy.

"Just treat it as any other holiday. Do the things you would normally do or would want to do on holiday. Take the pressure off. The rest will follow. We took up scuba diving on our honeymoon. Haven't looked back since. As a matter of fact, we've just come from a week of diving the Great Barrier Reef."

"Scuba diving, hey? Always wanted to try it. Might just do the trick. Thank you very much for the advice," says Mrs O'Connor.

70

Suite 4.
The one the honeymooners,
The O'Connors,
Are in.
No "Do not disturb" sign out.
Taps on the door,
Gently.
Hopes no one answers.
Hopes she can enter the room,
Clean up,
Tidy up,
Change the bed linen,
And make good her escape,
Undetected.
A woman opens the door.
The cleaner tuts,
To herself.
Knew it.
"Clean room please?" asks Tan, the cleaner.
"Oh yes please. Do come in. We've been scuba diving today and I'm afraid the room is in a bit of a mess," replies the guest.
"No problem, Mrs O'Connor," replies Tan.
The cleaner enters the suite.
Hopes the guest will leave
And let Tan clean the room,
In peace.
Woman sits down
On sofa
In the middle of the room.

Knew it.

Not proper

To talk to guests.

They don't like it,

Usually.

Work quickly.

Do not say a word

And soon she will be on her way.

Bathroom first.

Out of sight,

Maybe the woman will leave

By the time she finishes.

Bathroom cleaned.

Back

In the main room.

Woman

On sofa,

Still.

Knew it.

"What a lovely silver necklace you are wearing!" asks Mrs O'Connor.

Have to reply.

Disrespectful not to.

"Thank you, Madam," replies Tan.

"May I ask where you got it from? Is it local?"

"I make it, Madam," replies Tan.

"My word, you have a real talent. Do you make lots of jewellery?"

"Yes, when I can, I do. Usually for my family."

"Well, I think it is wonderful. You should start a business."

"Oh no, you are joking! No one would buy any," replies Tan, a little embarrassed.

Not used

To being the centre of attention.

But enjoying it,

All the same.

"I would buy one. Your necklace is so special."

"Really? I never thought so."

"Really."

"Thank you, Madam. No one ever said that to me before."

"Are you working tomorrow?" asks Mrs O'Connor.

"Yes, Madam."

"Would you bring some of your jewellery with you? I'd love to see more and maybe buy some off you. Provided you are happy to sell?"

"That would be good," replies Tan.

"Great! I can't wait to see more of your work. May I ask your name?"

"Of course. It is Tan."

"Tan. What a beautiful name. I am Trudy. It is lovely to meet you."

"Lovely to meet you too, Madam Trudy. I look forward to seeing you tomorrow."

Smiles at Mrs O'Connor.

Retrieves her trolley.

Leaves the suite,

Still smiling.

71

Still in the room.
Must get out,
Before the cleaner arrives
To avoid having to make embarrassing small talk.
Must meet people.
Must see the sights.
Must go to the beach.
It is Bali,
After all.
Paradise.
For couples maybe.
Not for single women,
Especially,
Shy single women,
Like her.
Jackie Lee.
Flew in from Hong Kong
Two days ago
For a holiday.
Hasn't had a single conversation,
At least no meaningful one
With anyone,
For two days now.
Might as well have stayed at home
And saved her money,
A lot of money.
Her fault,
She knows.
But that is how she is.

Too shy.

Too lonely.

Knock on the door.

The gentlest of taps.

"Clean room please."

Blown it.

Should have left the room earlier,

When she had the chance.

"Thank you," she says, as she opens the door.

"How are you today, Madam?" asks the cleaner.

"Fine, thank you."

"You enjoy Bali?"

"Beautiful island. You are lucky to live here," Jackie replies, forcing herself to speak.

"Oh yes, I know. Where have you visited since you arrive here?" asks the cleaner.

"Actually, I have not done much site-seeing yet," admits Jackie.

"Oh, but you must see more of Bali than this hotel."

"I find it a bit of a challenge to go out on my own sometimes," Jackie reveals, surprised at how honest she is being,

With a stranger.

"I finish work in an hour. I show you around my village and our secret beach if you want?" offers the cleaner.

Unsure.

Moment taken,

And another.

Courage summoned.

Decision taken.

"That would be lovely. But only if you are happy to?"

"Of course, I am. My name is Tan. I will meet you here in an hour, yes?"

"Thank you, yes please."

72

Great concert.
Great performance.
Great singer.
Heart said
Stay until the end.
Head said
Leave early
To beat the crowds.
Everyone will want to get home
From the Hong Kong Coliseum
At the same time.
Decision made.
Leave early,
Better chance
Of hailing a taxi.
Vivian and her boyfriend wanted to stay
To the end.
So Nina left
The lovebirds to it
And left
On her own.
Taxi spotted
In all its red and white glory.
She calls out.
"Taxi!"
Starts to run
Towards the cab.
Not fast enough.
Beaten to it

By a woman
By a matter of yards,
If that.
Woman opens the door
Of the taxi.
Turns around.
Looks at Nina.
"Where are you going?" she asks.
"Hong Kong Island," replies Nina.
"So am I. Would you like to jump in and share the ride?"
"Oh yes please. I left the concert early so that I could beat the rush."
"So did I!" exclaimed the woman, wearing a beautiful silver necklace.
Laughing,
The pair get into the cab.
"What a singer."
"The best."
"My name is Nina, by the way."
"I'm Jackie. Very pleased to meet you."

73

Hot,
Sweaty,
Feet aching,
Back sore.
Small price to pay
The traveller thinks to himself,
After all,
He has journeyed
From the other side of the world.
Enters the Smuggler's Inn
On the south side
Of Hong Kong Island.
Very busy.
Full of customers
All being served
Beer,
Food
And more beer
By an army of staff.
Wonders how he will find her
In this crowd?
All he was told
Was that she works
In the Smugglers Inn,
The famous pub
Where people
Come from all over the world
To see for themselves
The wooden beams

And the wooden stools
And the wooden tables
Made from ancient barrels.
A taste of olde England
On the other side of the world
In Hong Kong.
"Excuse me. I am looking for a Ms Nina Chan?"
The man asks a young woman.
Nina looks up.
A young man with red hair and lots of freckles,
Standing on the other side of the bar.
"I am Nina. Can I help?"
"Oh hi, Nina. My name is Mark," reveals the man in an English accent.
"Hello Mark," replies Nina.
"I am a friend of Sarah Powers, and she said I should look you up. I have just flown in from London. Hoping to spend a bit of time here and Sarah said you might have a spare bed for me for a night or two."
"How is Sarah? I haven't spoken to her for ages. We shared an apartment together for a year while she was living in Hong Kong," says Nina.
"She's great. Enjoying London. I think she has finally settled down."
"Be good to catch up with her soon. Been way too long. Listen, I have to finish my shift. More than happy to put you up for a few nights until you find your feet."
"That would be amazing. Thank you so much."
"Can I get you a drink while you wait for my shift to end? Fancy a beer on the house?"
"That would be great," says Mark,
Relieved
And thankful
For the good reception
And the warm welcome.

74

10am,
Only,
But
Three hours
Already
Clocked up
In front of the computer,
On top of his desk,
One of the many desks
In the open plan office,
In one of the many
High rise buildings
In Central, Hong Kong.
Just popped out for a coffee,
But,
Must be quick,
Has a few minutes,
Only
Before he needs to be back
In front of his screen
Reconciling trades
And transfers.
Fresh air.
Breathes it in,
Slowly.
Not so fresh air.
Too many cars.
Crosses the road
To the kiosk,

The one that brews
His favourite coffee,
Just the way he likes it.
Small queue.
Should be ok.
Moving fast.
Makes it to the front,
In double quick time.
"Cinnamon Dolce Latte please," asks the man, called Sam.
"Coming up," replies the barista.
He wonders
At the alchemy,
Performed
Before his very eyes
On this dreary morning
On this dreary street
In Central, Hong Kong.
Cinnamon Dolce Latte presented,
A work of art,
He thinks
To himself.
Hands over cash,
The exact amount.
Picks up
The cup
Full of the barista's magic.
Makes space
For a young man
With a shock of red hair
And freckles on his face
So that he can place his order
With the barista.
Moves to
The side
To get a stirrer
And a cardboard cup holder.

All in order,
Time
To head back
To the office.
No time
To waste.
Hurries off.
But oh no!
Shoe catches an edge
On the pavement.
Sam lurches forward.
The cinnamon dolce latte lurches forward.
Both land
On the pavement.
Angry,
Not about falling,
But about losing his coffee.
No time
To queue up
And get another.
Gets up.
Brushes himself down.
Picks up
The now empty cup.
Shoves it
Into a bin.
Shoves hands
Into his trouser pockets.
Trudges off
To his office.
Red light
At the crossing.
Has to wait
To cross the road.
More bad luck.
Going to be one of those days.

A nudge

On his arm.

"Hello there. I saw you had a little accident and thought you could do with one of these."

Sam turns around.

The young man with the red hair and freckles,

Holding two cups of coffee.

"The barista said you had ordered a cinnamon dolce latte. So I bought you another."

"Wow, that is so kind of you. I'm speechless. Here, let me pay you for it," says a very grateful Sam.

"No need for money," replies the young man with red hair and freckles.

"Thank you so much," says Sam.

"No problem. Enjoy."

75

Tired.
Why?
Long week.
That's why.
Looking forward to the weekend.
One more day to go.
One more day to get through.
Then a well-deserved lie-in.
No having to commute.
No having to be at her desk,
By eight in the morning.
Like she does
Monday to Friday.
No having to be anywhere.
Can stay in bed,
All day,
If she wants to.
But she won't.
Would be a waste
Of a day
Off work.
A well-deserved day
Off work.
Can't wait
To get off the subway.
Too hot,
Too stuffy.
Wall Street.
Her stop.

Finally.

Get the day over and done with.

Then enjoy the weekend.

Off the train,

Through the turnstiles,

Up the staircase,

Into the land

Of the living,

Or the corner

Of William Street and Wall Street

To be precise.

Wrong exit.

Got caught up with the flow.

Got caught up in her thoughts.

Turns down Wall Street

Towards number 60.

Into the atrium,

Into the lift,

Up to her floor,

Quickly,

Terrifyingly quickly.

Before she knows it,

She is back

At her desk.

Screen on.

Username:

Jodie Sharpe.

Password:

****

Logged in

With a minute to spare.

Phew.

Checks her emails

33 arrived overnight.

Looks like a busy end to the week.

Disappointed.

Was hoping for a quiet end to the week.

Suddenly,

She finds herself smiling.

An email,

From Sam

In the Hong Kong office.

She clicks it open.

"Been a long week. Thought you could do with a joke from the other side of the world to get you through the day."

Scrolls down.

To the joke.

"What do you call a man floating in the water?"

Scrolls down

To the punchline.

"Bob! Have a great weekend, Jodie. It'll be the weekend for me when you read this. Don't worry; you'll have your revenge on Sunday evening when I am back at my desk."

Jodie smiles.

Maybe today won't be so bad,

After all.

76

"Evening Frank."
That's three 'evenings',
This evening.
"Evening sir," replies Frank.
A handful of evenings.
That's all he's come to expect.
No time.
No one has any time,
These days,
To stop
And chat
To Frank,
The security guard,
While he is on duty,
In his navy-blue uniform
And his wide-brimmed blue security guard cap
In the atrium
Of number 60 Wall Street.
"Evening Frank."
Four.
"Evening madam," replies Frank.
Alright for them.
They are off home
To start their weekends.
He has to stay
For a few hours more
Until his shift ends.
No records going to be broken tonight.
Only four evenings.

Only stragglers left.

"Hi there, Frank."

The guard,

Thrown

Off balance,

Swivels

To his right.

"Hello, Ms Sharpe."

"Got any nice plans for the weekend, Frank?"

"Quiet one, Ms Sharpe. Taking junior to Little League tomorrow. That's about it, I think. Though the Mrs might have other ideas. What about you?"

"Oh, nothing planned. Going to take it nice and easy this weekend. Not going to think of work."

"That's the way it should be, Miss. Leave work behind in the office."

"Absolutely, Frank. How long have you got till your shift ends tonight?"

"Just a couple more hours."

"Weekend will be here before you know it. And when are you back on?"

"Not till Monday, Ms Sharpe."

"Well, you have a relaxing one."

"I will. And same goes for you, Ms Sharpe."

"Thank you, Frank. Have a good evening and see you on Monday."

"Good evening, Ms Sharpe," replies Frank with a big beaming smile on his face,

And perhaps,

Standing just that little bit easier.

77

No need to rush,
For a change.
No deadline to meet,
For a change.
No one waiting,
At the other end
For a change
For the man
In the blue suit and red tie.
Not like the early morning panic
To get to the office in time
To avoid the walk of shame,
That is
Passing the rows and rows
Of desks,
Manned
By those colleagues
Who made it in
On time.
Nine hours later,
He is going home
For a quiet evening,
After a hard day's work.
Enters the subway station,
Down the staircase,
Through the turnstile.
Taking it easy,
He walks towards the platform.
Hears a train approaching.

His pace quickens.
He does not know why.
Instinct?
He can always wait
For the next train.
But,
For a reason he cannot fathom,
The urge to catch this train
Builds inside of him.
Sees people walking
In the opposite direction,
Passengers who disembarked,
He presumes.
Means the train will be leaving soon,
He presumes.
He starts to run,
Towards the platform.
Train lies in wait
On the platform.
His train,
The one he needs
To get home.
Appears everyone is on board.
Appears the train is set to depart.
The train doors start to close.
It dawns on the man,
He is not going to make it.
Disappointment
Envelops him,
Even though
He is in no rush,
Even though
He has no appointment to keep to,
Even though
He has no one to meet.
"So why disappointed?" he asks himself.

"Hey buddy. Do you want to hop on?"
The man looks up.
Sees a security guard
Wearing a navy-blue uniform
And a wide-brimmed blue security guard cap
Holding the double doors open
With both his arms.
The man hops on.
The security guard lets go of the doors.
The doors slam shut.
The train departs.
"Thank you," says the man in the blue suit and the red tie.
"No problem. Saw you were in a rush," says the security guard.
"Yeah, thanks, I was," replies the man.
Feeling slightly embarrassed,
But grateful all the same.
He made the train,
The one he didn't need.

78

Young woman,
Red beret
Fixed at a slight angle
On her head,
Green blouse
Loose fit
With wide yellow sleeves,
Blue skirt
Billowing,
Ankle-length,
Earrings,
Large gold circles
Dangling from her ears,
Case
Upright
By her side.
Humming
To herself,
Quietly,
The young woman waits
On the platform
Of the New York subway
For the next red line train.
Let the last train go,
Too packed.
Never mind,
There's always the next one.
Before she knows it,
The next one

Enters the station.

Slows down.

Grinds to a halt.

Front carriage doors open,

The young woman clambers on board,

Dragging her case behind.

No free seats.

Never mind,

There's always the chance one will become free.

Carries on humming,

Quietly,

To herself.

"Excuse me, Miss."

She turns.

Man with a blue suit and a red tie

Stands up

From a seat.

"Would you like to sit down?"

"Oh, I will be okay. But thank you for being so chivalrous."

"No, please go ahead."

"How thoughtful of you. Thank you."

Sits down.

Carries on humming.

79

Man stands on a subway train.
New York Yankees baseball cap
On his head.
White t-shirt
With 'Pizza My Heart'
Emblazoned on the front
In faded red letters.
Dark blue shorts
Knee-length
With a white stripe
Running down each side.
Black trainers,
Well worn,
Laced up
With a double knot.
Small dark green rucksack
Cradled
Between his legs
On the floor.
Gym should start to empty soon,
He thinks to himself,
As the usual scramble
To get a workout
Under the belt
Before the weekend
Eases off.
Go to the gym,
Workout,
Collect weekend long licence

To indulge.
Standard procedure
For a Friday night
For many.
Not for him.
Two-hour workout
For him
Tonight,
At least two hours,
Maybe more.
Same again on Sunday.
After a swim on Saturday,
If he gets the chance.
Important part of his life,
Exercise.
Always has been,
Always will be.
Clears his mind
From the stress of work,
From the stress of life.
Train arrives
At his stop.
Grabs rucksack
From between his legs.
Steps off train.
Heads for the exit.
Slings one strap
Over his left shoulder,
Without breaking his stride.
Reaches back for the right strap.
Can't find it.
Arm in awkward position.
Where is the strap?
Can't have just disappeared.
Frustration
Builds,

More and more.

"Here let me help you with that."

Young woman,

Red beret

Fixed at a slight angle

On her head,

With a case in tow,

Approaches him from behind

Frees up the right strap,

Allowing the man's arm to loop through.

Rucksack falls into place,

The correct place.

"Thanks very much for that," says the man wearing the New York Yankees baseball cap.

"Not at all," replies the young woman with the red beret.

Got a feeling

It's going to be a good gym session,

Thinks the man.

80

Four miles.
15 minutes.
Halfway.
Four down
Four to go.
Not bad going.
But hurting.
Body soaked
With perspiration.
Legs aching
Badly.
Heart pumping
Rapidly.
Was never this hard,
Was it?
10 miles
Without breaking
Into a sweat,
Once upon a time.
Consigned to the history books.
Bald man on exercise bike
In a gym
In Queens,
New York.
Thinking,
About anything he can,
To distract him
From looking at the display
On the exercise bike.

Like waiting for paint to dry
Ticking off the miles.
2.5 miles to go.
Disappointed
With himself
For looking
So soon.
Legs heavy.
Head light.
Stitch in his right side,
As if he has been stabbed
With a sharp knife.
Out of shape.
Too many commitments
These days
To exercise regularly
These days.
Must try and do more,
Somehow.
Would make an 8-mile cycle
That much easier.
1.5 miles to go.
Getting closer.
Almost smell the finish line.
Wave of nausea
Hits the man.
Not convinced he can make it.
Not going to give up.
Less than a mile to go.
Looks around.
All the bicycles in use.
Man wearing blue New York Yankees baseball cap
And a white t-shirt
With 'Pizza My Heart' printed on the front
Standing close by,
Waiting for David,

The bald man,
To finish
And free up the bicycle.
0.2 miles.
Almost there.
Praise the Lord!
Man in cap still there,
Loitering,
Waiting.
A bit too close for comfort.
Uncomfortable.
8 miles
Done.
Thank goodness.
Dismounts
From the bicycle,
Slowly.
Legs unsteady,
Feel like jelly.
Feels like being sick.
"Here pal. Drink this glass of water."
Baseball cap man hands David a drink.
Very grateful,
He takes it.
Very quickly,
He drinks it.
Better,
Already.
"Thank you."
"Not a problem. It can get hot in here."

81

Round the Reservoir,
Along the Great Lawn.
Halfway round
The Central Park full loop.
Time for a drink
To keep herself hydrated.
Water bottle lid off.
Quick swig.
Disaster.
Bottle slips
From her fingers.
Bottle falls
Onto the ground.
Water spills out
Onto the path.
Bottle retrieved
Almost empty.
Bad news.
Another three miles to go
Without water.
The young woman with curly brown hair
Curses.
Always needs lots of water
When she runs.
What will she do?
Nothing
She can do
About it now.
Starts jogging again.

Struggles

To find her

Rhythm again.

Going to be a long three miles,

She thinks to herself.

"Hi there."

A runner,

A bald man,

Comes up beside her.

"Hi," she says.

"I saw you dropped your bottle back there," says the bald runner.

"Yes, I'm a clumsy klutz. Always dropping things," admits the woman,

As they both continue running.

"I have an unopened bottle of mineral water, would you like half of it?" offers the bald man.

"Really, would that be okay?" she asks.

"Absolutely. Important to stay hydrated in this heat."

"That would be amazing. I was wondering how I was going to cope with the rest of the run."

"No problem at all."

The bald man

Stops running.

Breaks the seal

Of the new bottle.

Pours half

Of the contents

Into the woman's empty bottle,

Carefully.

"There you go," says the man.

"That is so kind of you."

"No problem at all. Have a good run," adds the man as he streaks away.

"I'm Kathy, by the way. Might see you around someday," she yells before having a well-earned drink.

"I'm David!" he says, while running.

82

Whole Foods Market
In Brooklyn,
New York.
A mother
With a trolley,
Half full
Of groceries,
And two young children,
A boy,
Aged five,
And a girl,
Aged three.
Both children screaming
Their heads off.
Have been ever since they arrived in the store.
Tried ignoring them.
Tried reasoning with them.
Tried comforting them.
Tried shouting at them.
All in vain.
Still they scream,
In a head-splitting chorus
Of pure rage.
Sweets.
All started with sweets.
Walked past the confectionary counter
And all hell broke loose.
The children wanted sweets.
The mother said no.

The children started screaming.

Can't back down now.

A battle of wills

She cannot afford to lose.

Need to get them home,

As quickly as possible.

Bunch of bananas

And that's her lot.

Heads straight to the checkout

With children in tow,

Both still screaming.

"Oh dear. What's wrong with the little ones?" asks the young checkout assistant with curly brown hair, as she starts to scan the groceries.

"Sweets. They wanted sweets," answers the mother, as she unloads the contents of the trolley onto the counter.

"I've got an idea that usually helps. Mind if I try?" offers the assistant.

"Please go ahead. I'm out of ideas," admits the mother.

"Hello there, my name is Kathy. Would you both like to stand here and help me scan these items?"

Both children nod,

Sheepishly,

Both children move to the other side of the counter next to the assistant,

Excitedly.

Magic wand waved.

The screaming stops,

As the children put all their energy

Into helping the assistant.

"I can't believe it," says the mother.

"You have two adorable children," smiles Kathy.

"Please come home with us. Please," pleads the mother.

Half joking,

Half serious.

83

Always difficult to park.
Should have known better.
Big car.
Four-wheel drive.
Good for going up mountains,
Or over rough terrain,
Or navigating the jungle.
Not so good
When trying to find a space
To park
At a Whole Foods Market store
In the middle of New York.
One circuit completed.
Nothing.
Aside from one space
Large enough
For a small car,
Not large enough
For her gas-guzzling beast.
Woman,
With large red spectacles,
Drives round
The parking lot again.
A second circuit,
All she can do,
Aside from giving up all together.
Spots a woman pushing an empty trolley
Towards the shop.
Likely just arrived,

Likely be a while.

Drives passed.

Movement

In her rear-view mirror.

The driver turns around.

Catches an eye.

Woman with the trolley

Waving at her.

She stops.

She opens her window.

Woman trots over towards her.

"You looking for a space?" she asks.

"Yes, I am. All full it seems," says the woman with the red spectacles.

"Thought so. I'm just returning this trolley and then I will be on my way. I've got the big blue car over there. The one with two terrors in the back. Actually, they are much better than they were a few minutes ago, thanks to the lovely checkout girl."

"Been there myself many a time. Awful, isn't it? Thanks so much for taking the trouble to tell me you are leaving. I was about to give up," admits the woman with red spectacles.

"It's nothing. Just glad I could help. Be on my way shortly."

"Thanks again."

She closes her window.

Drives to the big blue car,

The one with two small children inside.

Both happily at peace

With the world,

For the time being,

At least.

84

Why do they have to move things around?
They:
Grocery stores.
Things:
Well, one thing in particular,
His favourite granola.
Home,
For the granola,
For as long as he can remember,
Has been a spot
On the middle shelf
In the central aisle
Of the Whole Foods Market
In Brooklyn, New York.
Not anymore.
Two weeks ago,
He would have been standing right in front
Of a wide selection of tasty cereals,
Including his favourite granola.
Fast forward to today
And all the man with curly brown hair
And four days' worth of stubble sees
Are rows
And rows
Of nuts
And seeds.
Can't be too far away
The granola,
Can it?

Nuts and seeds.

Go hand in hand

With granola and cereals,

He reasons.

Walks up and down the aisle.

Scans the aisle behind.

Scans the aisle in front.

No sign of the granola.

No sign of any cereals

For that matter

Unless he's missed them.

Missed them not once,

But twice.

Looks around

For an assistant.

Spots one

Helping a customer.

"You look lost?" asks a woman wearing red spectacles.

"Struggling to locate the granola. It was here two weeks ago, but I think they have had a shuffle around," replies the man.

"Oh, granola and the other cereals are now at the far end of the store. Second last aisle facing the wall. Easily missed. Let me show you."

Woman heads off with her basket.

Man with curly brown hair and four days of stubble follows.

Granola located.

"Thank you very much," he says,

All calm again.

85

Lost
In Brooklyn, New York,
Man in green overalls.
Mud under his fingernails,
Mud on his hands,
Mud on his arms,
All tell-tale signs
Of his job
As a landscape gardener
For the municipal authority.
The man stops
On the sidewalk
Of a street,
A street he has never been to before,
A street he will probably never go to again.
Only bricks
And concrete
As far as the eye can see.
Not a patch of green in sight.
How awful
It must be
To live
Without flowers,
To live
Without plants,
To live
Without colour.
But where is the red brick apartment block
Where a lady,

Called Miss Kennedy,

Lives?

Spoke to Miss Kennedy two days ago

About buying a collection of old books,

History books

About America.

Needs to settle up,

Collect the books,

And get back to the park

In time for his afternoon shift.

Going to be tight.

Needs to find the block,

Soon.

Rubs his now muddy chin

With his muddy hands.

"You look lost."

He turns around.

A man with curly brown hair and stubble on his face,

Cradling two paper bags

From Whole Foods

In both his arms.

"As a matter of fact, I am," replies the gardener.

"I live around here. Where do you need to get to?" asks the other man,

As he shifts the two bags higher up his chest.

"Block 316 Acacia Avenue. It's a red brick apartment block. Supposed to be meeting a woman there to collect some books."

"That's sort of on my way. Don't mind taking a little detour to take you there if you like."

"Oh, that would be great. I have to get back to the park soon so I'm cutting it fine."

"No problem. It's really close. Let's get going."

The two men head off together,

At a brisk pace.

"What are the books about?" asks the guide.

"They're on American history, specifically the Civil War. I'm really interested in the subject and these are old books I've been looking for, for some time."

But before the man in the green overalls
And mud on his face
Has time to describe the books
In more detail,
The red brick apartment block comes into view.
Couldn't have been more than two minutes away,
It turns out.
"Here you go," says the man with curly brown hair and stubble on his face.
"Thank you very much."
"No trouble at all. Enjoy the books," says the man,
As he doubles back the way he came
To go home.

86

Teenage boy.
Red baseball cap,
On back to front
On his head,
Black satchel,
Slung
Across his shoulder,
Pair of baggy denim jeans,
Barely cover
His underwear,
Nearly cover
His bright white trainers,
Headphones planted in both ears,
Music playing,
Loudly.
Soft rock from the 1980s,
Bands his dad used to listen to
When he was his age.
Walking back home
From high school,
After a pitstop
At the mall
With his friends,
He crosses
To the other side
Of the road.
Passes a red brick apartment block.
Spots a man ahead
In green overalls

On his knees
Digging up
A small patch of earth
In the sidewalk.
Bag of compost
And a cardboard box
By his side.
Can't make out
What's inside.
Removes one of his headphones,
The one in his left ear.
"You looking for something, mister?" the teenager asks.
"Oh no. Just planting," replies the man in the green overalls.
"Planting what?" asks the boy.
"Zinnia today. I was walking here the other day and noticed there are no flowers
anywhere. Thought I'd plant some along the street to brighten up the place."
"You gonna plant flowers along the whole street?" asks the boy in surprise.
"Yeah, why not? At least wherever I can find a patch of earth big enough. Might
plant some more on other streets too."
"Are the city authorities going soft or something?" the boy asks.
"No chance."
"So who is paying for it?"
"Me, I guess," answers the man in green overalls.
"So you are doing this for free?" the boy asks.
"Yes."
"Wow, that's awesome."
"You can help out if you want sometime. Provided your folks are okay with it."
"Love to, man."
"Well, if they say yes, I'll be back here this time tomorrow."
"Cool. Might see you then," says the boy.
He walks off,
While at the same time
Placing the dangling headphone
Back in his left ear.

87

Stuck
At home,
All alone,
Again.
She'll never get used to it,
Being alone.
Misses the days
When the house was full
Of family,
Of friends,
Of laughter,
Of life.
Seems like yesterday.
But more yesterdays now
Than she cares to remember.
Children all grown up now.
Children have children of their own now.
Thinks of her dear Giuseppe
Her dear, dear Giuseppe.
How she yearns
For his touch,
For his company,
For his reassurance,
For his love,
For his humour.
Glances at the side table,
At a silver frame
With a photo
Of her with her beloved Giuseppe

Standing together,

Arm in arm,

Gazing at one another,

As only lovers do.

A knock on the door.

"Grandma. Are you there? It's Joey."

The woman opens the door.

Face lights up

At the sight

Of her grandson,

The eldest son

Of her own son.

A teenager already.

Wearing a red baseball cap

Back to front

With headphones in his ears.

He removes one,

The left one.

"Hi Grandma."

"Hello dear. What a lovely surprise."

"Thought I'd see if you're okay. Sorry, it's been a long time since I visited."

"Oh, don't worry, my dear. I expect you are terribly busy with school and growing up. Come in please. Would you like a bite to eat? You must be hungry. You teenagers are always hungry."

"Thanks Grandma. That would be great. Oh, before I forget. I've got you something."

Retrieves a small pot,

Carefully,

From his satchel.

"I've been helping a guy plant zinnia along the street and he let me have one. So, I thought you might like it."

"What a thoughtful young man you are, Joey. I know just where to put it," she says,

As she closes the front door.

88

Five minutes
Before eight o'clock
In the morning,
Chemistry research scientist
At the University of California,
Santa Cruz
Arrives back
At his digs
After an all-nighter
At the lab,
Another one,
Third this week.
Working too hard
For his PhD,
He knows that.
Can catch up
On sleep
And R&R
Later,
But first
Needs to complete this latest test work
On synthesising
$Fe(III)$ complexes with ligated carboxamide nitrogen.
Been working on it for years.
Sacrificed much
To get to this point,
To what could be
The breakthrough moment.
Moved away from his family

In New York
For what could be
This breakthrough moment.
Doesn't see them much,
Anymore
Or any of his friends
Back home
Anymore.
Hasn't been back
Since Christmas.
Five days
In just twelve months.
That's all.
A low return.
"It's only temporary,"
He keeps telling himself.
Cell phone rings.
Thinks he'll ignore it.
Deal with whatever it is later.
Too exhausted to speak.
Looks at the screen.
Smiles.
Answers the call.

"Grandma! So good to hear from you."

"Hello, my dear. Am I calling you too early? Are you still in bed?"

"No, not at all. Been up for a while now. It's great you called. How are you?"

"Oh, I'm fine. Thank you. Just wanted to tell you how proud of you I am."

"Thanks, Grandma. That means so much to me."

"I'm so proud of all my grandchildren. Saw your cousin Joey yesterday. He came by with flowers for me. He's been planting flowers all over the neighbourhood to bring some colour to people's everyday lives."

"Wow, I'm impressed! What a good guy."

"Now tell me how are you over there in California? You looking after yourself, Josh?"

"Yes, Grandma. No need to worry about me. Was just thinking about you all in fact. Need to come over and visit soon. Been way too long."

"It has, dear. Would be wonderful to see you but I understand you are doing important work, Josh. You come and visit when you are ready. I'll have your favourite macaroni al' forno waiting for you."

"Can't wait, Grandma. Miss you very much."

"I miss you too, dear boy. Now I expect you have a lot of things to do so I will say goodbye now."

"Okay, Grandma. Love you."

Goes into his room.

Lies on his bed.

Falls asleep.

89

Going to be tricky,
Getting away from the lab,
Tonight.
Been working long hours,
All week.
Heading out this evening,
Or at least,
Supposed to be
Heading out this evening,
With her boyfriend
For a weekend
Of camping and hiking
At Yosemite National Park.
Five-hour drive,
If they are lucky.
Want to hit the road
By seven o'clock,
At the latest.
Knew the test work
Would run over
Into the weekend,
The one weekend
When she and Sean had plans.
Hopes Josh,
The project leader,
Won't mind,
When she asks to leave
Early,
Well early for those working in the lab,

Not early for the rest of the world.

Doesn't want to let the team down.

Doesn't want to let Sean down.

Torn.

"Aren't you supposed to be heading down to Yosemite this weekend, Anna?"

"That's right, Josh."

"What time are you planning on heading out? It's already getting late," asks the project leader.

"Was hoping to hit the road at seven, at the latest."

"You better get a move on then!"

"But I don't want to leave you in the lurch," replies Anna.

"Don't worry about that. You've been working late all week. You need to get away and have a break," says Josh.

"What about you?" asks Anna.

"I will be alright," replies Josh.

"But it's not fair on you."

"Really, I'm fine. As soon as this test is over, I plan to take a few days off and visit my family in New York. Want to see my grandma. Haven't seen her for ages."

"That sounds lovely. Okay, but I am going to hold you to that."

"Okay, Anna. Now go. You've got a weekend to enjoy!"

"Yay. Thanks, Josh. You're an angel."

90

Yosemite Creek Campground,
Three hours later
Than planned.
Already dark
And tent not up yet.
What's more,
No torch,
Or at least a torch that works.
Should have checked
Back at home.
Stupid mistake.
Will have to make do
With the headlights
Of the car
Until morning.
Found a spot
Next to a blue, two man,
Or two woman,
Tent.
Lights on inside.
Green with envy.
Wish their tent
Was up too.
Wish they were safe and snug
In sleeping bags too.
Wish their food was stored
Away from the bears too.
Car headlights on full beam,
The couple set to work,

Unloading the car,

Unfolding the tent,

Unwinding the guy lines.

Slow progress.

Pegs misplaced.

Poles missing.

Holes hard to find.

Slow progress.

Too slow.

Frustration building.

"Takes 10 minutes to put up. That's all."

That was what the man at the camping shop had said.

45 minutes,

And still the tent is not up.

Not even close.

"You guys need a torch?"

The couple look up.

Hard to see

Where the voice is coming from.

"Yes, we do. I'm afraid our one doesn't work."

"Here, have this one. We've got a spare."

"You're a lifesaver. Thank you."

"No problem. Do you need a hand? My boyfriend and I are happy to help. Aren't we, Sean?"

"Absolutely!" answers Sean, presumably.

"Thank you so much. We're new to camping. Haven't got a clue really. My name is Todd, by the way."

"And mine is Jo," says his girlfriend.

"Well, you know my name is Sean. And this is Anna."

"Nice to meet you guys. And thanks again."

10 minutes pass

And the tent is up.

The shop assistant at the camping shop was right,

After all.

91

El Capitan.
Tick.
Half Dome.
Tick.
Glacier Point.
Tick.
Glad they made the detour,
To Yosemite.
Started off at San Francisco.
Cruised down the Pacific Highway.
Last minute change of plan.
Head inland
To the National Park.
Can re-join the Highway
Once they have had their fill
Of Yosemite.
Two friends from Kent, England.
No schedule to keep to.
On a Californian road trip.
Big Sur,
Monterey,
Los Angeles,
San Diego,
All still to come.
The road trip of all road trips.
"What are you boys going to do today?"
Asks their neighbour,
A woman named Jo,
Camping

With her boyfriend Todd

In a green tent,

Pitched not too far from their own.

"Planning on doing the Four Mile Trail today," answers Toby, one of the two friends.

"Spectacular!" replies Jo.

"What about you guys?" asks Will, the second friend.

"Heading back today. So, we have tons of spare food and we wondered if you guys would like it?"

"That's so generous but why don't you just load it in your car and take it back with you?" asks Toby.

"Reckon you boys will need it more than us. You still got a whole load of miles ahead of you."

"We'll be alright, but thank you," says Will.

"Please take it. See it as a show of our legendary American generosity."

"Well, that is incredibly kind of you. Thank you very much," says Will again.

"No problem at all. Hope you guys have a safe trip."

"You too," replies Toby.

92

RV,
Just about
Parked.
Space,
Just about
Big enough.
Found it,
Eventually.
But only after
A long, frustrating search.
Much needed pit stop
In Monterey
On their way
To San Francisco
To visit their daughter
And her family.
Thought they'd travel in style.
Thought they'd get a taste of life
On the road.
Hired an RV,
One with all the bells and whistles.
Two grandparents,
Rediscovering their taste for adventure
After a lifetime
Of work,
After a lifetime
Of responsibilities.
Making up for lost time.
Making use of their time.

Couldn't stop in Monterey
Without a visit to the world-famous aquarium.
World famous for a reason.
Sea lions,
Pelicans,
Dolphins,
Rays,
Whales.
All just a piece of glass,
Or Perspex,
Away.
A quick bite
To eat
And a quick soda
To drink
At a café
In Fisherman's Wharf
Before hitting the road again.
Enjoying a chat
With their neighbours
On the table
To their left.
Two young men,
Will and Toby,
From Kent, England.
On a road trip
Down the Pacific Highway.
Back on track
After a detour
To Yosemite.
"Have you been to San Francisco before?" asks Will.
"Never. Shocking, isn't it? It's taken us almost 50 years and then only because our daughter has moved there," replies Carly Murray.
"It's an amazing city. Lots to see. Have you got a good map of the city centre?" asks Toby.
"Actually, we don't," admits Ben Murray, rather sheepishly.

"You must have ours then. You need a map to get around, especially if you are in an RV," adds Will.

"We have Satnav. We'll be okay," says Carly.

"Still, you can't be sure the Satnav will get it right when it comes to an RV. Please take ours. We don't need it anymore and we have a map covering the remaining part of our trip," explains Will.

"We're very touched, thank you. You are both charming young men," says Carly.

"Yes, absolutely charming," adds Ben.

"Think nothing of it. We've been blown away by the kindness of you Americans. It's the least we can do."

93

"One café latte with a sprinkling of cinnamon please."

"Of course, can I have your name?"

"Sandy."

"No problem, Sandy. That's three bucks fifty," says Mary Lou,

Proud owner of Mary Lou's Coffee Shop

In downtown San Francisco.

Money handed over by Sandy.

Change handed over by Mary Lou.

"Great, thanks. If you just wait over there, we'll have your coffee ready in a couple of minutes," explains Mary Lou,

As she writes 'Sandy 4'

On the side

Of a cardboard cup

With a thick black pen

Before passing it to Jamie,

Part-time barista,

Part-time student.

"Can I help you please, sir?" she asks the next customer.

"Two café mochas to go, thanks," replies one of two men standing,

On the other side

Of the counter.

"Of course, can I have your names?"

"Bill and Scotty."

"Great stuff. That'll be seven bucks please."

Money handed over by Scotty.

Change handed over by Mary Lou.

"Great, thanks. If you just wait over there, we'll have your coffees ready in a couple of minutes," explains Mary Lou,

As she writes 'Bill 2'

On the side
Of one cardboard cup
With a thick black pen
Before passing it to Jamie
And 'Scotty 2'
On the side
Of a second cardboard cup
With a thick black pen
Before passing it to Jamie.
Looks down the queue,
The long queue.
Another busy day
In her little coffee shop.
Seats 12,
At a squeeze.
Might need to get some more help,
Might need to get a bigger place,
If trade continues to roar.
"Can I help you, mam?" Mary Lou asks a woman with long grey hair tied in a bun,
Standing next to a man with thinning grey hair combed neatly.
"Yes please; can we have one Americano, two café lattes, a chicken sandwich and a bag of chips."
"Of course, can I have your names?"
"Ben for the Americano. Carly for one of the café lattes and I'm afraid we don't know the name of the woman for the other one."
"Sorry, I don't follow you?" asks Mary Lou.
"We want to buy the woman sitting on the sidewalk across the street a coffee and a bite to eat," explains Carly.
"How very nice of you. I tell you what, I'll mark hers with a big heart shape," says Mary Lou.
"Oh, how lovely. How much do we owe you?" asks Carly.
"Let's just call it ten bucks for the lot," replies Mary Lou.
Carly picks out a ten dollar note
From her handbag
And hands it over to Mary Lou.

"Great, thanks. If you just wait over there, we'll have your order ready in a couple of minutes," explains Mary Lou,
As she writes 'Carly 1'
On the side
Of a cardboard cup
With a thick black pen
Before passing it to Jamie,
And 'Ben 3'
On the side
Of another cardboard cup
With a thick black pen
Before passing it to Jamie,
And draws
A big heart shape
With the number 1 in the middle
On another cardboard cup
With a thick black pen
Before passing it to Jamie.

94

Long day
In the office.
Time for a well-earned drink
And a little music
At Ronnie's Jazz Bar
In downtown San Francisco.
Plays the piano himself,
A little.
Listens to his prized collection
Of the greats
At home,
A lot.
Still,
Can't beat
Sitting at a small table
Nursing a small bourbon
Listening to a small band
Playing live music
In the dimly lit bar.
Can't think of a better way
To end the day.
Finds himself humming
A Blue Note classic,
As he walks
On the sidewalk
Towards Ronnie's.
"Sorry to bother you."
A woman
Bags in her hands,

Bags on her shoulders,

Bags clamped under her armpits.

Bags everywhere,

It seems,

All with 'Mary Lou's Coffee Shop' printed

In big red letters

On both sides.

The man stops.

"How can I help you?" he asks.

"Do you know where St Jude's shelter for the homeless is? I looked it up earlier but I'm hopeless at directions," asks the woman.

"Yes, I know where that is. Actually, it is on my way. I can show you if you like."

"That would be great. Thank you."

"Can I help you with some of your bags?" asks the man.

"Well, aren't you a dear," replies the woman. "Thanks."

"Are you dropping these off at the shelter?" he asks.

"Yes. Spare food from my coffee shop that could do with a home before it passes its sell by date," reveals the woman.

"That makes you Mary Lou, I guess."

"That's right."

"I'm Jay, by the way."

"Nice to meet you, Jay. Where are you off to?"

"Off to Ronnie's Jazz Bar, which is just a block away from the shelter. So how long have you been donating food to the shelter?"

"First time. Was inspired by a sweet elderly couple who bought a coffee and a sandwich from my shop for a homeless woman. Sometimes, I worry I am too busy to see what is sitting right in front of my eyes."

"Well, I think this is so kind of you," declares Jay,

As they arrive at the shelter.

"Here we are," he adds,

As he hands over the bags to Mary Lou.

"Thanks again, Jay."

"No problem. See you in your coffee shop sometime."

"Coffee on the house for the knight in shining armour who came to my rescue if you do!" Mary Lou yells back,

As Jay crosses the street.

Jay stops.

Jay turns.

"What are you doing after you drop off all that food at the shelter?" he asks.

"Haven't got any plans," answers Mary Lou.

"Fancy coming over to Ronnie's for a spot of jazz and a drink?" he asks.

Pause.

"Love to," answers Mary Lou.

"Great! I'll wait for you there," replies Jay,

As he walks off

To Ronnie's

While humming

Another tune

To himself.

95

Another hot day
In San Francisco.
Too hot
For the teenage boy
With pimples
Randomly dotted
All over his face.
Decided to spend the afternoon
At home
To escape the burning sun.
Alone
In the front room
But not alone
In the house.
His mother is around,
Somewhere,
Probably cleaning
Or tidying up,
Somewhere.
Sitting in a corner of the room
At a small desk
In front of a computer,
The family computer,
The boy checks his emails.
First time in a while
That he has done so.
Lots of emails to get through.
Most are junk,
Most are deleted,

Ruthlessly,
Efficiently,
With the click of a button,
Without even a glance.
Automatic pilot on,
Until that is
Eye caught
By a name
On top of an email.
"Jay Donnelly"
Uncle Jay,
His mother's younger brother.
Reads the title of the email:
"You're not going to believe this."
Intrigued,
The teenager opens the email.
Running a half marathon
In a couple of months' time
With a girl called Mary Lou
To raise money
For a charity,
St Jude's shelter for the homeless.
Brief description of St Jude's
Followed by a plea
For donations.
"Every little bit helps."
Uncle Jay running?
Got to be a first.
Jazz.
That's all Uncle Jay likes.
Jazz.
That's all Uncle Jay lives for.
Impressed,
The boy runs off
To tell his mother.

96

Clean the bathroom.
Put a wash on.
Do the hoovering.
Prepare supper
For all the family.
All before
Her parents arrive
To stay
For a few days.
Has three hours,
If she is lucky.
Will have to work
Non-stop
If she is to have any chance
Of doing it all in time.
Always like this.
Something has to give
At some point.
Can't go on like this.
Needs help.
From the children?
No chance.
From her husband?
No chance.
Professional help.
That would work.
Twice a week would do.
Won't happen though.
Can't afford it.

Will just have to struggle on.

Mind back on the job.

Shower still to do,

Once she has finished

With the sink,

Then bathroom done

At least.

"Hey Ma? You'll never guess what…" says her son.

"What's that, honey?" replies his mother, while she carries on cleaning.

"Uncle Jay. He's going to run a half marathon for charity," reveals her son.

"You're kidding me. Uncle Jay doing something that has nothing to do with jazz? Well, I've heard it all now. Which charity is he raising money for?" asks his mother.

"St Jude's homeless shelter. He's sent an email telling us all about it and asking for sponsorship. I think we should sponsor Uncle Jay, ma. I'm going to donate 20 bucks of my own money."

"That's generous of you, Jimmy. I will definitely sign up. Busy at the moment. Got to finish up here, hoover the house and still prepare supper."

"Let me do the hoovering for you, ma."

"That would be amazing, Jimmy. It would really help me out. I'm so overwhelmed by how much I have to do."

"You should just ask, ma. I'm happy to help. In fact, from now on, let me do the hoovering."

"What's brought this on, Jimmy, you've never offered before?" asks his stunned mother.

"Don't know. Uncle Jay's email, I guess."

97

Elbow broken,
In seven places.
Surgery required.
Metal plate required,
Countless screws required
To keep the metal plate in place.
Pain,
Like he has never felt before.
Glad the operation is over
So that the healing process can begin,
Finally.
Two weeks since his accident.
Knocked off his bike
By a cab
That drove into him
From behind.
Flew into the air.
Landed,
On both elbows,
And his head
In the middle of the road.
Got away with that one,
Apart from the elbow,
Apart from the bruises,
Apart from the splitting headaches.
Has the helmet to thank,
For saving his life.
A knock
On the door.

Who could that be?

Doesn't want to be disturbed.

Just wants to be left alone

To heal

In peace.

More knocking.

Ignore it?

Another knock.

"Dave. You in there? It's Suzette from next door."

Opens the door.

"Hey Sue. Sorry I took so long. Bit slow off my feet at the moment," explains Dave.

"That's alright, Dave. I thought I'd come around and see how you are doing and also give your house a bit of a freshen up, if you would like?"

"You don't need to do that, Sue. That's beyond the call of duty."

"No trouble at all. In fact, I'm at a loose end. I was going to do the hoovering over at ours, but Jimmy is doing it. Miracles do happen. So, I thought I would come over and help out at yours."

"That is so kind, Sue. You're a good neighbour."

98

Tips.
It's all about
The tips.
Wages
Not enough
On their own.
Hardly worth
Delivering pizzas
In San Francisco
If it wasn't for the tips.
Bad night tonight though.
Customers not in a generous mood.
Maybe twenty bucks
In tips
From 10 deliveries,
If he is lucky.
Usually more,
Much more.
Needs the job
To help pay the bills,
While he studies
At the University of San Francisco,
Majoring in biology,
In his second year.
Might have to consider another job
If things don't pick up soon.
Just one more pizza
To deliver
During this run,

Before he heads back

To the store

To collect more orders.

One pizza,

California-style,

To deliver

To a house

In a nice, quiet neighbourhood.

Van parked.

Pizza retrieved.

Door tapped,

Three times.

Waits

And waits.

Better not be a prank.

Always tricky,

Explaining pranks

To the manager.

Door opens.

Relief.

Man,

With an arm in a sling.

"One California-style, sir."

"Great, how much do I owe you?"

"18 bucks 50."

Good arm in pocket,

Cash retrieved.

"What happened?" asks Tim, the pizza delivery man.

"Knocked off my bike by a cab. Smashed my elbow."

"Ouch. That must have hurt."

"It did. Still does. Here, keep the change."

"Really? There's 25 bucks here."

"Yeah, absolutely. You guys need all the tips you can get. You a student?"

"Yes, I am. How did you know?"

"Did the same job to get me through college," reveals the man. "Used to hate bad tippers."

"Tell me about it. Before you, I think I clocked up a measly twenty bucks tonight."

"Well, hopefully this will set you up for a better night."

"Thanks very much, sir."

99

"Good day, sir."
"How you doing today, mam?"
"Going to be a lovely day today, gentlemen!"
A greeting
And a smile,
One that stretches
From ear to ear,
For everyone he meets,
While he cleans the floors
Of the corridors,
Of the rooms
Of the University of San Francisco,
Each day,
Every day,
As he has been doing
Ever since he arrived in the city
From Palestine
11 years ago.
Never been back home since.
Never seen the loved ones he left behind since.
Thinks about them every day.
Will go back,
One day,
When he has enough money
To pay for a flight.
When he can get time
Off work.
Pushes his trolley
Round the corner

Into the university café.
Only to find the café
Packed
Wall to wall
With students,
With lecturers,
With staff.
Must be an event,
He decides.
He apologises,
To no one in particular.
He turns around,
Quickly,
To make good his escape
With his trolley.
"Sami, wait up! It's Tim."
"Hello Tim. Everything okay?" asks Sami,
Embarrassed to be in front of the young man,
In front of his friends,
In front of a crowd.
"Really good, thanks. We wanted to have a word with you," says Tim.
"All of you? Have I done something wrong?"
"Absolutely not, Sami. The opposite. You put a smile on all our faces every day and we want to say thank you."
"You don't have to say thank you. I just want everyone to be happy," explains Sami.
"That's just it, Sami. We are all so grateful we wanted to show how much we appreciate you," explains Tim.
"No need, Tim sir," replies Sami.
"Too late, Sami. We've all clubbed together, students, lecturers, staff, the whole college, in fact, to buy you a return flight back to Gaza so you can visit your family. We know you miss them terribly," says Tim, as he hands over an envelope to the cleaner.
The cleaner looks inside.
A ticket
To Gaza,

Just as Tim said.

"I don't know what to say."

"Oh, and we have squared it with the dean who has agreed to let you have a month off to go home to Gaza."

"I don't know what to say apart from thank you from the bottom of my heart."

"No. Thank you, Sami."

100

No fish,
Or at least none worth keeping.
The sea is dead,
Or at least the stretch of water
Where they fish is.
Can't go on like this.
Many fishermen have already left.
How long can he last out?
Likely have to find another way to make a living too,
Again,
Soon,
Only a matter of time.
A job closer to where he lives
This time,
In Gaza city.
Trouble is
Not much work around.
Lucky,
To get the job on a fishing boat.
Has his cousin to thank for that.
Will have to get any job he can
And be grateful.
Back at home,
His children
Run around
And play,
Constant reminders,
As if he needed one,
Of his duty

To put food on the table,
To provide shelter
For his family.
Voices,
Excited voices
Coming from outside.
He gets up.
He walks out
Into the street
To see what the commotion is.
Prepared
For anything
But not prepared
For everything.
Backs of people
All he can see.
Until,
One by one,
The bodies
In front of him
Peel away
To reveal
A man,
Not just any man,
But the brother he hasn't seen
For more than 10 years.
"Sami! It's Sami. I can't believe it. It's Sami. Back home," he exclaims.
Sobbing,
He flings himself
Onto the man
In front of him,
His long-lost brother.
"Hello, Yassar. What a sight for sore eyes you are, my dear brother."
"I must be dreaming," says Yassar.

"No dreams, brother. I am here for a month. The students I work for at the university bought me a ticket home so that I could see you and the family again," reveals Sami.

"I am forever in their debt. Come in, brother. You must meet my family."

Tears of joy,

Excited laughter,

Firm hugs,

Warm kisses,

Slaps on backs,

As the brothers catch up

On so many lost years,

As the brothers reminisce

On so many long-gone years.

"I have something for you, Yassar," says Sami.

Opens his bag

Pulls out a shirt,

A San Francisco 49er's shirt.

"All the way from America. I also bring you this," says Sami.

Extends his right hand

Towards his brother,

A roll of notes

Sitting upright

In the middle

Of the palm

Of his hand.

"385 dollars, brother. It's all I can spare for now. But as soon as I can, I will send more."

"This is more than everything, Sami. I thank you with all my heart."

101

Will be tough.
Will be slow.
Will be exhausting.
Will cost money,
What little he can spare,
That is.
But still,
Couldn't be happier.
He is rebuilding his house,
Finally,
Bit by bit
By himself,
For the most part,
Apart from when the menfolk
Of his family
Are able to help.
Doesn't matter.
No deadlines.
The house will be ready
When it is ready.
Waited long enough
Since the bomb hit,
Waiting a little longer,
Not a problem,
Especially,
With the prize in sight.
"Need a hand?" asks a voice.
"Or four?" adds another.
Two men.

Doesn't recognise either of them,

At least not at first.

Look similar,

At least vaguely similar.

"That would be great," says the man.

"I'm afraid I cannot afford to pay you anything though," he adds.

"No need to pay us," says one of the men.

"We're just happy to help if we can," adds the other in a strange accent.

"Be great if you could. I could do with the company as well," admits the man.

"Let's get to it then. I am Yassar and this is my brother, Sami."

"Nice to meet you both. I am Rashid. We've met before, Yassar, I believe. Sami, I do not think we've crossed paths."

"No, I live in America. I have come home to visit my family. I'm here for a month but I will be happy to help as much as I can while I am in Gaza."

"That is very generous of you. I am a builder by trade. But I am on my own."

"You've got help now, Rashid," says Yassar.

102

No materials,
Or rather
No bricks
To be precise.
Needs bricks
To repair his house,
Or to rebuild it
To be precise.
Family lives
In the home
Of the parents
Of his wife.
Not much space,
Not much privacy.
Has to make do.
Has no choice,
But to make do,
Ever since his home
Was hit.
Still visits
The site
Where his house once stood
Every day.
Clears up the debris,
Though,
Truth be told,
No more debris
To clear up.
Bricks.

Just needs bricks

So work can start.

"Looks like you are ready to start work, Ali?"

It's Rashid,

A builder he knows.

"I am but still no bricks."

"But you are wrong. There are bricks, and more to the point, I have got some for you."

"Bricks? But how?" asks Ali.

"An incredible woman. That's how. Palestinian but went to America to study. She has come back to rebuild Gaza," says Rashid.

"I don't understand," says the man, not quite believing what he is hearing.

"She has invented a way of making bricks out of coal and ash. And it works. I am using them on my house."

"And you found some for me?"

"Yes, Ali. I'll take you to the yard and you can see for yourself."

"Thank you for thinking of me, Rashid," says Ali,

With tears in his eyes.

103

Nervous.
Last day
Before he starts
His residency
At Hadassah Ein Kerem Hospital
In Jerusalem.
Doesn't know what to expect.
Doesn't know how he will be treated.
A Gazan
Working
And learning
His trade
In a hospital
In Jerusalem.
"See the bigger picture, Amin," he tells himself.
Grandfather died
Of a heart attack.
Lack of interventional cardiology in Gaza
To blame.
Intends to put this wrong
Right
By learning from the best
In Jerusalem.
And then by bringing his skills
Back to Gaza
To give victims
Of cardiac arrests
A chance.
Grateful for the opportunity,

Very grateful,
But nervous.
Going to be a long commute
Each day
Twice a day
And that's before
The checkpoints are navigated.
Walks back
To his grandparents' house
Where he lives
With his family
Ever since their house was hit.
Enters the house
To a chorus
Of voices,
Of cheers,
Of singing.
"Surprise!"
His family,
His friends
All gathered
To wish him luck.
Hushes
From his father, Ali,
Drown out
The screams,
Eventually.
"Sssshhh! Let me say a few words," his father shouts above the din.
Peace reigns,
For now.
"Amin. I just want to say how so very proud of you I am. My son selected to learn in a hospital in Jerusalem. Jerusalem of all places! They clearly recognise what we have all known since the day you were born. That you are a special person, Amin, and that you are destined for great things in this life," declares Ali, as he hugs his son and showers him with kisses.

"Thank you, Father. This is a lovely surprise. I only wish I could rewind the clock two years earlier so Grandfather would be here with us still," says Amin. "Jid would be as proud as I am, my son. Now let's enjoy ourselves and have a great party. A celebration."

Nerves banished,

Only joy

In his heart,

As an image enters his head,

Of his grandfather,

With that mischievous,

Toothy grin

Of his

On his face.

104

For as long as Gila can remember,
She has dreamed of being a doctor.
Practised all sorts
Of operations
And medical procedures
On her younger brothers
When they were all children.
Happiest day of her life
When she got in
To medical school,
Not just any medical school,
The Hadassah Ein Kerem Hospital,
One of the few,
If not the only hospital,
To have been nominated
For a Nobel peace prize
In recognition for treating all patients
Equally,
Regardless of ethnicity,
Regardless of religion.
Heart set
On becoming
A heart surgeon,
Even before her current placement
In the cardiology department started.
Even more so now.
Inspiring.
The patients,
The work,

The staff,
Especially,
Amin.
A Palestinian
In an Israeli hospital,
What a man.
Makes the trip
All the way from Gaza
To Jerusalem
Each day
To learn the skills he needs
To save lives
Back home.
Takes it all in his stride.
Settled into hospital life well.
Always smiling,
Always helping,
Always listening.
Must be difficult,
Being a Palestinian
Learning
And working
In an Israeli hospital.
Must have worried
About prejudice,
About preconceptions,
About provocation.
Not at this hospital,
But he would not have known that,
Maybe on his commute.
But he does it,
Why?
For the greater good
Of his people,
That's why.
Inspiring,

Listening to him speak
About losing his grandfather
To a cardiac arrest
And how he wants to ensure
No one else in Gaza
Suffers the same loss.
A shining beacon,
An example.

105

Still doubts
They will come.
Everything packed,
Everyone dressed.
Just waiting now
For them to come.
If they come,
That is.
Supposed to be here
One hour ago.
Doubts grow bigger
And bigger,
As each minute passes.
All the excitement,
All the hope
He had felt in his heart,
Being quickly consumed
By doubt.
Last chance,
He fears,
For his son,
Fadi.
No one can help his heart
In Gaza.
Jerusalem,
His only chance of salvation.
Still not convinced
This is not all a joke,
A sick joke.

A group of volunteers from Israel
Crossing the border
Into Gaza
To bring sick Palestinians
Back to their land
To make them get better.
Can it be true?
Has he been a fool?
Looks out
From the entrance
Of his home.
Watches
The road,
Wondering which direction
They will come from.
If they do come,
That is.
A white van turns
Into the road.
Drives slowly
Towards his house.
Could it be them?
The van stops
Close by.
Two of them,
A man
Driving,
And a woman
Seated
In the front
Next to the man.
Both get out of the van.
The man and the woman stop a man on the street,
Who stretches out an arm
And points towards his house.
The man and woman approach.

Too excited,

He meets them halfway.

"Hello. My name is Gila and this is Shai. Are you Rani?" asks the woman.

"Yes, I am Rani."

"Good to meet you. We're here to take you and your son Fadi to the Hadassah Ein Kerem Hospital in Jerusalem. Are you all ready?"

"Yes, yes. Thank you. I will go and bring Fadi. Thank you," says Rani, as he heads back into the house for his son,

Believing again,

That dreams do come true.

106

"You stay here with Bubbe, Rachel. I am just going to pop out to speak to the doctor."
"Okay, Mama."
Quick glance
At her mother,
Her dear mother,
Lying in her bed,
Still
And peaceful.
Quick glance
At her four-year-old daughter
Standing by her dear mother's side,
Tending to her every need,
Like a dutiful nurse.
A picture
To treasure
Forever.
Leaves the room.
Hurries
Along the corridor
To Room 23.
Nervous.
Doesn't know what to expect.
Prepares for the worst.
Knocks on the door.
"Come in."
Enters.
"Hello, Doctor."

"Hello, Mrs Aaronson. Please take a seat. Don't worry; it is good news about your mother."

Spring in her step.

She skips back

Along the corridor,

In double quick time.

Opens the door

Of her mother's room.

Still asleep.

Wants to wake her

To tell her

The good news.

Knows she shouldn't.

Anti-climax.

Rachel.

Where's Rachel?

Checks the bathroom.

Checks under the bed.

No sign.

Panic

Builds.

Leaves the room.

Stops a passing nurse.

She hasn't seen her daughter.

No one has seen her daughter.

Runs along the corridor,

Head scanning every direction

For any sign

Of her daughter.

None.

She runs down

To the reception.

A queue.

Too long.

She jumps it.

"Excuse me, I have lost my daughter. She's four years old and her name is Rachel."

"Ah. We were about to make an announcement. A man found her and brought her to the desk a few minutes ago. She is in the back office. Let me take you there now."

"Rachel! My darling, there you are," bellows her mother,

As she runs into the back office

To her daughter,

Before swooping her up

Into her arms.

"Where did you go, honey?" she asks her daughter. "I've been so worried."

"I was scared on my own with Bubbe sleeping. So, I tried to find you. I got lost, Mama, but Rani found me."

Rachel points to a man standing behind her mother.

Mrs Aaronson turns.

"This is Rani. His son is being treated here in the hospital," adds Rachel.

"Rani. I am forever in your debt. Thank you so very much."

107

Central Bus Station
Of Jerusalem,
Not far now.
Man,
Bald
With greyish black hair
On the sides
And the back
Of his head,
Sun-kissed skin
Flecked
With dark brown freckles
On the hairless top
Of his head.
Sitting on his own
By the window,
In the second row
From the front
Of the bus,
Behind a mother
And her young daughter.
A blue holdall
And a carrier bag
Planted on the seat next to him.
Phone held in his hand
Close to his ear,
As he speaks to his sister in Tel Aviv.
Bus pulling into the station,
Prompts a quick goodbye

To his sister
Before he tucks the phone into his pocket,
Right front of his trousers,
Always right front of his trousers,
No matter which pair of trousers
He is wearing.
Bus stops
At the station.
Doors open
At the station.
Passengers disembark
Off the bus
One by one.
Man grabs his bags.
Steps off the bus
And heads off
Into the city.
"Excuse me."
Man with the blue holdall and carrier bag stops.
"I think you left this phone on the bus. I saw it on the seat," says the woman with
the young girl,
The mother and daughter who had been sitting on the bus
In the seats
In front of the man.
Phone does look like his.
Hand in pocket,
Right front of his trousers,
Confirms
Phone is his.
"Must have dropped out of my pocket when I got up. Thank you," says the man.
"Can we go now?" asks the little girl.
"Yes, we can, Rachel," the woman says to her daughter. "No problem at all. Glad
I was able to catch up with you."
"Thanks again to you both," says the man,
Relieved.

108

So much to do
Before his flight.
Important business trip,
Raising money
From investors
For a cocoa plantation
In Cote d'Ivoire,
West Africa.
Needs to collect
Presentations,
Brochures,
Business cards
From the printers,
Pack his bags,
Say his goodbyes
To his family,
Catch a train
To Tel Aviv Airport
To board a direct flight
To Paris.
Only then,
Will he be able to relax,
A little.
Until then,
100kmph.
On his way
To the printers now
On Jaffa Road,
Jerusalem.

Walking fast,
Not paying attention,
Right foot
Steps onto a wet tissue.
Right foot
Slides forwards.
Right foot
Flips into the air.
The man loses
His balance.
The man falls
To the ground,
Head first.
Dazed.
Shocked.
Sore.
"You okay?"
Asks a bald man,
As he helps the businessman
To his feet,
Slowly.
The bald man helps the businessman
Sit down on a bench,
Slowly.
"Yes, I think so. Thank you."
"You have a nasty gash on your head. Let me call the paramedics to check you over."
"No, that's okay. I have lots to do. Can't afford to waste time," says the businessman.
Too late,
Bald man already on his mobile phone.
"They'll be here in 5-10 minutes. So won't delay you too much. Best get it looked at. I'll keep you company until then," promises the bald man, as he tucks his phone into his trouser pocket,
The right front pocket,
Places his blue holdall down on the ground and a plastic bag onto the bench,

And sits next to the businessman.

"What is your name?" he asks.

"Ori."

"Good, at least you remember that. Think you'll live to fight another day, Ori."

The two men laugh,

Just as the paramedics arrive.

109

Feeling sick
On a Metro Line 1 train
In Paris.
Morning sickness.
10 weeks pregnant.
Not quite ready
To announce
To the world
That she is pregnant.
No seat,
No choice,
But to stand up.
Just left Concorde
Still ten more stops
Before La Défense,
Her stop.
Doesn't think
She is going to make it.
Less worried
About being sick,
More worried
About making a scene
In front of lots of strangers.
Take one stop at a time,
She tells herself.
Take up a position next to the doors,
She tells herself,
Just in case a quick exit is needed.
Rather be sick on the platform

Than on a moving train
In a dark tunnel.
Thinking about it
Makes her feel worse.
Brakes suddenly slammed on hard
By the unknown driver
In the front
For a reason unknown
To her
Or to all the other passengers
On the train.
The woman lurches forward
Onto a man.
"Pardon," she says to the man,
As the train comes to a screeching halt.
Spots a small bandage
On the man's head.
"Pas de probleme," he replies.
Not French,
She decides.
"Est-ce que tu vas bien?" the man asks.
She retches,
Three times.
Nothing comes out.
Fellow passengers move away,
Suddenly,
Finding space
That wasn't there
Moments before.
The man helps support the woman,
As the train starts moving,
Slowly,
Into the station.
Doors open,
He helps her
Off the train,

Even though it is not his stop,

Even though it is not her stop.

Leads her to a bench

On the platform.

Sits her down.

Heads off

To a vending machine

On the platform.

Buys a bottle of mineral water.

Returns.

Opens the bottle

"Un peu d'eau?" the man asks.

"Merci," says the woman before taking a sip.

Stomach already settling down.

"You're not French," the woman asks in broken English.

"I'm from Israel. Here on business. My name is Ori."

"Pleased to meet you, Ori. My name is Pia. Thank you. I don't know what came over me," she lies.

She knows what has come over her

These past few weeks.

"Should take it easy today maybe," Ori suggests.

"Supposed to be at work in La Défense. I'll be okay. Thanks to you. Feeling much better already," says Pia.

110

Man with bright blond hair
Not feeling bright today,
Not at all.
Tooth aches.
Head throbs.
24 hours,
Since he bit the olive,
The one with the stone inside.
Thought it was pitted,
Supposed to be pitted,
Just like all the others
In the jar.
Result?
A day of pain,
Excruciating pain.
A day he will never get back.
Wants it to stop,
Now.
End in sight,
Now,
At least,
At last.
Sitting in the waiting room
Of the dentist
In a quiet street
Close to where he lives
In Porte de Saint Cloud,
Paris,
Counting the minutes

Until his turn.
Door opens.
Another patient enters.
Door slams
Shut,
Again.
Too loud.
Bolt of sound
Shoots into his head,
And explodes,
As if he has been struck
By a hammer
Or how he imagines
It must feel like
To be struck
By a hammer
On the head.
Happens every time
The door slams
Shut.
Wish people would stop
Letting the door slam
Shut.
Wish people would stop
And just think
Of others
For a change.
Woman enters.
Braces himself
For yet another
Hammer blow
To his aching head,
But none comes.
Instead,
The door closes
Without making a sound,

As the woman keeps hold
Of the handle
To prevent
The door from slamming
Shut.
"Good woman," the man thinks to himself.
"Pia Lefebvre. S'il vous plait venez a salle quatre," announces the receptionist
sitting at the desk behind the counter.
No sooner does she sit down,
The woman,
The thoughtful woman,
Stands up.
Heads to the door she came in from
Just moments before.
Makes sure
The door closes
Without making a sound,
As she did
Just moments before.
"Thank you," the man whispers to himself.
"Monsieur Gilles Dupont. S'il vous plait venez a salle deux."
Monsieur Dupont stands up.
Time to end the agony.

111

Galeries Lafayette
In Paris.
With its ornate glasswork,
Intricate stonework,
Curvaceous arches,
A cathedral,
Not for worshippers,
But for shoppers.
Always a treat
To pop in
For a visit
Whenever she is nearby
And has ten minutes
To spare.
Likes to soak up
The history
And the buzz
Created
By all those people
Housed in such a beautiful building,
All buying and selling
Garments,
Accessories,
Food.
All luxuries
All in one place.
Couldn't resist
An expensive box of chocolates.
Can't really afford it,

But she'll cut back
On something else
When she next goes to the supermarche.
Time to head out
Before she buys something else.
Heads for the exit.
Approaches the heavy doors.
Braces herself
To push
With all her might.
No need.
A man
Just ahead of her,
With a shock of bright blond hair,
Naturally blond,
She notices,
Opens the door
And holds it open
For the woman
With the box
Of expensive chocolates
In her small Galeries Lafayette carrier bag.
"Merci beaucoup, Monsieur!" says the woman, as she passes through the door.
"Je vous en prie," says the man with bright blond hair.

112

Chest high wall
Built with uneven stones.
No problem.
No need to slow down.
No need to speed up.
Continues running,
At a constant pace,
Straight
Towards the wall.
At the very last moment,
And just before impact,
He leaps up,
Places both hands
On top of the wall,
Swivels both legs
To the side,
Together,
Pencil straight,
And pushes off,
Effortlessly.
Clears the wall,
Effortlessly.
Both feet land
On the other side
Of the wall
At the same time.
All done in one,
Fluid,
Dynamic

Motion.

Speed vault

Executed

To perfection.

Carries on running.

Sees a bench.

Runs towards it.

Dives for the arm rest

Furthest away.

Grabs it

With both hands.

Tucks both feet up

Between his arms.

Brings both legs through

To the other side.

Plants both feet

Onto the ground.

Carries on running.

Spots another wall.

High and smooth.

Too high

To vault.

But perfect

For a back flip.

Quickens his pace.

Plants one foot

Onto the wall.

Launches himself backwards.

Arches back.

Swings arms over,

Head,

Body,

Hips,

Legs follow

Until feet hit the ground.

Noise.

Movement,
All around him.
A phone,
A water bottle,
Coins,
All scattered
In all directions.
His phone,
His water bottle,
His coins.
Checks the red rucksack
On his back.
Zip open.
Scrambles around
To retrieve his belongings,
While cursing himself
For the schoolboy error.
A woman with a carrier bag
From Galeries Lafayette
Stops
To help him
Gather up
His belongings.
"Très impressionnant," says the woman,
As she hands
A handful of coins
She rescued
Back to the young man.
"Merci. Madame," says the young man,
As he puts his blue plastic water bottle
Into his red rucksack.
The woman picks up his phone,
Hands it
Back to the young man.
"Merci encore," says the young man.

113

One bag of asphalt,
One trowel,
One shovel.
All he needs
To fix the potholes
That blight the road
Where he lives
In St Denis
On the outskirts
Of Paris.
No one else will do it,
Not the local council
At any rate,
Despite all the calls
He has made
Over the past year,
Pleading
For the road
To be repaired.
Damage
To the front wheel
Of his car
Costing 200 euros to repair,
The last straw.
Need a job done?
Do it yourself.
His father used to say.
May he rest in peace.
Road maintenance.

Not his job.
Teaching sports
At the Lycee Paul Eluard
In St Denis,
His job.
Needs must,
He opens the bag,
Uses the trowel
To spread asphalt
Into the first hole,
The biggest
And deepest hole,
The one that causes the left front wheel of his car
To judder violently,
Every time
He drives over it.
Uses the shovel
To compact the asphalt
Into the hole.
Repeats the process
Until the hole is completely filled.
One down
Four to go.
Moves to the next hole.
"Do you need any help?" asks a passing young man,
Carrying a blue water bottle in one hand
And a red rucksack on his back.
"That would be great, thanks," says the man. "The council does nothing about
the holes. Do you live here?" asks the man.
"Yes, I do," replies the boy. "I do parkour here too."
"It is very good of you to help," says the schoolteacher,
Impressed by this young man
Who has volunteered
To help him.
Puts a lot of the children
He teaches,

At the school,
To shame.

114

Eight teenagers
Penned inside a 10-metre-high metal cage
Kick a white heavily scuffed football around
On a five a-side pitch,
A concrete pitch
Guaranteed
To leave its mark
On anyone who falls
To the ground.
Open to the public
It may well be,
But only those
Who live
On the nearby estate
Are brave enough
To play
On the pitch,
Which lies in the shadow
Of the Stade de France.
The national stadium of the French football team,
A beacon
To the promised land
Of fame and fortune,
A beacon
That points to a way out
For the eight young men
From a lifetime
On the estate.
None go to school,

None have jobs,
All live with their families,
Their extended families.
Every day
They meet up
On the pitch.
Football,
Their only anchor.
Football,
Their only routine,
Football,
Their only release.
A man
With two carrier bags
Watches the teenagers play
From behind the fence.
Catches the eye
Of one of the teenagers.
Beckons the footballer to come towards him.

"Salut. I walk past here often on my way to and from work and see you all playing here. You are all very talented. Do you play in a league?"

"No, monsieur," replies the teenage boy. "We can't afford to buy shirts, let alone the fees to join a league."

"I thought that would be the case. I teach at the Lycee Paul Eluard and I thought you might want to have these old school rugby shirts. I know they are not football shirts but hopefully, they will do," offers the man.

"Thank you, monsieur, that is kind. But we only kick a football around with each other. We have no use for them," explains the teenager.

"Ah, but you could if you joined a league," says the man.

"But we can't afford the fees, monsieur," repeats the teenager.

"I have looked into it and there is a league not far from here. Teams play every Friday night and it costs 200 euros to join, that's all. Look, it says so on these registration forms."

"We can't afford even half that amount, monsieur."

"I will pay your fees. Give it a try. Test yourselves against others and see where it takes you," says the teacher from Lycee Paul Eluard.

"Wait one moment, monsieur."

The teenager runs over to speak with his friends.

One quick,

Animated,

Discussion later,

He returns.

"Okay, monsieur. We'll do it. Thank you."

"Genial," says the teacher as he hands over the two bags with the rugby shirts.

"They are all clean. I will fill in the form and hand it in to the football centre along with the fee. I need the name of one of you to put on the form. Should I put your name on the form?" the teacher asks.

"Yes, put me down. My name is Patrice Thuram."

"Fantastic," says the teacher, as he fills out the form.

"Monsieur, can I ask why you are doing this for us?" asks Patrice.

"Everyone deserves a chance, Patrice."

"Thank you, monsieur."

"All you have to do now is come up with a name for your team."

115

Teenage boy
Leaps over
A flight of stairs,
All six steps
Cleared
In one jump.
Uses his hands to stop himself
From crashing
Into the wall ahead.
Quickly turns,
Runs down
The next flight of stairs.
Hears voices,
Not far
Behind him.
Confident
He can outrun anyone.
Always was
The quickest,
Still is.
Best to keep running though
To get well away from his pursuers,
Otherwise
They will show him no mercy,
If their threats
Are to be believed.
Four more flights of stairs
Before he makes it
Out of the block

And into the open air.
Slows down,
But keeps on running,
More like jogging.
Looks back.
No sign of them.
Probably gave up on him
Or decided to pick on someone else.
Heart pounding,
He starts walking.
Hears shouts
And screams
Full of venom
Come from behind,
Not far behind.
He turns.
Sees the four young men,
Rage
And violence
Etched onto their faces.
They sprint towards him.
He starts running again,
This time
Faster.
Scared now.
Down one ally,
Across a stony patch of grass,
Over a small concrete wall
Towards La Cage
Where a group of boys are playing football.
Shouts
Seem louder.
Can hear the threats.
Can hear what they intend to do to him,
More clearly,
To teach him a lesson.

For what?

For refusing to do an errand for them?

For running?

He reaches La Cage.

Stops to look around.

For a place to hide.

"You okay?" asks one of the boys in La Cage.

Catching his breath,

The boy says nothing,

Just looks over his shoulder,

As the gang run

Towards him.

"Come in here, quick!" says the boy in La Cage.

He does

What he is told.

"Put one of these shirts on. And play football with us. What is your name?"

"Thierry," the boy says, as he puts on the shirt.

"I'm Patrice. Everyone, this is Thierry. He's our new player."

116

Last day
Of a four-day trip
To Paris.
A couple,
Bjorn
And Agnes,
From Oslo,
Norway,
Not old enough
To retire,
But old enough
To go on romantic breaks
By themselves
Again.
Children grown up,
Settled,
And working
Back in Oslo.
Free now
To go on trips,
They are making up
For lost time.
Louvre,
Notre-dame,
Montmartre,
The theatre,
Shopping,
All as wonderful
As they hoped

They would be.
Now the Eiffel Tower.
Made it to the top,
With a stop,
Or two,
On the way.
At every viewpoint
Pictures taken,
Including a very unexpected one,
A special one,
Of a man
With short dark hair,
Holding a ring
In his hand,
Kneeling
On one knee
In front of a woman
With long dark hair,
With her hands
Clamped
On both sides
Of her head
And a beautiful smile
On her face.
Not wanting to intrude
On their magical moment,
The couple from Oslo
Head back down
To the bottom
Of the monument,
And wait
For the newly engaged pair
To appear
So that they can show them
And so that they can give them
A picture of the romantic proposal

Which they can treasure
For the rest of their lives.
Cradling her rucksack
Between her legs
Agnes waits
With her husband.
A gentle movement.
Rucksack tipped forward,
She supposes.
Stoops down
To right it
Once more.
Shock.
The bag is not there.
Turns around.
A man,
With her rucksack
Over his shoulder,
Running
Fast,
"Arretez! Mon sac!" she yells.
Agnes and Bjorn
Both set off
In pursuit.
Both lose ground,
Fast.
Then out of nowhere,
A young man,
No more than a teenager,
Springs into view
And starts to give chase.
Quick on his feet,
He eats up the ground
Between himself
And the thief,
Who,

With increasing urgency

And with increasing frequency,

Anxiously

Glances back

Over his shoulder

At his pursuer,

As he runs.

Not fast enough.

The young man soon catches up

With the thief,

Who turns around

To face his pursuer,

Throws the rucksack

At the younger man

And runs off.

The younger man gathers up the bag,

And walks back

Towards the couple from Oslo.

"Merci merci beaucoup," says Agnes.

"Tu es notre héros," declares Bjorn.

"Pas de probleme," says the young hero, modestly.

"Do you speak English?" asks Agnes.

"A little," answers the young man.

"What is your name?" asks Bjorn.

"Thierry," replies the young man.

"Well, thank you very much for saving our holiday," says a grateful Bjorn.

"Please, take this as a reward."

A 50 euro note.

"Wow! Merci bien," says Thierry.

117

Dinner eaten.
Table cleared.
Dishes washed.
Time to relax
On the sofa
With a glass of red wine
And her tablet.
Always likes catching up
With what her family have been up to,
And her friends,
And even friends of friends
And friends of friends of friends.
Always amazed
By the number of friends she has
On social media,
Especially those
She has never spoken to,
Let alone met,
In the flesh and blood,
As far as she can remember,
At any rate.
Scrolls down.
Posts of hope,
Posts of frustration,
Posts of humour.
Scrolls down
Stops.
A post.
From Agnes and Bjorn Olsen.

Doesn't know them.

One friend in common.

A handsome man from Oslo

She met while travelling in Asia.

A Norwegian

And a Dane,

The most natural of travelling companions.

Looks at the post.

Titled: "Wanted"

"Please help us find this couple in the picture. We captured the moment when the man proposed to his girlfriend while on the Eiffel Tower. We didn't manage to show them the picture when it was taken and we'd love to get in contact with the happy couple so that we can send it on to them."

She looks at the picture.

A man with short dark hair

On bended knee

In front of his girlfriend

With long dark hair.

With a lump

In her throat

And a tear,

Of happiness,

In her eye,

She clicks 'Like'

Before sharing it with her friends.

Who knows,

One of them

Might just recognise

The happy couple

In the picture,

Maybe even

A friend

Of a friend will.

118

Morning rush over
At the Happy Rambler Hostel for Travellers
In Goa,
India.
Breakfast
Served
And ended
An hour ago.
Dorms
And private rooms
Being cleaned
Right now.
Time to catch his breath.
Time to catch up on admin
In his small office.
Anton Baptista,
The manager
Of the hostel,
Sits at his desk
In front of his computer
About to check the bookings for the day.
Tricky keeping tabs
On all the travellers
Coming and going
To and from
The hostel.
A ping from his computer
Catches his attention,
Alerts him to a new post

On his social media page.
Could be an enquiry
Or a booking
From a customer
Or a message
From a friend.
Hopes it is a message
From a friend.
Breaks up
The routine of work.
Clicks on the alert.
It is from a friend,
Agathe,
A Danish woman,
Stayed at the hostel
Two summers ago.
Travelled with a Norwegian boy.
Can't remember his name.
Got on well with Agathe,
He remembers.
Sees she has shared a post
From a Norwegian couple
Trying to track down
A couple in a picture they took
At the Eiffel Tower
Of a man proposing to a woman.
Want to give them the picture.
"Lovely thought."
He thinks to himself.
"Isn't that what social media is all about
Bringing people together?"
Shares Agathe's post
With all his friends.
"Hope this helps,"

He thinks to himself.
Before getting back
To the bookings.

119

Children dropped off.
House tidied up.
No sign
Anywhere,
Anymore,
Of the morning panic
That is
Getting the children
Off to school,
In good time.
Quick coffee
And a biscuit
Before she resumes her errands.
Mind wonders
To the family
She left behind
In Goa
Many moons ago now,
When she married her husband,
A Canadian,
And settled down
In Vancouver.
What are they doing right now,
Her Goan family?
She asks herself.
Doesn't get to see them much,
Anymore.
Costs too much
To fly all that way

For a visit,
Especially,
With three children in tow.
Powers up her computer
To see if any of her family have been in touch
Since last night
When she last checked.
An alert
From her cousin,
Anton.
Not a message
But a post
He has shared.
About a couple
From Norway
Looking for another couple
To give them a photo they took
At the Eiffel Tower
In Paris.
Looks like the man is proposing to his girlfriend.
Romantic.
Clicks 'Like'.
Writes a message to Anton:
"You getting soft in your old age, cousin? How are you, Anton? Hope all is well at home in Goa. Miss you all terribly. Arkanj."
Clicks send.
Then shares the post
From the Norwegian couple
With all her friends.
Good luck,
She wishes.

120

Postgraduate
From Canada
Studying for a PhD,
In botany.
Still feels like a dream
To have secured funding
To spend a year
At the University of Brasilia,
Home to one of the largest biomes
In Brazil.
Brazil,
The place to be
For a botanist.
His knowledge,
His understanding
Have already soared
To a level
Much higher
Than he could ever have imagined possible.
Due to return home soon
To Canada,
To the University of British Columbia
To finish his studies.
Then
Decision time.
Continue in academia
Or get a job?
Is it time to join the rat race?
Tired of scrounging for funding

At the age of 26,
When all his friends
Have well paid jobs,
When all his friends
Have settled down.
Strong sense of unfinished business
Keeps him hooked,
Teases him
To pursue his studies further,
To take them as far as he can.
Sitting in a café
On campus
Laptop on.
Ping.
Post received
From Arkanj,
Wife of an old lecturer
He keeps in touch with
But hasn't seen for a while.
Sharing a post
From a couple
From Norway
Seeking another couple
To return a picture they lost,
Or something like that.
Asking to spread the word.
Ignore
And move on.
Looks at the picture.
Sees the excitement
On the woman's face,
As her boyfriend kneels
On one knee
With a ring
In his hand.
"It's not all about the money now, is it, Paul?" he thinks to himself.

Suddenly,
His big decision
Doesn't seem to be so big,
Anymore.
Clicks on 'Share'.

121

Meet interesting people,
Up to a point.
Meet interesting people,
Stuck.
Meet interesting people,
Still stuck.
A list of one,
Is that all?
Is that the only positive
About her job
She can think of?
A receptionist
For a law firm
In Seattle,
Weighing up
The positives
And the negatives
About her job.
Negatives,
No shortage of negatives,
Low pay,
Low benefits.
Hours and hours
Of sitting down
With not much to do.
Apart from,
Having to smile at strangers,
Not because she is happy,
But because it is her job

To meet
And greet
With a welcoming smile.
The quiet afternoons,
They are the worst.
Spends most of her time
Watching the clock
On the bottom right-hand corner
Of her screen.
What a life.
Came down from Vancouver
Looking for adventure.
Looking to travel around the US,
And beyond.
12 months on,
Barely made 150 miles.
Needs to get her act together.
Checks her phone,
Discreetly,
Under the lip of the counter
So no one can see.
Only half an hour
Since she last looked.
Could have missed something.
Who knows,
A friend might have added a post?
Anything to pass the time,
She scrolls down.
A post
Shared by an old school friend
From back home.
Tania.
A picture of her dancing,
Having fun.
Good on her.
Another post

From Paul,
Her brainy friend,
Studying in Brazil.
About a quest
To locate a couple
In a picture
Getting engaged.
One day
That will be her,
Getting engaged.
One day
Complete strangers
Will be tracking her down,
Jennifer Martin,
To give her a picture
Of the moment
Her boyfriend,
Whoever he may be,
Got down
On one knee
To propose.
Smiling,
Not because she has to,
But because,
Suddenly,
She feels happy.
She feels full of hope.
She clicks 'Like'.
She clicks 'Share'
Just in time,
As a party of four
Enters the building
And walks towards her desk.

122

A grandmother
Remembers the time
When keeping in touch
With relatives
Living in different countries,
Let alone different continents,
Meant airmail letters,
Meant postcards,
Meant telegrams,
Meant long distance telephone calls,
Expensive long distance telephone calls.
Not these days.
So many ways
These days
To communicate
With almost anyone
Anywhere
In the world,
Instantly,
Easily,
Cheaply.
Thank goodness,
With so many of her family
Living outside
Her beloved Galway,
On the west coast of Ireland.
A godsend,
That is what the internet is.
Never thought

For one moment
She would be able to master a laptop,
Let alone a tablet.
But needs must
And all that.
What do they call her tech savvy generation?
Silver surfers.
That is what she is,
A silver surfer.
Checks online
Whenever she can
To see what her family is up to.
Her children
In Canada,
Australia,
And England.
Her grandchildren
Two in Canada,
One in Seattle.
Her brother
In Scotland
And her sister
In Spain.
Feels she is still a part of all their lives,
Despite being so far away,
And all thanks to the internet.
Post received.
Her heart quickens
With excitement.
From her granddaughter
Jennifer,
Works in Seattle,
As a receptionist.
Supposed to be travelling around the US.
Seems to have been in Seattle
For a while now.

"How are you, Grandma? Thought you might like this post!" writes her Jennifer.

Scrolls down to the post.

Shared thousands of times.

Must be worth a read.

A couple

Got engaged

On top of the Eiffel Tower,

Both look so happy.

How romantic.

Strangers

Took a picture of the moment.

Now they are seeking help

To locate the happy couple.

A noble cause,

A heart-warming cause.

Deserves a like

And a share

And a message

To her sister in Spain,

"Does this bring back memories, Aoife?"

123

Message received
From her dear sister Eileen.
Still lives in Galway,
Been there
All her life.
Hardly ever
Been outside Ireland,
All her life.
Expects she will stay in Ireland
For the rest of her life.
The only one
Of her siblings
To still be in Ireland,
The country of their birth.
Brother moved to Scotland.
She moved to San Sebastian
On the north coast of Spain
With her husband,
Her beloved,
Her late,
Husband.
Almost 20 years gone
Since he passed away.
Thought about moving back to Ireland,
Many times,
To live with Eileen.
Couldn't bare being so far away
From her beloved Serxio,
From their beloved marital home,

Surrounded by all the memories,
Surrounded by all the photos,
Surrounded by all the possessions.
"Does this bring back memories, Aoife?"
Writes her sister Eileen
About a post
She shared,
About a man
On bended knee
Proposing
To his girlfriend
On top of the Eiffel Tower.
Just how her Serxio proposed
To her
On top of the Eiffel Tower
All those years ago.
A tear drops down
From her left eye
And runs all the way down
Her cheek
To the corner
Of her mouth.
"Good to see romance isn't dead!"
She writes to Eileen,
Before sharing the post
With her friends,
With her family,
With a lump in her throat.

124

"Come look at this post, Pieter," says Johanna.
"It's been sent by dad's cousin Aoife in Spain," she adds.
"Very romantic," she continues.
Reluctantly,
Her husband stands up
From the table
Where he had been happily seated
Reading the newspaper.
Grunts,
Quietly,
To himself,
As he walks over
To his wife
To have a look.
Better be good,
He thinks
To himself.
Was reading an interesting article
About the growing international trade dispute.
The UK in the thick of it.
Language
Between the two governments
Becoming more and more heated.
Threats
Being met
With more threats.
Ante
Being upped
At every turn.

Both sides overreacting,

He thinks.

Cool heads needed,

He thinks.

Forget about international affairs.

Johanna wants him to look at something,

Something much more important

On social media.

Spends a minute

Reading the post.

Sighs.

"Is that it?" he asks.

"Don't be such a grump. I think it is very sweet."

"Can't believe you got me to come over to read that," Pieter says.

"It's a lovely thing they are doing, trying to locate a couple to give them a picture of the moment they got engaged," argues Johanna.

"If you say so," says Pieter.

"I do. Have you forgotten you were once a romantic? Remember how you proposed to me?" asks Johanna.

"Of course I do," replies Pieter defensively.

"Can't think of a more romantic way to propose, writing 'will you marry me?' in the sand on the beach at Durban."

"It was romantic, wasn't it?" Pieter, fishing.

"Very," Johanna, taking the bait.

"I suppose it would be nice for the couple to have the picture," admits Pieter.

"I'm going to share it with all our friends. You never know; it might help track them down," says Johanna, before she clicks on Share.

"Worth a try. Sorry for being a misery guts before," Pieter apologises, as he hugs his wife.

"That's okay, my love," she replies,

Content.

125

Woman
At her desk
In the Johannesburg branch
Of an international real estate agency.
New instructions received.
New properties to market.
Apartments,
Houses,
Villas.
Business is booming.
Two properties ready for marketing,
Now.
First things first,
Properties need to be listed.
Not just a matter of placing them
In the local paper,
Like the old days,
Or even on the corporate website.
These days
Social media
Plays a key role.
Uses two profiles,
A corporate one,
And a personal one,
To advertise the properties
And reach as wide an audience
As possible.
Logs on
To the corporate profile first.

Copies the details
Of the first property
From a file
On her computer.
Pastes the details
Of the first property
Onto a pre-prepared post.
Shares the post
With the agency's network
Of contacts
And customers
All around the world.
Job done.
Logs onto her personal profile
To do the same.
Post received from Johanna,
An old school friend,
Lives in Bloemfontein
With her husband
And children.
Hasn't seen her for a while.
Shared a post about a couple
Looking for another couple
To give them a photo
Of the moment
The second couple
Got engaged.
What a lovely proposal,
She thinks to herself.
What a lovely gesture,
She thinks to herself.
Shares it with her friends,
300 or so.
Decides to share it
On the corporate profile too
With customers,

With colleagues,
With contacts
All around the world.
Who knows,
Someone might know
The happy couple,
Someone might be able to help
Track down
The happy couple.

126

All she ever dreams about
Is owning a portfolio
Of properties
In far flung places of the world.
Jet setting
From one bolt hole
To another.
A life of luxury,
A life of adventure.
She wishes.
Has to make do
With her one-bedroom apartment
In Rome, Italy,
For now.
Window shopping
Will have to do,
For now.
Sees the South Africa Office has sent a post
About two new properties
That have come onto the market.
Both in Johannesburg,
Never been there.
Would like to go there,
One day,
To visit.
Not for her though
Either of the two properties.
Oh well,
Will have to continue looking.

Another post shared
By the South Africa Office.
About a man
Proposing to his girlfriend
On top of the Eiffel Tower.
Just like how her friends,
Joe and Sarah
From Malta,
Recently did.
Joe,
An estate agent,
Works for a local agency
In Valletta, Malta
Which she uses to help market properties
On the Mediterranean island
From time to time.
Post includes a picture
Of the moment
When the girlfriend realises
What is happening.
Her heart quickens,
She looks at the picture
One more time,
More closely,
This time.
Joe and Sarah.
Without a doubt.
Reads the post again.
An appeal
By a husband and his wife from Norway
For anyone who knows the couple
To get in touch
So that they can forward them the picture.
103,206 likes later

104,328 shares later
And the quest
Is over.

127

Still can't believe
He is getting married
To the woman of his dreams.
Trip to Paris was perfect.
Everything went according to plan,
Like clockwork.
Better than he could have ever imagined.
The long walks
Around the famous city,
Taking in all the famous sights,
Seeing all the priceless works of art.
The romantic meals,
The evening strolls
Arm in arm.
Then the piece de la resistance,
The trip to the top of the Eiffel Tower
Where he went down on one knee
To ask Sarah,
His girlfriend
Of three years,
For her hand in marriage.
Confident she would say yes.
But one never knows,
Not for certain.
Has been pinching himself
Ever since
They arrived back in Malta,
Just to convince himself
It was not all a dream,

A beautiful dream.
No sitting on laurels.
Wedding to plan,
Wedding to pay for.
Both sets of parents will help,
Up to a point.
The engaged couple will have to fund their share though.
Need to sell some properties.
Need to earn some commission,
That would do the trick.
Time to do some work.
Sitting at his desk
In his office
In the heart of Valletta,
He picks up the phone
To make some calls.
A two-bedroom apartment in the city,
Proving hard to shift
So far,
Surprising.
Determined to drum up interest.
Email alert pops up
On the bottom right-hand corner of his screen.
Catches his eye.
From Aurelia
A friend from Rome, Italy.
A fellow estate agent.
Probably another property
For him to market in Malta
On behalf of her agency.
Always happy to oblige.
Might generate a little commission as well.
Every little bit helps.
Email not work related,
But personal.
Very personal.

Includes a link
To a post
With a picture
Of a couple
Getting engaged
On top of the Eiffel Tower.
Not just any couple.
It's them!
Can't believe it.
The one thing
He and Sarah had thought was missing from Paris,
A picture of the magic moment.
Turns out
There is one.
Turns out
Strangers took a photo with their phone.
Turns out
They have been trying to track them down ever since.
And thanks to over 105,000 shares
They have.
Can't wait to tell Sarah
About the photo,
Can't wait to tell Sarah
About the kindness
Of strangers.

128

Two years,
And counting,
Since they started looking
For a house to buy
In Rabat,
The ancient city in Malta
Which stands on the doorstep
Of the ancient fortress of Mdina.
Home to the knights
For many, many years,
Mdina is a must-see
For many, many tourists
Visiting the country today.
Tired of renting.
Tired of looking at countless properties.
Tired of having hopes raised,
Only for them to be dashed
For one reason or another.
Just wants to settle down
And make a home
For her and her family.
Thought house-hunting would be easy.
Thought house-hunting would be enjoyable,
Up to a point.
Far from it.
Lack of properties on the market
On the one hand,
Lots of buyers
Fighting over the same properties

On the other,

Combine to make real estate in Malta

A seller's market.

Key is getting to see houses,

As soon as they come on the market.

Easier said than done.

Signed up with every agency.

Scours the internet every day,

More than once a day,

To try and get ahead of the pack

And see properties first.

Still no luck.

Needs that little bit of luck,

That's all,

She keeps telling herself.

Phone rings.

It's Joe Faruggia

From a small agency,

In Valletta.

Better answer it.

"Hello, Mrs Vassallo, it's Joe here," he says.

"Hello, Joe. Please call me Lara."

"Will do, Lara. I know you've been looking for a while so I thought I'd give you a heads up about a four-bedroom house in Rabat that is about to come onto the market. Think it could be right up your street," he says.

"Sounds interesting," she replies, trying not to get too excited.

"I think I can arrange a viewing before marketing begins in earnest. I know the vendors and I expect they would be happy to let you see it before anyone else does."

Excited now.

"That would be great," she says.

"Okay, when would be good for you?"

"Name the time, Joe, and I will be there."

129

Three months
Since they left their home,
Since they left their life
In Germany.
Opportunity for her husband Florian
To set up,
And run,
An international financial services business
In Malta,
Too good an opportunity
To turn down.
Good salary,
Good place to live,
Good weather.
All positives.
Leaving friends,
Leaving family,
Leaving school.
All negatives.
Big upheaval,
Especially,
For the children,
Matthias
Aged 12,
And Claudia
Aged 10.
Florian is happy.
Work is going well,
But takes up most of his time.

Hardly sees him.

Children are happy

Settled into school well

Made lots of friends.

She seems to be the only one

Who is unhappy

And struggling to make friends.

Misses the children terribly

During the day

While they are busy

At school.

Homesick.

Lonely,

So much so

She counts the hours

Until she picks up the children from school.

Almost that time of the day now.

Her happy hour.

Parks the car.

Walks to the school entrance

And waits for her children.

A woman,

About her age,

Approaches her.

"Hello. My name is Lara Vassallo, I believe my daughter Mia is in the same class as your daughter. Claudia, is it?"

"Yes, that is right. I am Hannah Weber. Nice to meet you, Lara," she says.

"Nice to meet you, Hannah. How are you finding Malta? You settling in okay?" asks Lara.

"Okay, thank you. Malta is so beautiful and the weather is great. It has been a big change but I think we are getting there," replies Hannah.

"Well, please do feel free to get in touch if you need anything. Happy to help. Been meaning to introduce myself properly but I've been so busy trying to find a house for the family."

"That's okay. I know how stressful moving can be. Have you found one that you like?"

"I think so. Just had an offer accepted on a house in Rabat. Fingers crossed. Oh, before I forget, a couple of the other mothers are meeting up for a coffee tomorrow after drop-off. Would you like to join us? Would be a good opportunity to meet some new people," suggests Lara.

"I would love to. Thanks so much for thinking of me," replies Hannah.

130

Volunteers.
Need more
Volunteers
To watch
Over the eggs,
The loggerhead turtle eggs,
Buried in the golden sands
Of Golden Bay,
A beach
On the west coast of Malta.
Imperative
The eggs are not disturbed
By anyone.
Vital
The eggs are protected
From predators.
Crucial
The turtles have a chance
Before they even hatch.
As soon as he heard about the turtle and the eggs,
He answered the call
From Nature Trust
For volunteers.
Spends a couple of hours
In the afternoon
At the beach
Whenever he can.
But his pastizzeria in Zebbug
Won't make pastizzi,

Malta's traditional savoury pastry,
On its own.
If enough people did their bit
Each shift
Could be shorter.
More volunteers,
That would do it.
He turns
From the sea.
He walks
Back to his chair
On the beach.
He spots
Two children,
A boy and a girl,
And their mother,
He presumes.
He watches them approach the gazebo
Next to the part of the beach
Where the eggs were laid.
They stop
In front of a notice
Pinned onto a makeshift board.
They read
Information on the turtle
And the hatching process.
They read
The appeal for volunteers.
They read
About Nature Trust's work.
The mother approaches the man.
"Hello. Could you tell me how long will it take before the eggs hatch?" asks the
mother in a German accent.
"A little while longer," replies the pastizzeria owner.
"Are you still looking for volunteers?" asks the woman.
"Oh yes. Why, are you interested?"

"Yes, I am. I can spare a couple of hours during the day, when my children are at school," says the woman.

"That would be great."

"Also, I'll see if any of the other mothers from our school are interested in volunteering," adds the woman.

"Fantastic. My name is Chris, by the way."

"Mine is Hannah. And these are my children, Matthias and Claudia."

"Pleased to meet you all. Do you live here?" asks Chris.

"Yes, we recently moved from Germany," replies Hannah.

"Well, thank you very much for moving from Germany and volunteering!" says Chris.

131

Back on the front steps
Of Tony's Café
Opposite the Church of St Philip of Agira
In the heart of Zebbug, Malta.
Sat there yesterday
With the others:
Tony,
The café owner,
Pippo,
One of his oldest friends,
Paulo,
His cousin
And Pizu,
Another old friend
He has known all his life.
All five
Have been sitting on the same front steps
Together
Every day
Since they retired,
Some 20 years,
Or so,
Ago.
Talking,
Laughing,
And joking,
Reminiscing about the past,
Putting the world to rights,
Watching the world go by,

Or at least,
The townsfolk of Zebbug,
His hometown.
Old friends
And family
Stop to chat
To the old men
On their way
To wherever they are heading.
Suddenly,
The five men break out
In laughter,
In unison.
Pizu managed to slip
Off the step
He had been sitting on.
Regaining his composure,
After what seemed like an age,
Mikey spots a man,
Crossing the square,
Walking towards them,
With a tray in his hands.
Can't make out who it is.
Eyes not what they were.
Probably Chris,
From the pastizzeria.
It is Chris.
"Bongu," greets Chris.
"Bongu," shout out the old men,
In unison.
"Thought you boys could do with some food," says Chris,
As he offers them each a pastizzi,
One cheese,
One pea.
"Thank you, Chris," say the old men,
In unison.

"Mikey was just saying how hungry he was, weren't you, Mikey?" claims Pizu. "Yes, that's true," replies Mikey, while tucking into a pastizzi. "I am always hungry."

132

Too many bags,
Too much shopping,
Too heavy.
Arms aching,
Almost burning.
Always the case
After she's been to the market.
Having to stop
For a break
Every few metres
It seems.
Will take an age
To get back home,
At this rate.
Was never like this
When she was younger,
That's for sure.
Makes it to the church,
Eventually.
The halfway marker
To her small house.
The church,
A good place,
To take a breather.
A good place,
To call for divine intervention
To help get her back home,
As quickly as possible,
And with both her arms

Still intact.

"You look like you could do with some help, Ella."

Ella turns around.

It's Mikey.

Standing upright

For a change.

Usually planted firmly on the front steps

Of Tony's Café.

"Oh, Mikey. That would be so great if you could. But only if you feel strong enough. These bags are so heavy," says Ella.

"Nothing I can't handle. Besides, Chris gave us all free pastizzi earlier. I have energy to burn," says Mikey.

"That was nice of Chris. He's a good man. I could do with the help but please don't feel you have to carry the bags all the way to my house," replies Ella.

"Of course I will. I'm not going to leave you in the lurch," promises Mikey.

133

Quick glance at his watch,
Again.
30 minutes
Before band practice
Starts.
Desperately needs to practice
Ahead of the festa
This weekend.
Plays the trumpet
In the local brass band.
Plays a key role
In the celebrations.
Doesn't want to miss practice.
Feeling nervous already.
Just wants to play now
Until the weekend,
To get it right.
Terrible timing,
The worst.
His turn on the roster
To clean the Church of St Philip of Agira
In Zebbug.
Not on his own,
Thank God.
There will be other volunteers,
Like him,
Thank God.
Enters the grand church,
Hoping the others will be happy

To cover for him,

Just this once,

So that he can make practice.

Looks around.

Sees only one volunteer.

Ella,

A widow

In her 60s,

Lived in Zebbug

All her life.

Should be five volunteers.

Plus him.

Six in all.

Can't leave Ella on her own,

Unless the others are around,

Somewhere,

Or the others are running late,

Somehow.

If not,

He will have to stay

And miss practice.

"Bongu, Julian," says Ella.

"Bongu, Ella," replies Julian.

"Looks like it is just you and me today," reveals Ella.

"No one else around?" asks Julian, hopefully.

"No, at least not yet. You look disappointed," replies Ella.

"I have band practice for the festa. Was hoping someone could cover for me," admits Julian.

"Oh, I'll be alright here on my own. I was half expecting to be by myself anyway before you turned up," offers Ella.

"I couldn't let you clean this church all on your own, Ella, but you are sweet for offering," answers Julian.

"Don't be so silly, my dear, I don't mind at all. I haven't got anything else to do this evening. Besides, I've done it plenty of times before on my own and I like the peace here. Now, off you go," orders Ella.

134

Bad day.
Another one.
Hardly any customers
And those that did come
Through the door
Of his convenience store
Were out of the door,
As fast as they had entered,
Often without
Uttering a single word,
Often without
Looking at him in the eye,
Even those who made a purchase.
Maybe a grunt.
Maybe a thank you,
If he was lucky.
Maybe a question
Asking if there were any papers left,
Or for directions to a café.
What he would give
To talk
About anything
With anyone
Even a complete stranger.
Bored of his own company.
Bored of wishing the hours away,
Until it is time
To close the shop for the day.
And then what?

Go upstairs
To the apartment
Above the shop
Where he lives?
A prisoner,
That is what he has become,
A life sentence,
That is what he is serving.
The door opens.
Knows the man's face
Can't remember the name,
Not at first.
Julian,
That's the name.
"Bongu, Edward. How are you today?" asks Julian.
"Had better days, to be honest," replies the shopkeeper.
"Oh no, that's not good. What's wrong?" asks Julian, as he picks up a bottle of cold mineral water from the fridge and brings it to the counter.
"Wondering what the point of it all is, that's all."
"Well, that's enough to send anyone into a spin. Must be tough working every day without much of a break. You need something to look forward to. Can't you get someone to run the store one day a week? Give you a chance to have a break and relax?"
"Can't afford to. Struggling to make ends meet as it is," says Edward.
"Everyone has to have a break. I tell you what. Why don't you let me look after the shop sometimes? I can spare a few hours one day every fortnight and I would be happy to do it, and you can pay me with a newspaper. I have a lot more time on my hands these days since I retired."
"Really. You would do that for me?" asks Edward.
"Yes, of course. Always wanted to work in a shop. I have to go to band practice now for the festa, but I'll pop in tomorrow and let's sort out the details."
"That would be great. Thank you so much, Julian. Let me give you your money back for the water."
"No way, Edward. You have a business to run," replies Julian, as he walks out of the door.

135

Torture.
Going to the shop
With his mother
After school.
Always hungry
After school.
Last thing he wants
After school
Is to go to the local store
With all those tasty things
To buy
With all those tasty things
To eat.
Fruits,
Ripe
And juicy.
Breads,
Freshly made
That day.
Biscuits,
All the best-selling brands
And flavours.
Snacks,
Savoury
And sweet.
All tastes catered for.
And then there are the chocolates
And then there are the sweets.
So many,

They send him into a spin,
Every time his eyes fix on them.
How he would love to stuff his pockets
With a handful,
Or two.
But his mother never buys
Any chocolates
Or sweets,
Or at least,
Not the ones he likes.
Instead,
She always buys
The same old chocolate,
A bar with nuts and raisins.
Better than nothing
He supposes,
But how he would love to try
Just one
Of the weird and wonderful flavours
Lined up,
Enticingly,
In front of him.

"Hello, Mrs Attard. How are you this evening?" asks the shopkeeper.

"Fine, thank you. How are you, Edward?" replies the boy's mother.

"Good, thank you. Been a slow day, but things have picked up in the last hour or so," says Edward.

"That's good to hear," says the boy's mother.

"So much so that it has become a very good day. Would you mind if I gave young Simon a nice chocolate bar? He's such a good boy," offers the shopkeeper.

Thinks he heard what the shopkeeper just said,
But doesn't believe it.
His mother looks at him.

"I don't see why not, but that is very generous of you, Edward. Simon, what do you say to Edward?" asks his mother.

Eyes widen.
Mouth opens.

Allows himself to believe.

"Thank you so much, Mr Scibberas."

"No problem, Simon. Go over to the chocolate shelf and choose a bar that catches your eye."

Simon runs to the aisle.

Licks his lips

And grins.

136

New school,
New friends.
Well,
That is what his parents had told him.
New school,
No doubt
About that.
Struggling
To find his way around
The unfamiliar buildings,
The countless rooms,
The long corridors.
Constantly having to ask
For directions
To the correct classroom.
Already been late for class
On more than one occasion.
Luckily for him,
Teachers have been in a forgiving mood,
So far.
As for new friends?
Hasn't even made one.
No one seems interested
In finding out more
About the new boy in class.
He has a story to tell,
Just like everyone else.
Jonathan Zammit,
12-year-old boy

From Naxxar.

Switched from St Edward's College

Just outside Valletta,

To San Francesco Saverio School

In the north of the island.

Didn't want to change schools.

Was settled at St Edward's.

Parents made him move.

The school run,

They said.

Took too long,

They said.

How can it take so long

When Malta is so small?

17 miles long

And 9 miles wide

Or so he was told,

At junior school.

Going to be late for maths class,

Again.

Confused,

Again.

Lost,

Again.

Was never like this

At St Edward's.

No one would have let this happen

At St Edward's.

New students were always welcomed

At St Edward's,

With open arms.

"You lost, Jonathan?" asks a boy

In his maths class.

Can't remember his name.

"Er yes. Can't find my way around this place," answers Jonathan.

"Yes, it is a big old place, isn't it? Don't worry, come with me if you like," offers the boy.

"Thanks. I'm sorry but I can't remember your name."

"Don't worry, must be tricky with all the new faces and all the new names. My name is Simon."

"Of course. Sorry for not remembering."

"Don't be silly, Jonathan. Tell you what. A group of us are planning to kick a ball around at lunch break. Do you fancy tagging along?" asks Simon.

"Yeah, cool, thanks."

"Great. Now we better get to math or we will be kept in during lunch!" says Simon, only half-joking.

137

Five more minutes
In the cubicle
That ought to do it.
In five minutes,
The bell would have been rung
And everyone should be on their way
To their classes,
He hopes.
Too distracted
He hopes
To tease him,
To mock him,
To bully him,
Just as they do every day
Whenever they set eyes on him.
Prefers to lock himself in a cubicle
In a hardly ever used lavatory
In a quiet corner of the school,
Rather than
Run the gauntlet
Of the corridors
And the playground
Of San Francesco Saverio school.
Still has no idea
Why he is picked on,
Relentlessly.
There was a time
When he had friends at school.
There was a time

When he enjoyed school.
Something happened,
It must have,
To change all that.
Still can't put a finger
On what it was.
Something he said?
Something he didn't say?
Something he did?
Something he didn't do?
No idea.
Wish someone would tell him.
Put him out of his misery.
Maybe he could put right
Whatever it was
He did wrong,
If only he knew.
Thinks about his swimming club.
Has friends at his swimming club,
Many friends,
Good friends,
Go back many years.
What would he do
Without his swimming club?
Looks at his watch.
Time
To leave the shelter
Of the cubicle.
Time
To brave it
Outside.
Unlocks the door.
Steps into
The washroom
At the exact moment
When another boy enters

The washroom.

Not just any boy,

Robbie Bartolini,

His nemesis.

"Is this where you've been hiding all this time? Wet your pants did you, Dumb Dumb Dominic?" mocks the bully.

"No," is all Dominic can muster in response.

"Well, you have now!" adds Robbie as he hurls water that he had cupped in his hands from the tap onto Dominic's trousers.

Looks down.

Worst fears realised.

Large damp patch

Growing around the zip area

Of his trousers.

Great.

Can't go into class like that.

"And another one!" Robbie yells, as he repeats the prank.

"Leave him alone."

An unfamiliar voice,

Halts the bully

In his tracks.

New boy,

Called Jonathan.

"Why don't you just go back to your old school, Johnny new boy?" orders Robbie.

"You okay, Dominic?" asks Jonathan.

"Yes thanks," he replies.

"I'm talking to you!" shouts Robbie.

"Come on, let's get out of here. The sun will help dry your trousers. Let's stay in the playground as long as possible before class. Give your trousers a chance to dry. We can say I got lost and you showed me where to go," adds Jonathan, as he follows Dominic out of the washroom,

Leaving Robbie behind,

On his own.

"Thanks for that. You were great," says Dominic.

"No problem. The thing bullies hate the most is being ignored. Try it some time. Can be hard particularly if they push you around. But just be strong and ignore them and eventually, they'll move on."

"Thanks for the advice. I'll try that," says Dominic.

"And if that Robbie gives you any more trouble, just come and find me."

"I will," promises Dominic.

Strange feeling,

A feeling he hasn't felt

For a long time

At school.

What is it?

A feeling

Of not being alone,

Of maybe even

Having a friend.

138

In a cubicle
In the changing room
In the Tal-Qroqq Sports Complex
In Msida, Malta.
Out of a pink rucksack,
A woman pulls out
A dark blue swimming costume,
A yellow towel,
A pair of mirror lensed goggles
And a white swim hat.
Tries to swim
At the National Swimming Pool
At least three times a week.
Always comes at 12pm
On a Saturday afternoon
To spend an hour
In the water.
Finds the best time
Is when the children's lessons end
And everyone heads out to lunch.
Not her.
Lunch can wait.
Often gets a whole lane
All to herself
At this time of the day.
Bliss.
Hears the children
Enter the changing rooms.
Lessons finished.

Perfect timing,
She thinks to herself,
As she pulls the straps of the costume
Over her shoulders.
Hears the door
Of the neighbouring cubicle
Close.
A double cubicle,
Fits two people.
Hears two boys,
Joking with each other.
Loud,
As boys should be.
Starts packing her clothes
Into her rucksack,
Neatly.

"Well done today, Dominic. You left me for dust in the pool," says one of the boys.

"Thanks, Andrew. Felt stronger today for some reason," reveals the boy called Dominic.

"What are you doing this afternoon? Fancy hanging out at mine? Reckon my mum and dad won't mind," asks Andrew.

"I'll have to ask my mother. Hey, let's change on one side of the cubicle. That way we keep the other side dry so that the next person doesn't have to step into pools of water if they don't want to," suggests the boy called Dominic.

"That's a good idea," says the other.

"It truly is,"
Thinks the woman
To herself,
"And very thoughtful."

139

Valletta,
Capital city of Malta
And UNESCO World Heritage Site.
As beautiful,
As they were told
It would be
By the countless travel books
They devoured
Before they arrived
On the island.
The Baroque palaces,
The impregnable bastions,
The limestone buildings,
The elegant balconies,
The generous piazzas,
The grand churches,
The cafes,
The countless cafes.
But there is one cafe
Both have their hearts set on visiting.
Caffe Cordina
In Republic Street.
Full of Maltese delicacies
And specialties,
They were told.
Recommended
By just about everyone they had spoken to
Before they arrived
And by just about everyone they had spoken to

Since they arrived
On the island.
Want to taste Malta?
Go to Caffe Cordina
They were told.
A lot to live up to
Caffe Cordina.
Excited,
The elderly couple pass the Palace Armoury
And enter Republic Square.
The famous old cafe
Appears before them,
Just as the guidebooks
Told them it would.
Both feel a pang of excitement,
But the famous emporium
Of Maltese cuisine
Looks busy.
No free table outside.
No matter,
Was hoping for a table inside,
Despite the warm weather.
Not every day
One gets to eat
Inside an old palace,
After all.
Inside,
The cafe is just as busy
As the outside.
No spare tables,
As far as they can see.
Not wanting to give up
Without a fight,
Both look around,
To see if anyone
Is settling up

Or if anyone
Is about to leave.
No luck.
Everyone looks settled in
For a long stay.
Disappointed,
They turn
To walk out.
"Sorry, are you English?" asks an elegant older woman sitting at a table to the right of the entrance.
"No, we are from Denmark, but we speak English," replies the woman.
"I saw you looking for a table and wondered if you would like to sit here. There are two spare seats," offers the woman, as she picks up a pink rucksack from one of the seats next to her.
"That would be lovely. We heard so much of Caffe Cordina we were really looking forward to having a spot of lunch here," says the man with a big grin on his face.
"Thought you looked disappointed. Come and sit here and enjoy the delights of our Caffe Cordina."

140

She knew it would be a mistake,
To bring Coco to Valletta.
Never been good on a lead
Even when there are no distractions.
Never been good on a lead
On the busy streets of Valletta.
Too busy
To take her for a walk
This morning.
Had to go to the city
This afternoon
For a spot of shopping,
A birthday present
For her husband.
Kill two birds with one stone,
She thought.
Regrets it now.
Arm tired
From all the pulling
In every direction
By her very excited
Chocolate-coloured
Two-year-old
Labrador.
Tried puppy training.
Didn't work.
Waste of money.
Tried bribing her with treats.
Didn't work.

Gobbles them up
Before charging off.
Tried a special harness.
Didn't work.
The opposite.
Allowed her to pull
Even harder.
Shouldn't be so stressful,
Having a dog.
Dreading
Going into the jewellery shop
With Coco bounding around,
Chomping at the bit,
Straining at the leash.
Quick in and out
The only way.
Hoping a circuit
Around the Upper Barrakka Gardens first
Will take the edge off her
Before they head
To the jewellers
To look for a new watch
For her husband.
"What a beautiful dog. May we stroke her?" an elderly man asks in an accent,
Scandinavian maybe,
Standing next to an elderly woman,
His wife,
Presumably.
"Yes, of course. She's very friendly. But she is still learning her manners," warns
Coco's owner.
"That's alright. We love dogs. We have two back home in Denmark," reveals
the man.
"Aren't you beautiful," says his wife, while bending down and stroking Coco's
body all over. "Even though we are in this beautiful country with all its fantastic
distractions, we miss our dogs very much."

"I can imagine. Don't think you'd miss this one though. She's a puller," says Coco's owner.

"Oh, are you a puller?" says the man in a babyish voice. "How old is she?" he asks, in a grown-up voice.

"Two," replies the dog owner.

"She'll grow out of it soon, don't worry. All dogs go through a teenage phase. But it passes soon enough," says the man.

"I hope so," replies Coco's owner.

"It will. She looks like a very intelligent and loving dog to me," adds the man's wife.

"Yes, she is," agrees Coco's owner,

Suddenly feeling proud,

Suddenly feeling full of love

For her dog.

141

Less than 24 hours
Before he sets sail
For Cyprus,
And what does he do?
Lose his wallet.
Money,
Cards,
ID,
All gone.
Chances are
He won't see them again,
Especially,
As he is not a Maltese citizen,
Especially,
As he has no fixed abode,
Especially,
As he lives on a boat
In the marina.
No one would be able to get in touch with him,
Even if anyone had the inclination to.
Only hope,
An honest person has handed in his wallet
To the Police.
Doesn't care
If they pocket the money first,
As long as they leave the rest,
That will do.
Off to the police station
In Valletta

On the off chance
That some good soul found his wallet
And did the right thing.
Upper Barrakka Gardens,
Last time he remembers having his wallet
When he bought himself a cold drink.
Could turn out to be
The most expensive drink
He has ever bought,
He thinks to himself.
Arrives at the police station.
Enters the building.
Takes a deep breath.
Last chance,
He knows it.
If the wallet is not here
Cards will have to be cancelled.
Last thing he wants to do,
As he will be away
At sea
For who knows how long.
Walks up
To a police officer.
"Excuse me. I lost my wallet earlier today and wondered if someone has brought
it into the station?" he asks.
"Aha. You might be in luck. A wallet was handed in an hour or so ago. Follow
me," says the policeman.
Hopes raised,
He walks towards a counter.
Police officer bends down.
Opens a safe.
Brings out a box.
Opens the box
To reveal a treasure trove
Of lost items.
Police officer picks up a wallet.

The man recognises it

In an instant.

"Before I give it to you, can you tell me what is inside?" asks the police officer.

"ID with my name on it, Jake Whitehead, two bank cards and a bunch of receipts. There were about 120 euros as well, but I am not expecting them to still be in there," says Jake.

Police officer checks inside.

"It's yours alright and you're in luck. The 120 euros are still inside," says the police officer, as he hands the wallet over.

Checks it for himself.

"Wow. I can't believe the money is still there. What an honest person. Do you know who brought it in?" he asks.

"Yes, the wallet was found by a dog called Coco."

142

Good to be back
On the water.
Will miss his family,
The comforts of home,
His favourite food,
Of course.
Always does.
Will get better
When they get going.
Always does.
Not knowing
How long they will be away for
Doesn't help,
Though.
Never does.
Sailing the Oyster superyacht
To Cyprus
To pick up
Food,
Supplies,
Water,
And then,
The owner
Of the 123ft yacht himself
And his staff.
Followed by his guests.
Expecting eight.
Could be more,
Usually is.

Cruising around the Mediterranean
For as long as the owner,
And his guests,
Want to.
Everything
Has to be ship shape
Before the Russian billionaire
Comes on board,
Especially,
When he is entertaining.
So glad
They have a week or so
Sailing to Cyprus
To make sure
All is in order.
His responsibility,
As skipper,
To make sure
All is in order,
To make sure
The crew works well
Together.
Four crew.
Worked with two previously,
Jake Whitehead,
An experienced Australian,
Clocked up a lot of sailing,
Despite his young years.
Old Man Mike O'Malley,
An Irishman,
Been around forever.
Lives in Malta,
Regularly crews,
Reliable.
Two unknowns.
An American,

Bradley Donavon,
Learnt his trade
In the Caribbean
Crossed the Atlantic
A couple of months ago
Made his way to Malta,
To find work.
And Jen Masters,
An Englishwoman,
Been teaching youngsters to sail
In Malta
For over a year.
Keen.
Untested.
Something about her though.
A twinkle in her eye
That says
"I'm a winner and I'm going places."
Standing on the deck
Of the yacht
Moored at the marina
In Valletta,
He watches
The crew catch up.
He watches
The crew get to know each other.
Thinks they will work well together.
Nice balance,
At least he hopes
That will be the case.
The laughing and joking
Are all encouraging.
"Got something for you Skip."
Jake interrupts his thoughts.
"Me? I'm the skipper. No one gets the skipper anything," he jokes.
"Well, I have!" replies Jake,

As he tosses a bag over to him.

"What's this?" he asks, somehow managing to catch the bag

Without spilling its contents.

He opens the bag.

Full of packets of Twisties and Tasties

And a couple of cans of Cisk beer,

His favourite snacks,

And his favourite local brew.

Reminders of home.

"I know you always miss home when you are out at sea," says Jake. "So I thought this might help."

"Cheers, mate," he says.

143

Teaching
Young people to sail,
Fulfilling,
Rewarding,
Fun.
But there's nothing like
Being out at sea crewing,
Exhilarating,
Thrilling,
Liberating.
It is
What sailing is all about.
One concern,
A big concern,
Been weighing on her mind,
Ever since she took the job.
Worried,
She will be assigned the menial jobs
Cleaning,
Cooking,
Washing.
Happens all too often.
Just because
She is a woman,
Skippers assume
She can't handle
The physical aspects of sailing,
So she is treated differently.
Big mistake.

Can hold her own,
Will hold her own,
More than her own.
Ready to stand her ground.
Ready for anything.
Very much hopes
There will be no need
To fight her corner.
Skipper looks decent enough.
Talks a good game.
But jury out
Until he hands out
Duties.
Soon find out
If he treats her differently
To the men on board.
Won't be afraid
To stand up for herself,
If needs be.
But would prefer not to have to,
For a change.
As for the rest of the crew,
Lots of joking,
Lots of banter,
Just what she likes.
Can give
As good as she gets.
Intends to give
As good as she gets.
As for the boat,
Luxury on water.
Fit for a king
Or in this case,
An oligarch.
Packed with all the latest technology
And gadgets.

Takes some of the romance
Out of sailing.
Shame,
But that's progress,
Apparently.
"Jen!" yells the captain.
"Yes Skip," she replies.
"When we're out of Valletta, I want you on the main mast. Let's get the sail out and see what she's got."
"On it, Skip!" she shouts in reply,
Good man
That Skip.

144

Hard day.
Lots of sailing,
Lots of cleaning,
Lots of cooking.
Wouldn't change it for the world though,
His job,
Crewing.
Except for one thing.
The thing that is always there
In the back of his mind,
When he is distracted by work.
The thing that is always there
In the front of his mind,
When he has a moment to himself,
Like now.
Loneliness.
Loves sailing.
No doubt about that.
Much better than any other job
He can think of,
Especially,
A job that requires being chained to a desk
Nine to five.
But there is a price to be paid
With his job.
Loneliness.
Yearns for female company.
But,
Fears he'll never get a chance

To meet the woman of his dreams
If he sticks with sailing.
Sees his friends settle down
One by one
With the one,
The love of their lives.
All have normal jobs.
A desk
In an office
In a city
Or a town.
His turn next.
He always says to himself.
Never is.
A nomad
That is who he is.
Just a wanderer,
Sailing from one port
To another.
Maybe that is just his lot
And he just has to accept it.
Lovely girl on this trip though,
Jen.
Beautiful
And funny.
Way above his league.
Hasn't got a chance.
Takes a swig from his bottle of beer.
A Cisk,
The Maltese brew
The Skipper loves,
As he sits on the deck,
Taking a well-deserved break,
After cooking a meal
For the crew,
A mushroom risotto.

Crew seemed to like it.

Nothing left in the pan.

Likes cooking.

Glad he was assigned cooking duties

By the Skip.

"That was delicious, Bradley. Where did you learn to cook?" asks Jen, as she sits down opposite him.

"Just picked it up on the way, I guess," he replies. "Always liked helping my grandmother bake cakes when I was young."

"I hate cooking. Always see it as a chore," she admits.

"I see it as the opposite. I love combining wonderful ingredients with different flavours to create a tasty dish. Then watching others eat it and hopefully like it," he says, excitedly.

"I love it how you are so passionate about cooking," she adds. "So tell me, what's your story, Bradley? Where are you from, where did you grow up?" she continues after a short pause.

"Originally from Santa Cruz, California. Always loved the water. Name a water sport and I did it. Spent my childhood in the water at Steamer's Lane surfing. Or up the coast wind surfing at Scott's Creek. And of course, sailing. Gradually, sailing took over. Knew that's all I wanted to do from a young age. So when I left school, I didn't bother with college. Earned some money doing little jobs. Then headed down to the Bahamas to get a job on a boat. Any boat. Any job. Stayed there for the best part of 10 years. Sailing up and down the Caribbean. Then got a gig crossing the Atlantic to Ireland and worked my way to Malta."

He stops to take a swig of his beer before continuing, "That's basically me in a nutshell. What about you?" he asks.

"Pretty similar. Grew up in Dorset, south coast of England. Spent most of my childhood on the water sailing. Taught children to sail when I left school. Managed a couple of crossings but not enough. I headed to Malta to see if there was more work in the Med. Ended up teaching sailing for a year or so again. Until I got this job. So, is there a girl somewhere waiting for you ashore?" she asks.

"No, I wish. Hard meeting someone special in this job," he replies. "What about you?"

"Same. It's a nomadic existence, isn't it? Difficult finding someone who is on the same wavelength. Someone who knows what makes me tick. A lot of guys just don't get the pull of the sea."

"Exactly the same with me, but with women," he laughs.

She laughs.

He smiles.

She smiles.

145

Aching
All over,
Especially,
His back
And his joints.
Name it
And it aches,
And it has only been two days
Since they set off from Valletta
On the 'One Good Turn',
A 123ft luxury yacht.
Another five days or so
Before they reach
Cyprus.
Short stopover
Before they head off
Cruising
Around the Med
For who knows how long.
Doesn't know how his body will cope.
Getting too old.
A lifetime at sea
Catching up with him,
Finally.
Sailing,
All he has ever known
Since he was a boy
In Cork, Ireland.
Can't imagine life without sailing.

At least he lives
On the island of Malta
When he is not at sea.
Married a local girl,
Vanessa.
Met too late for children.
But they love each other dearly
And that is all that matters.
So, all not lost
When he finally swaps
Life on the sea
For life on terra firma.
Not there yet.
Not for a few years more.
Won't let a few aches and pains
Stop him
From doing what he loves.
And he loves it all,
Even scrubbing the decks
Like he is doing now,
Even though his back doesn't like it so much.
Decides to take it easy,
Decides to scrub gently
So that he doesn't pull a muscle
That takes an age to heal.
Has to manage his body these days.
Hopes no one will notice.
Hopes no one will think he is not pulling his weight.
"Is there a spare brush around Mike?" asks Bradley, an American.
Nice boy.
Getting on very well with Jen.
Nice gal.
Good match.
"There's another in the bucket," he replies in his thick Irish accent.
"Thought I'd help you out. A lot of deck to scrub," says Bradley.

"Never a truer word said there. You don't have to mind. Got it all under control," says Mike, though in truth he would love some help.

"That's okay. Happy to help," replies Bradley.

"That's grand of you, Bradley. Thank you."

146

Loves boats.
Spends as much time as he can
On boats
Or around boats.
Was always going to be that way.
Father is a fisherman.
Father gave him a boat of his own,
A small dinghy
With a small sail,
Which he shares
With his older brother.
Wants to work on large boats
When he is older.
Wants to own a large boat
When he is older.
Heads down to the Port of Limassol
On the south coast of Cyprus
Whenever he can
To watch the boats
Come and go.
Leisure craft,
Fishing boats,
Ships.
Heads down to Limassol Marina
Whenever he can
To see the luxury yachts
And dream
About which one he will own
One day,

One day.
Spots a large yacht
Moored,
A superyacht
Must be over 100ft long.
Hasn't seen it before.
Walks over.
Reads the name of the boat
Slowly,
"One Good Turn"
Doesn't know what it means.
Crew still on board,
Stowing away equipment,
Cleaning the decks,
Coiling lines.
"Speak English?" asks one of the crew,
An old sailor wearing a blue cap,
Speaks in a funny accent.
"A little, sir. Where have you come from?" asks the boy in broken English.
"Malta," answers the old sailor. "Do you know where that is?"
"Yes. West. Not too far away," he replies.
"That's right. What is your name?" asks the old sailor.
"Andreas."
"Nice to meet you, Andreas. My name is Mike. Do you like boats?" asks Mike.
"Yes, I do, Sir," replies Andreas.
"Do you want to come on board and look around?" asks Mike.
"Yes please!" answers Andreas,
Trying to contain his excitement.

147

Good catch,
For a change.
Mullet,
Sea bream.
All
Already sold
To local restaurants
And local markets.
Someone will enjoy
Freshly caught fish this evening,
He thinks to himself.
Kept a few back
For his friends
And his family,
Like he always does.
Back at his boat
He cleans his net.
Hard work,
Especially,
After an early start,
Especially,
After a long day
At sea.
Might be a chore
But a necessary one.
The net is his livelihood,
After all.
Has to look after it.
Has to clean it,

This evening.

No one else will.

"Papa!" yells his son, Andreas.

"Yes, son," replies his father.

"I saw a 123ft yacht. Sailed in from Malta. You have to see it."

"Where is it?" asks his father.

"At the marina. The crew let me look around and stand at the wheel. It was amazing. You have to come and take a look."

"Too busy. Maybe later if there is time."

"Do you have lot's still to do, Papa?"

"Yes, cleaning the net. Always takes a long time."

"Let me help you, Papa," offers Andreas.

"What? You have never cleaned the nets before!" says his father.

"First time for everything, Papa. It's time I learned."

"Nothing would make me happier than helping you, Papa," he adds.

"Nothing would make me happier than you helping me, son," says his father.

Father and son,

Working together

On the nets,

Laughing

And joking together.

148

Busy day
In the restaurant.
Lost count
Of the number of meals she prepared.
Mezes mainly,
As usual,
The most popular dish
By far.
A lot of hard work
Goes into each serving.
A lot of ingredients
Go into each serving.
Olives,
Black and green,
Marinated.
Tahini,
Humus,
Taramasalata,
Tzatziki,
All homemade,
All served with strips of freshly cooked bread
And a bowl of mixed salad.
Then there are the various servings,
Fish,
Halloumi cheese,
Grilled,
Keftedes,
Kebabs,
Skewered.

Followed by fresh fruit,
Diced
And sliced.
Cooking doesn't end
When she leaves the restaurant,
Unfortunately.
Hungry mouths to feed
At home.
Last thing she wants to do,
More cooking
At home.
But husband never cooks.
Spends all his time with his boat.
Sons never cook.
Andreas is too young
To do it on his own,
Kostas is too old,
Has a life of his own,
Spends less and less time
At home
These days.
Down to her
To feed the hungry mouths.
Home,
A small house
On a quiet street
In Limassol.
Reaches the front door,
Finally,
After a long hard day.
Opens the door.
Strange smell.
Cooking,
Fish?
That's it.
Must be coming from next door,

She tells herself.

No.

From the kitchen,

From her kitchen.

Enters the room.

Her husband.

"What's this?" she asks.

"You'll never believe what happened, Maria. Andreas came by to the boat and offered to help me clean the nets. We finished up early so I thought I'd cook dinner tonight. Give you a night off. You must be sick of cooking," says her husband.

"Very much so. I love you, my husband. You sweet man," says Maria.

149

Tired now.
Three trips already,
Transferring cases of drinks
From his car,
Parked near the Promenade
In Limassol,
To the bar
He manages
A couple of streets away.
Not the most efficient way
To restock,
He admits
To himself.
Must find a distributor,
A reliable one,
This time.
Would save
A lot of time,
A lot of energy,
A lot of stress.
Walks back to his car.
Picks up two crates of beer.
Heavy,
Too heavy.
Knows he should take one crate
At a time.
Decides to risk it
To save time
And his arms.

With a swing of his hips
He slams the door of his car shut.
Crosses the street.
Walks
Fast,
Almost
Runs.
Needs to get to The Tavern
Before his arms give way.
Hopes someone will open the doors for him
When he arrives
At the bar.
Tricky on his own,
Especially,
With two crates
In his arms.
Moment of truth.
Arggh!
No one around.
Now what?
Stops
In front of the doors,
Trying to figure out
What to do.
"That looks heavy. Let me help you."
He turns around.
Sees a middle-aged woman.
"That would be great. Thank you," he says.
"Happy to help," she says.
Doors opened,
Quickly.
Bar entered,
Quickly.
Crates set down,
Quickly,
Onto the floor.

The man turns to the woman.

"Thanks again. If you ever come here for a drink, it will be on the house. Just ask for Nico."

"That's kind, thank you. My husband and I might just take you up on that. My name is Maria."

"Nice to meet you, Maria. Absolutely, bring your husband too."

150

Furry feeling
In his mouth.
Can't figure out why.
Parched.
That's it.
Water.
That's it.
Needs water,
Badly.
Head thumping,
Badly.
Can't get out of bed.
Can't open his eyes.
Can't lift any of his limbs.
Can't even get a glass of water.
Beads of sweat
On his brow,
On his back,
On his arms,
On his legs.
All over.
Still wearing his clothes
And his shoes,
It seems.
Never made it under the covers,
It seems.
How did he end up in bed?
Remembers hitting the town
With the rest of the troop.

Remembers walking on the Promenade
In Limassol.
Remembers visiting as many pubs
As they could find.
Remembers drinking as much beer
As they could manage.
The rest of the night?
One big blur.
Not every night
They get permission
To leave the barracks.
Had to make the most of it.
Seemed like a good idea,
At the time.
Who knows
When they will get another chance
To have a blowout.
Doesn't seem like a good idea now though.
Being transported
Back to the UK
This afternoon,
Along with the rest of the lads,
For exercises
On Salisbury Plain.
Last minute change of plan.
No idea why.
Not his place to ask.
Her Majesty's Government
Been throwing the baby out of the pram recently.
Big spat
Been brewing for some time,
Tensions rising.
Something to do with that,
Most likely.
"Get up, Smithy, you lazy bastard!"
A shrill voice rouses him

From his slumber.

Owner of the voice must be close.

Felt drops of spittle

Fall into his ear.

Words still rattling

Around in his head,

He gently turns around.

Sees a familiar face

With a big grin on it.

Belongs to Gaz,

His roommate.

"What happened last night?" asks Smithy softly.

"Dunno. You disappeared, mate," replies Gaz.

"How did I get back to the barracks?" asks Smithy.

"Turns out a local found you. Manager of The Tavern, in fact. Chap called Nico. You were paralytic, mate, but he somehow got you in his car and drove you back here," reveals Gaz. "Top bloke, that Nico."

"Got away with that one, didn't I?" says Smithy.

"Won't argue with you there. Now get your backside in gear, we've got a plane to catch."

151

Been staring
Out of the window
Ever since
The plane took off
From Cyprus.
Nothing to see,
Except endless clouds,
Punctuated,
Every now and then,
By snatches of blue,
By glimpses of the sea.
Doesn't care.
Not looking
At anything,
Only thinking
About his grandmother
In hospital,
In Bath, England.
Very sick.
Doctors do not know
If she will pull through.
How he would love to see her.
Might be the last time
He sees her.
Doubts he'll get a 24-hour pass
To see her though.
Too much going on.
Needs to be on exercise
With the lads.

Not convinced

It is even worth asking.

Loves the army.

Proud to be a soldier,

Proud to do his duty,

But wishes

He was on civvy street

At this moment in time.

Would be able to see his gran

And comfort his family,

Especially,

His mum.

Being so close

In Wiltshire

Will only make it more frustrating.

Thought about sneaking out

For one brief moment

Before common sense prevailed.

"Private." The voice of Captain Fraser stirs him

From his thoughts.

The Captain sits down

In the free seat

On his right.

"Sir," he replies.

"Smithy tells me your grandmother is seriously ill in hospital in Bath. Very sorry to hear that, Davies."

"That's kind of you, sir," replies Davies.

"You know, we are due to go on exercise tomorrow, don't you?" asks the officer.

"Yes, sir," replies Davies.

"We're due to land at 1300 hours so we have a few hours to spare. By my reckoning, that will give you a good crack to leg it over to Bath to spend some time with your grandmother and the rest of your family," suggests Captain Fraser.

"Certainly will, sir," says Davies, suddenly alert.

"But you've got to be back at 0600 hours tomorrow morning, Davies. Make sure you are."

"Of course I will, sir. Thank you very much for this, Captain."

"That's okay, Paul. I think you've got Smithy to thank though. Really pleaded your case," reveals Captain Fraser.

Good old Smithy,

He thinks to himself.

152

Young girl
Sitting on a chair,
Beside a bed.
An old lady,
Her granny,
Lying still
On a bed.
Sleeping,
Peacefully.
Young girl swings her legs
Back and forth,
Under the chair,
In front of the chair,
Again and again,
As she watches
The adults
Whisper to each other,
Hug each other,
Hold each other's hands.
A machine beeps
Every now and then.
Has no idea
What it is trying to say
Of if she should say anything
To someone,
To anyone.
Sees her mother.
She looks tired,
Very tired.

Sees her auntie.
She looks worried,
Very worried.
Sees her brother,
He looks strong,
Very strong.
So good seeing her brother again.
Misses her brother,
Terribly.
So proud of her older brother,
Paul,
Her brave soldier.
Surprised everyone
He did,
When he turned up
At the hospital
Out of the blue.
Swept her up in his arms,
He did,
As soon as he saw her.
Swung her back and forth
For an age,
He did,
Just as he always used to do.
Wishes he still lived with them
At home
In Bath.
Watches her brother walk over
To her.
"Boring, hospitals, aren't they?" he says.
She nods in agreement.
"Fancy a burger?" he asks his sister.
"Yes please! A Schwartz Brothers burger?" she asks.
"Can't believe you had to ask, Ems! Of course, Schwartz Bros," he replies.
"Oh great!" she says.
She smiles.

She hops off the chair.
She runs to her mother.
A kiss,
A hug,
Before she runs back
To her big brother.
Grabs his enormous hand,
And walks out of the ward.

153

A girl,
Eight years old,
School uniform on,
Breakfast eaten,
Teeth brushed,
Time to check
All her teddies,
All her cuddly toys,
Are safely tucked up in bed.
Says goodbye
To each and every one of them
With a warm kiss
And a loving cuddle.
Puts on her shoes.
Grabs her rucksack.
Walks out of the front door
With her mother.
Off to school.
Catching up with friends
In the playground
After the weekend,
She spots a youngster,
Daniel in Year 1,
Sees him fall over.
Rushes over
To the stricken boy.
Helps him up
Onto his feet,
As he fights

Back tears.

Puts her arm

Around his shoulders.

Whispers comforting words

To reassure him.

Walks him

To his mother.

"Oh Daniel, what happened?" asks his mother.

"I saw him run and fall over," explains the girl. "It was quite a fall."

"Oh dear. Thank you, Agnes, that's very kind of you for looking after him," says the mother.

"That's okay, Mrs Collins. You'll be okay, Daniel, but if your knee hurts during playtime, come and find me and I will look after you," she says.

Runs over to her friends.

Resumes the important business

Of catching up

On everyone's weekends.

"Agnes!"

At once,

She recognises

The voice of her great friend.

"Ems!" she yells.

Runs over.

Gives her friend a hug.

"I have something for you," reveals Ems. "You know my duffel coat, the one that you love?"

"Yes," says Agnes.

"I'm too big for it now and my brother Paul bought me a new one on Saturday. So I thought you might like it," says Ems.

"Oh, that is so kind. I don't have a proper coat. But is it alright with your parents?" asks Agnes.

"Absolutely. We'll be like twins when the weather turns cold," she says.

"Oh, I can't wait," says Agnes.

The pair walk off

To class
Arm in arm,
Chatting away.

154

A boy,
10 years old,
Lies on his bed
In his room
At home,
Reading a book
About teenage spies
Saving the world.
Dreams about saving the world himself,
One day.
Beating the odds
To defeat dastardly baddies
Up to no good.
Or,
Failing that,
Coming up with a device
That will save the planet
From overheating.
Started the book yesterday evening,
One more chapter to go.
Fast reader,
Always has been.
Beats his dad
In a read-off
Hands down,
Every time.
Teenage spy saves the day
Once again.
Another book finished.

Must lend it
To his best friend,
Nathan,
He'll love it.
Must get the next
In the series,
Soon.
Goes downstairs.
Home alone
With his dad.
Mum and younger sister
Out shopping
In Bath
For a coat
For Agnes.
Or at least they were.
A clink of keys,
A lock unlocked,
A front door opened,
All herald the return
Of his mum
And Agnes,
His sister.
No bags.

"Didn't you buy anything?" he asks.

"Agnes said she doesn't need a coat this winter after Ems gave her an old one she had outgrown. So instead, Agnes asked to spend the money on a duvet for a homeless man we came across in the street," explains his mum.

"That's very generous of you," says her brother, giving his sister a hug.

"Thanks, Ambrose."

"It really was a generous act," agrees Mum.

"He looked ill. Poor man," says Agnes with a shiver.

"He was very grateful," says Mum.

"Wish we could do more for him," says Agnes.

"Maybe there is something more we can do," adds Ambrose.

155

Last pitch booked for the evening
At the St Agnes Camping and Caravan Park
On Cornwall's north coast.
Full house,
Again.
32 caravans
And motorhomes,
18 tents,
All add up
To 100 plus campers.
Summer shaping up
To be a good one.
Best one yet,
Fingers crossed,
Since she
And her husband
Bought the business
On a wing and a prayer.
Five years of hard graft later
And the benefits are only
Now being reaped,
Finally.
Had their fair share of doubts,
Lots of doubts.
Upped sticks
From Kent
On the other side of the country.
Moved to Cornwall
Without a job,

Without an income,
Without a clue.
Stumbled across the campsite
By accident.
Love at first sight.
Glad they stuck at it.
Wouldn't swap it
For the world,
Now.
Thinking about closing up the shop
Now
For the evening
For a well-earned break.
Won't be too far,
In case she is needed,
In the house next door
With her feet up,
A glass of sherry close by
And a good book.
The door opens.
Looks up.
Pitch 17.
Father and son
From Bath.
Arrived a couple of hours ago.

"Are you all settled in?" she asks.

"Yes, thank you. Took a while to get the tent up in this wind. But we got there in the end, didn't we, Ambrose?" asks the father.

"Almost blew me away like a parachute," jokes his son, Ambrose.

"All part of the adventure. Are you both walking far?" asks the owner.

"We're walking 100 kms of the South West Coastal path in five days," replies the father, "this is our fourth day. One more to go."

"We're raising money for a homeless charity in Bath and we've already raised over £1,000," adds Ambrose.

"That's incredible. Well done and what a great cause. Can I just ask how old you are?" asks the owner.

"I'm 10 years old," replies Ambrose.

"Not bad for a 10-year-old, is it?" asks his proud father.

"Not bad at all," agrees the owner.

156

Eight kilometres clocked
Since they headed out of Perranporth.
Eight kilometres
Of spectacular scenery,
Of dramatic cliff tops,
Of shear vertical drops to the sea,
Of long abandoned tin mines,
Of the South West Coastal Path.
One more kilometre to go
Before they reach their destination
For the day,
St Agnes Camping and Caravan Park.
Wished his wife had managed to call ahead
To book a pitch
For the night.
Couldn't get through,
Bad reception.
Small price to pay
For the raw beauty
That is the North Cornish coast.
Expects there will be a pitch for them both,
Always is,
In his experience at least.
Must be close now.
Quick check of the map,
Quick swig of water,
Quick chat with his dear wife.
Both feeling grand.
Been meaning to walk the path together for years.

Countless excuses,

Eventually dried up,

One by one,

Until there was nothing left

To prevent them from walking

The first of a number of legs.

Plan to cover the whole length of the path,

Together,

Over the next few years.

Blue signpost spotted,

By his wife.

Always had the better eyesight.

"St Agnes Camping and Caravan Park, Turn left."

With a spring in their step,

They obey the instruction.

Enthusiastically,

They enter the campsite.

They locate the reception building.

They press the bell on the counter.

They wait,

Until a middle-aged woman,

Not much younger than the couple,

Appears.

"Good evening. We are hoping you have a pitch for us for the night," says the man.

"I'm afraid we are fully booked for the night," replies the owner.

"Oh, that is a shame. We tried to call earlier but couldn't get through," reveals his wife.

"Yes, bit of a black spot around here for mobile phones. Where have you walked from?" asks the owner.

"From Perranporth today. But we started out from Newquay a couple of days ago. Planning on walking to St Ives," replies the man.

"That's a fair old way. Tell you what, how about you pitch your tent in our front garden? Wouldn't want you not to have a spot for the night," offers the owner.

The couple look at each other.

"That would be fantastic. Thank you so much for putting us up," says the man.

"No problem. Just let me know your names and where you are from and I'll fill in the registration form for you," says the owner.

"Sebastian Grainger," says the man.

"Margaret Grainger," says the woman, "And we're from Devon, just outside Barnstaple."

157

Long weekend
Camping in Gwithian
On the North Cornish Coast.
Just what the doctor ordered
After a long week
In the office
In the big city.
Campsite found.
Pitch located.
Car unloaded.
Tent unpacked.
Groundsheet laid out.
Poles lined up.
Pegs spread out.
Instructions read,
Instructions not understood.
Instructions read again.
Still confused.
Not their tent.
Borrowed it from a friend.
Bigger than their own.
The promise of more room
Comes at a price,
It seems.
Too complicated.
Far too complicated.
Wish they had brought their small two-man tent.
Would be up by now.
Would be on the beach by now.

Spirits sinking.

Frustration growing.

The two friends look at each other

Help!

Written on both the faces

Of the two young men.

Not a good start to their weekend

Of surfing,

Of kayaking,

Of drinking.

"Need a hand with your tent?"

They turn around.

A man

In his late fifties,

Or early sixties,

And a woman,

His wife,

Presumably.

"Can be very complicated, these big tents," says the woman.

"Yes, we're stumped. Can't make head nor tail of the instructions," admits one of the young men.

"Here, let me have a look. I expect between us, we can get it up," declares the woman.

"Thanks, that would be great but only if you have time," says the other young man.

"No problem, we're walking the South West Coastal Path and we've done our leg for the day. So we've got lots of time on our hands now. My name is Sebastian and this is my wife, Margaret," reveals the man.

"Nice to meet you. My name is Matt," says one of the young men.

"And I'm Jeremy," says the other.

158

Clothes
Soaked,
Feet
Aching,
Shoulders
Sore.
Feeling
Wonderful.
Porthmeor Beach in St Ives
To Gwithian
In just over seven hours,
Seven hours of bliss,
Despite the rain.
Rained
All day.
Only makes the achievement
All the more
Satisfying.
16.5kms chalked up in one day.
55kms chalked up in three days.
90kms still to chalk up
Before he reaches Padstow,
His final destination,
For now.
Will be back.
Made a promise
To himself.
Recover from the surgery
To his heart

And he will walk
All the great walks in the UK,
Starting with the South West Coastal Path.
Plans to finish the entire path
In one year
Before he moves on
To the Coast to Coast Walk.
Starting at St Bees in Cumbria
On the Irish Sea,
Just as Wainwright suggested,
Finishing in Robin Hood's Bay,
On the North Sea.
Already looking forward to it.
Before then,
A lot more walking to do
On the South West Coastal Path.
Before then,
The tent needs putting up.
Usually takes minutes,
Not so today.
Struggling to push the pegs
Into the stony hard ground.
Four bent already.
Palms red with anger already.
A mallet,
That would make life easier.
Chose not to bring one,
A luxury,
He could not afford
To carry,
He had decided.
Had to travel light.
He had decided.
Tried using large stones.
Tried using the heel of his right boot.
Tried using a large piece of wood he found.

But the pegs are not for budging.

A mallet,

That's what he needs.

"You having trouble there?" asks a young man from the tent next door.

"Struggling to get the pegs into the ground. Too hard to push them in with my bare hands," replies the man.

"Hang on. We've got just the answer," says the man.

Walks over to his car.

Disappears inside.

Reappears in seconds,

With a mallet.

"This should sort you out," he says.

"Thanks ever so much," says the happy camper.

"No bother. Did you walk here?" he asks.

"Yes, walking the South West Coastal path from Land's End to Padstow."

"Met a few walkers doing just that this weekend. Must try it one day," says the young man.

"Highly recommend it. I'm Andrew, by the way."

"I'm Jeremy and that ugly mug over there is my friend, Matt," says Jeremy, as he points to another young man walking towards them.

"You been here a few days?" asks Andrew.

"Yes, last night tonight. Then off back to London tomorrow."

"Well, thank goodness you are here now. Would have struggled to secure my tent without your mallet," says Andrew.

159

Woman,
Walking her dog
On the section
Of the South West Coastal Path
Just outside Newquay
That lies within a stone's throw away
From her house.
Walks the same route,
Every morning,
With Alice,
Her springer spaniel.
Takes about an hour,
Usually.
Not today,
Unfortunately.
House keys lost.
Used them to lock her front door this morning,
As she always does,
Before setting off with Alice.
Thought she had put them in her trouser pocket,
Her right front,
As she always does.
Not there now.
Went back to her house
On the off chance
She would find them
Still dangling
From the keyhole.
No luck.

Decided to retrace her steps
On the off chance
She would stumble across them
In a field.
No luck.
At least not yet.
Lucky Alice,
Double walk this morning.
Needle in a haystack,
Springs to mind.
Must stay positive.
She'll find them,
Eventually,
Won't she?
As long as she follows her own footsteps,
She should be alright,
Won't she?
Two heads down,
Four eyes peeled,
Six legs walking,
Owner and dog
Follow the well-beaten track
Side by side.
Not for long though,
For soon Alice decides to sprint off ahead
To greet a walker,
A little too enthusiastically.
"Down, Alice," orders the woman, "sorry for that."
"That's quite alright," says the man with a large rucksack on his back.
"I don't suppose you've seen a set of keys on the ground?" asks the woman,
hopefully.
"As a matter of fact, I have. About two fields away. Saw them by a kissing gate.
I tied them to the gate with a spare piece of red string I had on me in the hope
the owner would return to retrieve them," reveals the man.
"What a relief! Thank you ever so much," says the woman.
"No problem at all. Happy to have helped," says the man called Andrew,

A man on a mission
To walk the South West Coastal Path
In a year.

160

Never thought
It would be this difficult
To walk the South West Coastal Path.
Go to the coast,
Find the path,
And just follow it round.
Simple.
If only.
Forks in the path,
Concealed turns,
Multiple tracks,
Lack of signs,
All conspired
To throw them off course
On more than one occasion.
Thought they would spend a day or two
Of their holiday in Cornwall
Walking,
A family day out.
Children signed up
After the promise
Of a burger and fries
In Newquay
At the end of the hike.
A well-earned feast
Before the short train journey
Back to Par
To retrieve their car
Before heading back

To the hotel.

Turning out to be anything but

A walk in the park.

Well and truly lost now

Among the dunes,

Among the labyrinth of paths

That run off

In every direction.

Soft sand

Tough on the calves.

Long grass

Prickly on the legs.

Father knows they are lost.

Mother knows they are lost.

Neither wants to admit it

In front of the children.

Need to find someone

To ask for directions.

Haven't seen anyone,

For ages.

Until now,

Or at least a dog,

A springer spaniel,

Sprinting

Towards them.

Or,

To be more precise,

Towards their youngest son,

Charlie.

Always had a soft spot for dogs,

Charlie.

A breathless woman

Appears

Over a dune.

"Alice, get down. So sorry. Alice, get down," orders the woman.

"It's okay, I love dogs," says Charlie.

"Could you possibly help us?" asks his mother. "We're trying to find the coastal path, but there seem to be so many tracks, we don't know which is the correct one."

"It's so easy to get lost in these dunes. Tell you what, it's probably best if I take you to the path myself. We need to go this way," says Alice's owner, pointing to her right.

"Really, it's not out of your way?" asks Charlie's father.

"Don't worry. I thought I was going to be out all day looking for my house keys until a kind walker found them for me," she replies.

161

Four hundred metres
Until the next marker,
An Ordnance Survey Trig Point
On a cliff
Between Newquay
And Watergate Bay
On the North Cornish Coast.
Head down,
Arms swinging,
Man marches
Towards his target
With purpose,
With determination.
Green backpack,
Army issue boots,
Khaki trousers,
Camouflage top.
All very familiar
To the ex-Royal Marine.
Just what he wanted,
Just what he was looking for,
From the four days of hiking
On the South West Coastal Path
From Hayle to Padstow.
Misses the structure,
Misses the comradery,
Misses his mates,
Misses the Royal Marines.
Hardest decision

Of his life,
To leave
The Royal Marines,
After 25 years' service.
Joined straight from school
When he was just 17 years old.
All he has ever known
Is being a Green Beret.
Struggling,
To adapt to life
On civvy street.
Struggling,
To find a purpose.
Struggling,
To find a role,
Something worthwhile to do
With the rest of his life.
Were the marines as good
As it is going to get?
Is it only downhill
From here?
Regrets leaving.
Would go back
In a second,
If he could.
Wonders
If he could.
Picks up the pace,
Like the old days,
As if he was on a yomp
With the lads,
With the troop
Like the old days.
Kept to a fast pace
These last few days.
Walked long hours

On the path.
Slept short hours
In his bivouac
On the cliff edges,
Hidden from view.
The boys would be proud.
Trig Point reached.
Civilians swarming all over it.
A family.
Stops a little way off.
Doesn't want to speak to anyone.
Never wants to speak to anyone,
Not even his friends and family,
Especially,
His friends and family.
They wouldn't understand.
Time to rehydrate.
Pack off.
Water bottle retrieved.
Long, thirst-quenching drink.
"Are you a soldier?"
Looks down.
A boy,
Not more than eight.
"I was," he answers.
"Which regiment did you serve in?" asks the boy.
"I was a Royal Marine," he reveals, proudly.
"Wow, a marine," gasps the boy in awe.
Water bottle
Stowed away,
Pack
Back
On shoulders,
The veteran
Starts walking.
"Did you do lots of fighting?" asks the boy, running to keep up.

"Charlie, stop harassing the man," yells his father.

"Don't worry, he's no bother," the old soldier yells back.

He means it.

He stops.

He pauses.

He takes off his pack.

"Which way are you guys heading?" he asks the boy.

"Towards Watergate Bay. We're staying in a hotel near there," he answers.

"That's the direction I'm going. Tell you what. If it is okay with your folks, I can tell you all about life in the marines while we walk to Watergate."

"Is it okay, Dad?" asks Charlie.

"Only if this gentleman really doesn't mind having company?" replies Charlie's mother.

"Yes, I am happy to have a little companion," answers the marine

With a hint

Of a grin

On his face.

First time

He has smiled

In a while.

They all head off.

Ex-marine and young boy in the front,

Ambling along,

Talking the whole way,

To Watergate Bay.

162

Lost count
Of the number of steps
It took them
To get down
To the beach
At Bedruthan Steps.
Will get another chance
To count
The steps
When they go back up
To the path.
Not looking forward to that.
Worth it though.
Spectacular,
The huge outcrops of slate
Lined up,
Perfectly,
For the giant
Bedruthan
To skip across the bay,
Or so the legend goes.
Makes for a backdrop,
Like no other.
Glad they took the detour
From their walk
To climb down.
Glad they were able to
Thanks to the low tide.
Perfect timing.

Perfect moment.
Holding hands,
They walk
Along the golden sand,
Weaving between
The giant's steps.
No one else to be seen.
All alone,
A teacher
And his wife,
Also a teacher.
Teach at the same school
Back home
In Berlin.
Picture moment.
Outstretched arm,
The husband's.
Two beaming grins,
Photo snapped
With a phone,
The husband's.
Another for luck.
Both keepers.
Except,
A figure
In the background.
Hadn't noticed the man on the beach
Until now.
Dressed in army fatigues and boots,
Big pack
On his back,
Big bag
In his hand.
Bending down,
Bending up.
To a rhythm

Of sorts.

Exercises?

They walk closer.

Rubbish.

Picking up litter

From the rocks

And the beach

On his own.

The giant,

Bedruthan,

Would be pleased.

163

Hot summer's day
In Berlin.
Only one place to be.
The beach
By the lake
At Wannsee.
Schoolboy arrives
For another lazy day
By the water
With his friends,
As he has done
Almost every day
Since school broke up
For the summer.
The whole of Berlin,
It seems,
Has the same idea today.
How will he find
His group of friends?
First things first,
Shoes off.
Feels the fine grains
Of the warm golden sand
Fill the gaps
Between his toes.
Buries
His feet
Deep into the sand.
Looks

In both directions.

Thinks

He spots his friend,

Christian.

Starts

Walking

Towards the boy lying

On a bright yellow towel.

False alarm.

Stops.

Performs an about-turn.

Reckons they must be in the crowded section

Of the beach.

Stops.

Spots

His teacher,

Frau Mayer,

With her husband,

Herr Mayer,

Also teaches at the school.

Both look very out of place.

Not because they are teachers,

But because they are both fully clothed

And carrying

See-through plastic bags.

"Hallo, Frau Mayer," says the schoolboy.

"Oh hallo, Peter. How are you? Are you having a good summer?" asks his teacher.

"Yes, thank you. How about you?" replies Peter.

"Oh, we had a lovely time in England, walking around Cornwall. You should go there one day," suggests Frau Mayer.

"Would love to. May I ask what you are both doing?" he asks.

"While we were in Cornwall, we saw a man picking up the rubbish on a remote beach all on his own, and we thought we should do the same at Wannsee," reveals Frau Mayer.

"That's a great thing to do," says Peter, "can I help you?"

"You don't want to spend your summer picking up rubbish. Go and spend time with your friends. Long term ahead, you need to relax," she says.

"Oh, I can spare five minutes or so," says Peter as he grabs a plastic bag and heads off to find rubbish.

164

Sous chef,
Second in command
In the kitchen
Of the world famous
Hotel Adlon Kempinski,
In Berlin,
Falls
Onto her bed
Finally,
At 2 am,
A spent force.
Another exhausting evening
At the hotel,
Supervising,
Cooking,
Trouble shooting.
Always a fine line
In any kitchen,
In her experience,
Between disaster
And glory.
Always manages to avert disaster,
Somehow.
Makes the glory
Even more glorious,
Somehow.
Still,
Not good for the nerves.
Got through today though

So can rest easy tonight,

At least.

Eyes close.

Eyes open.

Alarm clock buzzing.

9 am already?

Hauls herself upright

In an instant,

For fear

Of falling back to sleep.

Slippers on,

Dressing gown on,

Glasses on,

Shuffles to the kitchen

For her first coffee of the day.

Shuffles down the corridor

To her son's room.

Probably still sleeping.

That's what teenagers are supposed to do,

After all.

Not this one.

Not today at least.

"Morgen Mutter," says her son, all dressed.

"Morgen Peter," she replies, as she looks around his room,

His clean room.

"What happened to your room?" she asks.

"I decided to have a clean-up," answers Peter.

"Ach, you never tidy up your room! What's happened to my Peter?" she jokes.

"Bumped into Frau Mayer from school at the beach yesterday and helped her pick up rubbish. Got me thinking that I should do the same with my own room. From now on, you will never have to tidy up for me, Mutti," he promises.

"You are a sweet, sweet boy, Peter, and I am so lucky to have you," she says before planting a gentle loving kiss on his forehead.

165

Demoralised.
Exhausted.
Lost.
And that's after only two days
As a trainee chef
At the world famous
Hotel Adlon Kempinski
In Berlin.
All the excitement,
All the pride,
All the positivity,
He felt
After his appointment,
All vanished
Without a trace
The moment
He walked into the kitchen
For the first time
Yesterday.
Only yesterday.
Forget steep learning curve,
More like vertical learning curve
With no holds to cling onto,
With no ropes for support.
Thrown in at the deep end
After only the briefest
Of introductions,
After only the briefest
Of instructions.

Then all became a blur,

A maelstrom

Of non-stop activity,

Of unbearable heat,

Of constant shouting,

Of total pressure,

Pressure like he has never felt before.

Do this!

Do that!

In double,

Triple,

Quick time.

Barely time

To breathe,

Let alone have a break.

Not sure how long

He can survive this.

Not sure if

He wants to survive this.

Mistakes.

Made lots of them today.

Sous chef had to takeover

Several times.

Wishes he could go home

And cry.

Can't.

Still has to scrub everything clean.

"Tough evening."

He looks up.

He sees the sous chef.

"Yes, Chef. Sorry you had to step in a few times today," he says.

"Oh, don't worry about that, Friedrick. It was only your second day. I made a tonne more mistakes on my second day," lies the sous-chef.

"Thank you, Chef, it is good to hear you say that," says Friedrick.

"Not at all. Now let me help you clean up so that you can get home to bed," orders his sous-chef.

"Thank you very much, Chef," replies Friedrick, suddenly not feeling so sorry for himself anymore.

166

Luggage
Lots of it.
Small bags,
Large bags,
Large cases,
Medium-sized cases,
Small cases,
Hat bags,
Shoulder bags,
And other containers
Of intriguing shapes.
All matching,
All with the same brown and gold pattern,
All belonging to the same owner.
Always amazes him
How much the wealthy
Bring with them
On their travels.
Must have enormous wardrobes
In their homes,
He thinks
To himself.
Must have enormous homes,
He thinks
To himself.
One o'clock in the morning
Outside the main entrance
Of the Hotel Adlon
On Unter den Linden,

Berlin's celebrated boulevard
That runs from the City Palace
To Brandenburg Gate.
Guests arrived already.
Checked in
Before they had even arrived,
Or at least their help
Checked in
On their behalf.
Feet up and relaxing now
After their trip
No doubt.
Luggage arrived separately
In a large van.
Had to,
He imagines,
No room for the guests otherwise.
Needs help
With all this luggage.
On his own.
Karl-Heinz,
His fellow porter,
Busy
With another job.
Could be gone a while.
What to do?
Can't leave the luggage on the street.
Can't bring the luggage in
All in one go.
"Evening, Gerhard."
It's the new chef,
Friedrich,
Started this week.
Good to see
He came from the side entrance
Rather than the main entrance

He used

On his first day.

Not for staff,

The main entrance.

"That's a lot of luggage. Need a hand?" offers Friedrich.

"Actually, that would be fantastic. I'm on my own and need to deliver this lot. Would you mind staying here for a moment just so I can get a trolley?" asks Gerhard.

"Of course, I will," answers Friedrich.

Quickly,

The porter disappears into the hotel.

Quickly,

The porter reappears from the hotel

With a trolley.

"Thanks Friedrich. I'll be okay now."

"Here, let me help you load all this up," offers Friedrich.

"But aren't you tired after a long hard day in the kitchen?" asks Gerhard.

"I will be fine," replies Friedrick.

"Well, thank you very much," says Gerhard.

167

A bell boy,
18 years
And a handful of months old,
Youngest member
Of the staff
Of the Hotel Adlon
In Berlin.
Proud of his job,
Proud of his uniform,
Proud of his hotel,
Proud of being part of the history,
Even though
He knows
He is on the lowest rung
Of the ladder.
Only time
Anyone speaks to him
Is to give him an instruction,
Or an order,
Or a deadline.
Doesn't bother him.
Accepts there has to be a hierarchy,
A chain of command,
But he does wish someone
Would talk to him
About anything
Other than hotel business
Every once in a while.
There is a person

Underneath the uniform

With his own story

To tell,

Just like everyone else.

Spends so much time

With all these people,

And yet,

No one knows who he is.

"Hallo, Jurgen."

Gerhard,

One of the porters.

"Hi there, Gerhard," he replies.

"Do you need me to do anything?" he adds.

"Not at the moment, no. Quiet for now," he says.

"Won't last," he replies. "Better enjoy it while it lasts."

"That's very true. You have a wise head on those young shoulders. I bet you did well at school," he adds.

"Actually, no. Never was for me, the classroom. Left school at the first opportunity."

"And joined us at the Adlon?"

"Yes, that's right."

"Why a bell boy? Why the Adlon?" he asks.

"My father worked here for 27 years. Always wanted to work at the Adlon but I knew I had to start at the bottom and work myself up."

"Can be hard following in your father's footsteps. How are you finding it?" he asks.

"A lot to learn. But I am loving it. Want to rise up the ranks. Just like my father did," he reveals.

"Reckon you will, Jurgen. I have a good feeling you are going to go far here," he says.

"Thank you. That means a lot."

"Not at all. I must get back to my post, but I will be keeping an eye on your amazing progress, Jurgen."

Gerhard heads off.

Jurgen smiles to himself,

Now that's more like it.

168

Where is it?
The elusive,
The wonderful,
The heart-lifting,
Good deed of the day.
It will come,
Always does.
Just has to keep her eyes open,
Just has to be receptive,
That's all.
Keeping her waiting today though,
That's for sure.
Could always make one up
If,
However unlikely it is,
One does not appear.
Or rather,
Could always pluck one
From the database
She has built up
Over the years.
Full of good deeds
She has witnessed
But,
For one reason or another,
She has never used.
Timing might be a little off,
No bother.
Good deeds are timeless.

What is important,
Is to give her readers
What they want:
Warm stories
Of good deeds
That are carried out
Each and every day
Right under everybody's noses
By ordinary folk
From all walks of life,
Just like the readers.
A repository of good news
That is what she set out to build.
An antidote
To all the bad news and deeds
One gets bombarded with
By the mainstream media.
What started as a small-scale website
With a readership
Of mainly family
And friends
In Berlin,
Has grown,
And grown
Into a readership
Running into the thousands,
Including readers from across the globe.
Feeling proud
Of what she has achieved,
She walks
Through the Brandenburg Gates
Onto Unter den Linden.
Passes the museum.
What's this?
A bell boy,
From the Hotel Adlon,

Helping an elderly woman,
It seems.
She crosses the road.
She stops.
She watches
The bellboy
Find the woman a seat
On a bench
Then sit next to her
And then chat to her.
Pleased,
She knows
This is it.
This is what she has been waiting for.
Still,
Wants to double check
For her own peace of mind,
Wants to double check
Her sixth sense
Is still working.
Walks up to the bell boy and the old lady.
"Is everything okay?" she asks.
"Oh yes," answers the old lady, "this lovely young man called Jurgen helped me cross the road and when I said I needed to rest my legs, he not only found me a seat, but he decided to keep me company."
"Wunderbar!" exclaims the woman. "Do you work at the Hotel Adlon?" she asks.
"Yes. I'm a bell boy. I was out on an errand when I came across Frau Fischer," says Jurgen.
"Well, Frau Fischer and the Hotel Adlon are both very lucky to have you," says the woman.

169

Her favourite lunch.
Salad,
With all the trimmings.
Potatoes
Boiled in their skins,
Eggs
Hard boiled,
Tomatoes
Large and ripe,
Salad leaves
A selection of various types,
Parsley,
Just a sprinkling on top,
Olive oil,
A generous dollop all over,
Lemon,
A couple of squeezes.
Settles at her desk
On the third floor
Of an office block
In the Lisbon Metropolitan Area.
Phone
Off the hook,
Favourite website
On the screen.
The Kindness of Strangers,
A blog
That chronicles every day good deeds.
Reads the English version every day.

Always raises her spirits,
Reading about all the good
There is out there
In the world.
'The Lady and the Bell Boy',
Today's story,
About a young bell boy from the Hotel Adlon
In Berlin
Who helps an old lady
Cross the road
Then sits down
To have a chat with her.
Story ends
With a call to arms:
"To all the young folk out there
Be inspired by the bell boy.
The elderly are not invisible
They are funny,
Interesting,
Intelligent,
And what's more
They could do with your company."
Mr Fonseca
In the apartment
Below hers
Springs to mind,
As she eats a salad leaf
And half an egg.
Will make a point
Of popping in
On Mr Fonseca
A lot more often
Than she does.

170

New day,
Same old routine.
Finds it difficult
Remembering
What day it is.
Every day the same
As the last,
These days.
Gets up at 0600 hours,
Every morning
Without fail.
Plants a long and loving kiss
Onto the lips
Of his late wife
In the picture
In the silver frame
That stands on his bedroom windowsill.
Takes a cold shower
To wake himself up,
Properly.
Gets dressed,
Smartly,
Always smartly.
Downs a large glass of water,
Usually in one go.
Skips breakfast,
Always has done.
Apart from a small banana,
Always a small banana.

Heads out
To the newsagent
Round the corner
To buy the paper,
Always Publico.
Goes back home.
Reads the paper,
Always from cover to cover.
Then,
As if,
Penance has been served,
It is time,
Finally,
To bring out
His pride and joy,
The reason
For his very existence,
His violin.
Plays
For hour
After hour
Until he is exhausted.
Plays
Not only to hear the beautiful music
He once performed
As part of the national orchestra,
But also,
To transport himself back
To happier times.
When his beloved Maria was with him.
When he was not so alone.
When he was young.
When he had most of his life
Ahead of him.
A knock
On the door.

Never gets visitors.

A voice

Outside

Calling his name.

"Senhor Fonseca. It's Ana from the flat upstairs."

Excited to have a visitor,

For a change.

He opens the door.

"Ola, Ana."

"Ola, Senhor Fonseca. I was wondering if you would like a slice of this cake I have just made?" asks Ana.

"That would be lovely thank you very much. Do come in."

Cake cut

Into slices.

Slices laid out

Onto dishes.

Cake eaten

With fingers.

Sat round the blue Formica kitchen table

The pair talk.

Ana asks questions

About Senhor Fonseca's life.

Senhor Fonseca tells Ana

All about his Maria,

All about his childhood,

All about his work as a music teacher,

And all about his music.

"I hear you playing when I am upstairs. You play beautifully. Would you play me something now?" she asks.

"I haven't played in front of anyone for years. But why not?"

Mendelssohn's Violin Concerto.

Takes him back decades

To a concert

In the Coliseu de Lisboa

In front of an audience of thousands.

"Bravo!" yells Ana, clapping her hands excitedly, after Senhor Fonseca lowers the violin from his shoulder.

Back

In the present,

Senhor Fonseca takes a bow.

"You should play more often," suggests Ana.

"I play all day every day, Ana," he replies.

"I mean, in front of people."

"Oh, I can't do that anymore. I am well past my sell by date. Do you know I am 84?"

"You don't look a day older than 70! Well, it's a shame no one gets to hear you play anymore," she says.

"You're welcome to come by and listen to me play anytime, Ana. All I ask..."

He pauses,

"Is you bring another delicious cake with you."

"It's a date!" she replies.

171

Today,
The day,
He has been waiting for,
Ever since
He first saw
The notice
Outside the church
In Caparica,
On the outskirts of Lisbon.
"Free music lessons,
For children.
All welcome."
Loves listening
To classical music
On the radio.
Loves playing
All the masterpieces
In a big orchestra,
In his dreams,
That is.
Parents can't afford lessons,
Let alone an instrument.
School doesn't offer lessons,
Let alone provide instruments.
Heart beating
Faster
And faster,
As he walks
With his mother

To the church.

A woman,

Standing

At the entrance

Of the make-shift music school,

Greets them.

"Ola, my name is Ana, can I have your name please?" she asks the boy.

"Joao Costa," he replies nervously.

"And how old are you, Joao?" she asks.

"12."

"Great. Do you want to walk down the aisle and introduce yourself to the teacher, Senhor Fonseca, who is standing at the end by the music stand? Meanwhile, I am going to ask your mother to fill out this form for me."

Looks at his mother,

Waits for her reassuring nod,

Before he marches

Down the aisle

And introduces himself

To Senhor Fonseca.

Warm shake of hands

With the teacher,

Before he goes to find a seat

In the front row

Next to half a dozen other children.

"Welcome, boys and girls. As you know, my name is Senhor Fonseca. I was about the same age as you when I started playing the violin and piano and I have never stopped playing since. I was nine years old when I first started. That was 75 years ago, so how old does that make me?"

"84!" yell out his charges in unison.

"Yes, 84 years old. Music has been my life. I have played in orchestras; I have taught music in schools; and I still play the violin every day. After talking to my friend, Ana, whom you all met at the entrance, about the joy music has given me all my life, I thought the least I could do was to share it with others, like you youngsters."

He pauses.

Quick sip of water.

He continues,

"Now I have brought some old violins and a keyboard with me. Sadly, I do not have enough to go around for everyone. But every other week, each child will get to take an instrument home with them to practice with. I wish I had more instruments but hopefully, these will do for the time being. Now, who wants to come and choose one? But don't worry, whoever misses out today, can play on my violin or the church piano!"

Great excitement,

And a mad scramble

Signal the start

Of lesson one.

All traces of shyness

Gone.

172

Thought there would be a lot more screeching
Than there has been.
Perhaps,
He really does have an ear
For music.
Two days since
His first music lesson
With Senhor Fonseca
In the church.
Hardly seen her son, Joao,
Since.
Hardly left his room
Since.
Hardly stopped practising
Since.
Except now.
Silence.
Feels strange.
Goes to check on him.
Enters his room.
Boxes.
Three of them
On the floor
Full of toys,
His toys.
Old ones
And new ones.
"What are you doing sweetheart?" she asks.

"I thought that seeing as Senhor Fonseca is being so kind teaching us music and lending us his instruments for free, I would sell my toys and give him the money so he can buy more instruments," he explains.

"That's very thoughtful of you, Joao, but you don't have to do that. Senhor Fonseca wouldn't want you to sell your toys," explains his mother.

"I want to, Mama."

"But you still play with a lot of these," she adds.

"They are just toys, Mama. Besides, I will not have much time to carry on playing with them."

"Why?" asks his mother.

"Because I just can't stop playing Senhor Fonseca's violin!"

"So how are you going to sell them all?" she asks.

"I thought you could take a photo of them and send your friends and work colleagues an email to see if any of their children would like them."

"I can do that. I will send them to my entire address book and let's see what happens."

"Thanks, Mama," says Joao.

173

The owner
Of Del Rosario & Sons,
A musical instrument shop
In Lisbon, Portugal,
Sits by his workbench
In a room
At the back
Of his store.
One ear
On the front door,
In case someone enters,
Both eyes
On the trumpet
Lying on the bench
In front of him.
Almost finished cleaning
And polishing
The old instrument.
Been at it
For two days now.
Buys old, neglected instruments.
Gives them the love
They deserve.
Then finds them the homes
They deserve.
Been doing it for years.
Just like his father did
Before him
And his father's father

Before him.

Third generation business.

Hopes his children

Will keep it going,

One day.

That is,

If the youngsters find the time to play

Musical instruments

Rather than just play

Games on their computers.

Door opens.

A customer entering the shop?

He puts down the trumpet

And enters the shop.

A woman

And her daughter,

He presumes.

"Bom dia, Senhora," he says.

"Bom dia," says the woman.

"How can I help you?" he asks.

"My daughter is learning to play the guitar and her teacher has asked us to buy her a book. Classical Guitar for Beginners Volume One. He said to come to you."

"Yes, we have this," he replies,

As he plucks the book

From a stand

In the centre

Of the shop.

"Great, how much do we owe you?"

"12 euros."

20 euro note handed over

By the woman.

Eight euros in change,

Along with the music book

In a brown paper bag,

Handed over

By the shop owner.

Mother follows her daughter
Out of the shop
And into the street.
Owner goes back
To his desk
And sits down.
Logs on to the office computer
To record the sale,
As he always does
After making a sale.
An email
Catches his eye.
From a Senhora Costa.
Doesn't know her.
Reads the email.
An appeal
Inspired by her son
Selling all his toys
To raise money
To buy an instrument
For an old musician's classes,
The retired maestro Senhor Fonseca,
Who is teaching children music
In a church
For free.
Appealing to music shops
For any old instruments
To be donated
To the cause.
Would be much appreciated.
Great idea
Introducing the young to music.
Already has an idea
Regarding which instrument he will donate.
Another idea.
He'll forward the email

To all his fellow music shop owners
And musicians
In Lisbon,
Across Portugal,
Across the rest of the world
That he has stored
In his address book.

174

Favourite hour of the day,
12pm to 1pm.
The hour,
When students perform
In the hall
At the Conservatory of Music of Oporto.
Tries to sit in
For the duration
Of the performance,
Whenever he can.
Best lunch hour
There is.
A perk of the job
He loves.
Responsible for the school's collection
Of instruments.
All the usual suspects
Violins,
Violas,
Cellos,
Pianos,
Clarinets,
Trumpets,
French Horns,
And that is just
The tip of the iceberg.
Ensures they are all in good working order
And,
Importantly,

Ensures they are all well preserved
For future generations.
Will soon be losing
One of the instruments
From the collection though.
An old violin.
Not a valuable one,
But one that still makes a beautiful sound.
Going to a good home.
Going to the care of Senhor Fonseca,
A former student
Of the college,
Going back many years,
Introducing children in Lisbon
To the wonderful world
Of classical music,
Despite his advanced years.
School governors did not think twice
When he approached them
About an email received
From Del Rosario & Sons in Lisbon
About an appeal
For spare instruments,
Especially,
When they heard
About Senhor Fonseca.

175

Teatralnaya,
Theatre Square,
Her stop
On the Moscow Metro
And home to the Bolshoi Theatre,
Where she works
As a cellist
In the orchestra.
Performing 'The Marriage of Figaro'
Tonight
For three glorious hours.
No higher honour
For a Russian musician
Than to play
In Moscow's historic theatre.
Natalya Orlova,
Cellist at the Bolshoi.
Fills her with immense pride.
Exiting the station
She checks her phone
For calls,
For messages,
For emails,
For one last time
Before she turns off her phone
For the performance.
An email,
From her old music school,
The Conservatory of Music of Oporto,

In Portugal.
Sent to all its alumni,
She presumes.
Addressed
"Dear alumnus"
Rather than
"Dear Natalya Orlova".
An appeal
For donations,
Specifically
Musical instruments,
Not for the school,
But for a former pupil.
Turns out
A Senhor Fonseca,
An old musician now in his eighties,
Is teaching children
How to play the violin
And the piano
For free
In an old church
In Lisbon.
Has more students
Than instruments.
Can't afford to buy new instruments.
Students have to share
What few
There are
Between them.
The story
Of the old musician
Teaching children,
Who can't afford music lessons,
How to play
With his own violins
And keyboards,

Reminds her
Of her own story,
Of how she was taught to play the cello
By a friendly neighbour
For no charge,
Just like the children in Portugal.
Always wanted to return the favour
One day.
That day
Has arrived
At last.
Knows exactly which instrument to donate,
An old violin
She hardly ever uses
Anymore.
Will send it off to Lisbon
First thing tomorrow.
But now
She must perform.

176

First performance
As Conductor Laureate
Of the Tokyo Philharmonic Orchestra.
First Londoner
To hold the prestigious position.
Nervous.
Always is
Before any performance,
Let alone
A premier.
La Traviata
By Verdi.
Performed it
Many times,
Should help.
Musicians
All world class,
Should help.
Fabulous cast,
All experienced,
Should help.
Finds it strange
That even with
All his years of experience
Working with orchestras
All over the world,
Moscow,
San Francisco,
London,

Leipzig,
To name but a few,
He still gets nervous
Ahead of a performance.
Shows he cares at least,
That's what his old teacher,
At Oxford,
Used to tell him.
Not long to go now
At least
Before he takes to the stage.
All will be well then,
Always is.
No time
To think
About the nerves then.
Phone going crazy.
Messages
And emails
Of support
From his family and friends.
An email
From a cellist
He conducted
Last winter,
Plays for the Bolshoi Orchestra.
Natalya Orlova.
Very good cellist.
Wishing him luck
For tonight's opening performance
And forwarding an appeal
For donations
Of old musical instruments
For an old musician
Who is teaching children
Music for free

In a church
In Lisbon.
Great cause.
Will see what he can do about that
Tomorrow.
For now
He forwards the email
To his friends and family,
Before turning off his phone
And taking to the stage
To rapturous applause.

177

Relaxing
In his Victorian terraced house
In Islington,
North London,
After another
Fast and furious day
Working in the City
Trading Eurobonds.
Sitting
Comfortably
In his favourite armchair,
Feet
Resting
On the coffee table in front of him,
Glass
Of red wine
In his hand,
Faure's Requiem
Playing
Loudly
On the radio,
His idea of heaven.
Classical music,
Always been a big part of his life.
Always will be.
Excels with the violin
And the piano.
Won a music scholarship to Winchester
When he was 13 years old.

Won a place at Oxford University to study music
When he was 18 years old.
Graduated with a double first
When he was 21 years old.
Then it happened.
He came
To a fork
In the road.
Pursue a career in music,
Pursue a career in the arts.
Or earn big money
In the City.
Took the latter.
Regretted it
Ever since.
Doesn't get to play his violin
Much these days.
Wishes he could play more,
A lot more.
Alert on his phone.
Email.
Probably work.
Tries to ignore it.
Drawn to it.
Can't ignore it.
Picks up his phone.
Not work.
Thankfully.
An email
From an old friend.
Studied music together at Oxford.
The friend who took the path
He wishes he had taken
All those years ago.
Now a conductor
For the Tokyo Philharmonic Orchestra.

Doesn't get to see him much anymore.
But still a dear old friend,
Even though,
He is a constant reminder
Of what could have been.
Reads the email.
About an old man
In Lisbon
Introducing children to music.
More pupils
Than musical instruments.
Appeal for any old instruments
That can be spared
To be donated.
Doesn't have any spare instruments
To give away,
But something
About the story
Of the old musician,
Triggers something
Deep inside.
Feels an urge,
He hasn't felt
For a long, long time.
An urge
To spread
The joy
Of music.

178

Lost
Control
Of his mind,
Of his body.
A powerful force,
An invisible hand
Now at the controls
Of his mind,
Of his body,
Guiding him,
Inexorably,
Towards the station.
It is as if,
As soon as the decision was made,
He handed over
The reins
To his soul
To someone else,
To something else.
How did it get to this?
How did it get to be
So hopeless?
He knows how.
One by one,
The people he loved
And the people who loved him
Were taken away from him.
The cruel passing
Of his mother,

His beloved mother,
The last straw.
Cheated.
That's how he feels.
The one person,
Who was always there
For him,
Who always knew what to say
To him
At exactly the right time,
Who loved him
Unconditionally,
Gone,
Well before her time.
Hopelessly alone now,
So hopelessly alone
He no longer feels
He exists.
It is as if
He is invisible.
No one sees him,
Anymore.
No one talks to him,
Anymore.
Lost his identity.
It is as if
Ben Seymour is no more.
Might as well be John Doe,
For all he cares,
For all anyone cares.
Not long now.
No one there for him now.
No one there to stop him now.
No one there to sing Ave Maria to comfort him now,
Like his mother used to do
Whenever he had a nightmare

In the middle of the night
When he was a young boy.
Wishes so much
She was here.
She would never have allowed him
To get to this point,
To go to the station,
To go to Paddington Station.
Walks through the main concourse
Towards the underground,
And then,
He hears it.
Music.
Not just any music,
But the music,
Ave Maria.
Might be a man,
Standing by the information kiosk,
Playing the violin,
But he knows
It is his mother,
Singing to him,
Comforting him,
Saving him
From himself,
Once again.
Stops.
Listens.
Tears
Running down
His cheeks,
He closes his eyes,
Remembers the words,
Remembers the soft voice,
Remembers the gentle touch,
Remembers the warm embrace

Of his mother.

It is as if,

He was a young boy again,

Safe in his mother's arms again.

The music stops.

He opens his eyes.

He wipes away the tears.

He pulls out a note.

He looks for a cap

Or anything else

Where he can leave the money.

Nothing.

"That was beautiful," he says to the violinist. "That piece means so much to me. Where can I leave this?" he asks.

"Oh, I am not playing for money. Just playing for the fun of it," replies the violinist.

"But don't you need to earn money?" he asks.

"I work for a bank in the City. I play just to do my little bit to spread the joy of music."

"Well, sir, you have done a lot more than that for me today."

179

Needs to speak
To someone,
To anyone,
Now.
They are back,
Suffocating her,
Taking up all the oxygen.
Been away for a while.
Didn't miss them one bit.
Had started to think
They had gone for good.
Good riddance.
Wish she knew why
They come
When they do.
Then she could stop them
Before they wreak havoc
With her mind.
No escape
When they come.
They are everywhere
When they come,
Even in her sleep,
Even when she is busy at work,
Even when she is busy at home.
Too late
To call friends or family now.
Wouldn't call any of them now.
Wouldn't be fair on them.

Wouldn't want to scare them.
Needs to talk to someone,
Someone who can understand her.
Remembers her sister
Talking about an old friend
Who turned his own depression around,
Now training to be a Samaritan.
Fetches her phone.
Messages her sister.
Asks for her friend's number.
Phone rings.
It's her sister.
Doesn't want to speak to her sister.
Doesn't answer.
Phone stops ringing.
Phone rings,
Again.
It's her sister,
Again.
Still doesn't want to speak to her sister.
Still doesn't answer.
Phone stops ringing.
Message alert.
It's from her sister.
"Please speak to me, Janey."
She messages back,
She can't.
Asks for the name and number of her friend,
Again.
Received,
Finally.
Dials the number,
Immediately.
Hopes he picks up.
He does.
"Hello, is that Ben Seymour?" she asks.

"Yes, it is," he answers.

"So sorry to call you so late…"

She bursts out crying.

"It's okay, take your time. I am here to listen to you when you are ready and I will be here for as long as you need me," he says.

180

Dreading the next call.
Three calls made so far.
Three short calls made so far.
One brought him
A torrent of abuse,
The other two
Were hang-ups.
Barely had a chance
To introduce himself,
Let alone read the script.
Looks at the list
On his desk.
21 more names,
21 more numbers to dial,
And that is just the first page.
It's a numbers game
He was told
At training.
If it can be called training.
What was the stat?
One in a hundred,
Or something like that
Will be engaged.
Get a foot in the door
Then barge your way in
And make the sale.
Selling double glazing.
What a cliché.
Can't believe

He is selling double glazing.

Three months ago,

He was studying for his finals

At university.

For what?

For this?

A means to an end,

He keeps telling himself.

Earn some money

Then go travelling,

For as long as it takes,

Until he figures out

What he wants to do.

"Oi, you ginger-haired four-eyed twit! Why aren't you speaking on the phone?"

Bruce, his line manager, a most unpleasant man.

"Just dialling up the next one now, Bruce," he replies, but Bruce is already hurling insults at the occupant of the next cubicle.

Here goes.

Who's next?

A Ms Jane Buchanan.

Dials the number.

Mustn't take the abuse personally,

He tells himself.

"Hello."

"Hello. Is that Jane Buchanan?" he asks.

"Yes, that's me," she says.

"Great, my name is Jamie Stubbs and I am calling from Glazed Up. Do you have a spare five minutes for me to talk you through what great double-glazing offers we have?" he asks.

Curses himself,

Already he is off script.

Prepares himself

For a torrent of abuse.

Starts looking

At the next name on the list.

"Bless you, Jamie. I don't need any double glazing but thank you for taking the trouble to call me. I expect you have a tough sales target to meet, so perhaps you could put me down for a follow-up call in six months' time. That should help keep your manager off your back," she says.

"Gosh, that would be great, thank you so much," he says, still reeling from the shock that Ms Buchanan is talking to him pleasantly.

"I guess we better speak a little longer to make it seem authentic," she suggests.

"Only if you have time. Though I have to admit, it would help me no end to be on the phone for more than 10 seconds at a time for a change!"

"No problem at all," she replies. "So Jamie, tell me a bit about yourself."

181

Woman,
In her mid-twenties,
Shoulder-length brown hair,
Hazel eyes,
Running late.
Parents won't mind,
But she will.
Got home late
From work.
Had to have the quickest shower ever,
Before she was off
Out of her flat
In Wembley,
North West London,
And walking
The 15-minute walk
From her apartment
To the underground station.
Half runs,
Half walks,
Half in the hope
That she can make up
Five minutes
Or so.
Glance at her watch,
Wonders,
If she will make it
In time
For the show

In the West End.
Loves the theatre.
Has done ever since she was a girl.
Group of teenage boys ahead,
Going to hold her up.
Walking slowly,
Laughing loudly,
Taking up most of the pavement,
She slows down.
Sees one of the boys
Drop an empty can
Onto the pavement,
Just metres away
From a rubbish bin.
Would say something
If she had the time.
Or would she?
Sees a young man,
Red hair,
Glasses.
He passes the group
In the opposite direction.
Then,
Without a moment's thought,
Stops.
Picks up
The empty can.
Carries it
To the bin.
Deposits it
In the bin.
Walks past the woman.
If he found the time
To do a good deed,
She thinks to herself,
So can she.

182

Almost the end
Of his shift.
Another day
As Station Manager
Of Wembley Underground Station
Draws to a close.
12 hours
Since he left his home
This morning.
12 hours
On his feet,
Constantly checking
Everything
Is all in order.
12 hours
Since he came up
With the joke of the day.
Writes one every day
On the notice board
By the entrance
Of the station
With a blue marker pen
To cheer up the commuters.
Yet to think of tomorrow's one.
Always worries
He won't think of a good one.
Always manages
To come up with something,
In the end.

Sometimes has to wait
Until the last minute though.
Like this morning.
Still plenty of time.
Can always search for inspiration
Online
Back at home,
If needs be.
Standing by the station entrance,
Hands clasped behind his back,
He watches
Strangers scuttle
This way and that.
He wonders
Where they are going.
Home?
Most likely.
Will be his turn soon.
Sees a woman enter the station
In a hurry.
She hurtles towards the ticket barrier.
Pauses,
Before she carries on.
Pauses again.
Before she turns around
And rushes back
To the entrance of the station.
Curious,
He follows her.
Sees her bend over
To pick something up
Off the ground.
Then hears her call out
"Excuse me!"
At the top of her voice.
Good strong voice,

He thinks to himself.
A man walks towards her.
She hands over a card,
Or something similar.
The man raises his hand,
In thanks.
The woman then turns back
And re-enters the station.
"Everything okay, Miss?" asks the station master.
"Yes, thank you. I saw the gentleman drop his bank card and thought he'd miss it," replies the woman with shoulder-length brown hair and hazel eyes.
She walks off
To catch a train.
He smiles.
He doesn't need a joke,
Knows what he will write
On the notice board
For the commuters
Tomorrow morning.

183

"Once more unto the breach,"
Says a man,
Dressed in a navy-blue suit
And black polished brogues,
To himself.
Can't believe
He is walking,
With his small dark green bag
Slung over
His right shoulder,
To Wembley underground station
To catch a train
To work
Already.
Seems like it was just yesterday,
Since he was last there.
It was yesterday!
He smiles to himself.
Usual crowd gathers
To get through
The ticket gates.
Familiar faces,
But that's all.
Everyone so keen to get to work,
No time to get to know
Their fellow passengers.
He smiles to himself,
Again,
As he slowly shuffles

Towards the nearest gate.
Looks to his right
At the station notice board
To read the joke of the day
That some kind soul from the station writes
With a blue marker pen
Every day,
Without fail.
Never the funniest of jokes,
But it is the thought that counts.
"Old London Underground Proverb: one good turn deserves another."
No joke today,
It seems,
Just a piece of advice.
Good advice
Though.
His turn at the gate,
Finally.
Eyes drawn
To the gate
On the right
To a grey-haired man,
Holding an umbrella
With a wooden handle.
"Seek Assistance"
Pops up on the display
Of the man's gate
In red letters.
The dreaded words
All commuters fear
After their ticket
Goes through the machine.
Can mean having to go back
To the end of the queue
When all that is usually required
Is simply to try another gate.

He turns to the grey-haired gentleman.

"Would you like to try this gate?" he asks.

"That's awfully decent of you," says the grey-haired man.

Card accepted.

Gates open.

"The mystery of the London Underground ticket gates,"

The man in the navy-blue suit,

Says to himself.

184

Seems everyone
Had the same idea.
Leave work at six o'clock
On the dot
To catch a train home
From Bank station.
Date
With his girlfriend.
Doesn't want to be
Late.
Young man with blond hair
Tied into a ponytail,
Still dressed in the standard issue
Black and white
Checked trousers
He wears in the kitchen
Of the restaurant
Where he works.
Stands in one of several lines of people,
All patiently waiting
To get to a ticket gate,
To get to the platform,
To get a train home
Or wherever they are going.
Announcement
From someone,
Somewhere
In the heavens,
Informing all the would-be passengers

That a number of ticket gates
Have now been closed
To avoid overcrowding
On the platforms.
Looks ahead,
Looks above the heads,
Of all those ahead.
People shuffling
From the right-hand side
Towards the left-hand side.
Typical,
He thinks to himself.
The gates on the opposite side
Are open,
While the gates on his side
Are closed.
No choice
But to shuffle across.
Toe to heel,
Heel to toe,
Slowly,
He creeps
Sideways
And forwards,
Ever closer
To where the congestion is deepest,
To where the bottleneck is narrowest.
Eventually,
He makes it across
To the side
Of a gate,
One that is still open.
Still has to try
And make it across
To the gate.
Hopes someone

Will let him in.

Doesn't want to

Have to barge his way in.

"Would you like to go ahead?" asks a grey-haired man carrying an umbrella with a wooden handle.

"Cheers," says the man with the blond ponytail.

He walks through the gate.

Good man,

He thinks to himself.

185

Smile.
Someone smile.
No smile
Equals
Mayhem.
Man with shaven head
And black goatee beard
Made a deal with himself
Back in his room
In the bed and breakfast
He stayed at
Last night.
Board a carriage
On a Northern Line train
At Kennington.
If no one smiles
At him,
Or if no one talks
To him,
Pleasantly,
Before the train
Reaches Camden Town
He will take that
As his signal
To unleash his fury,
His rage,
On all those
In the carriage.
No one

Will be spared.

Opens his rucksack.

Checks everything is all there.

Pats the chest pocket

Of his jacket.

Came well prepared

For no smiles.

Smiles

To himself.

Euston station.

Flurry of people

Get off the train.

The lucky ones,

He thinks to himself.

Spots a free seat.

Takes it.

Looks around him.

Everyone busy,

Playing with their phones

Or reading the paper.

That's the problem,

He thinks to himself,

No one cares.

Everyone just living

In their own worlds.

Everyone just too busy

To take an interest

In other people's worlds.

Glances at the row of seats

Opposite him.

Catches the eye

Of a young man

With blond hair,

Tied into a ponytail,

Wearing trousers

With small black and white checks.

Must be a cook,
He thinks to himself.
Then it happens.
A smile,
A great,
Big,
Beaming
Smile
From the man
With the blond hair
Tied in a ponytail,
At precisely the moment
The train enters
Camden Town.
He smiles back
Before zipping up his rucksack.
He won't be needing that,
Anymore.

186

Made it,
Just.
Train already waiting
When the woman
With straight black hair,
Tied in a bun,
Reached the platform
At Camden Town.
No time to check
If it was the right train.
Needs a High Barnet train
To get to her flat
At Totteridge & Whetstone.
No bother,
If it stops
At Mill Hill East
She'll jump off
At Finchley Central
And wait.
Usually a train
Within five minutes.
Looks around
On the off chance
There is a free seat.
No chance,
Not during rush hour,
She thinks to herself.
Wishes she didn't have so many bags,
Handbag,

A large one
With far too many things in it,
Rucksack,
With all the gym gear
She used for her lunchtime workout,
And a carrier bag
From a supermarket
With tonight's supper inside.
Strategically,
She shuffles in between
Two rows of seats.
At least that way,
She thinks to herself,
She can put the rucksack
And the carrier bag
Between her feet
And,
At the same time,
Be in prime position
To grab a seat
Should someone get off
At the next station.
"Excuse me. Would you like to sit down?" asks a man with a shaven head and a
black goatee beard sitting in the seat in front of her.
"Are you sure?" she asks.
"Please," he answers as he picks up his rucksack and vacates the seat.
"You are so kind," says the woman with the bun, as she flops down onto the seat,
smiling her thanks.
The man with the shaven head and a black goatee beard
Smiles back.

187

Two men
In their early thirties.
One with dark brown hair
And a sprinkling of freckles
On his face.
The other with black hair
And thick black glasses.
Both men hang on
To the dark blue bar
That runs above a row of seats
In the middle carriage
Of a Northern Line train
To High Barnet.
Off to meet some friends
In a bar
In Highgate.
Struggling
To have a conversation,
Over the din
Of the train
And the hordes
Of commuters
Around them.
"Is this our stop, Harry?" asks the man with the black hair and black glasses.
"Yup," shouts back his friend.
Train enters the station.
Train comes to a halt.
Train doors open.
The two men

Step off the train.
The two men
Go up the escalator.
The two men
Go through the ticket gates,
Out into the fresh air.
Walking up the hill,
The two men
Hear a voice,
A woman's voice,
Shouting out
"Excuse me!"
They turn around.
A woman
With straight black hair tied in a bun
Carrying three bags,
A handbag,
A rucksack,
And a shopping bag,
Trots towards them.
Breathless,
She stops.
Facing Harry,
She says,
"I'm sorry. I saw you on the train just now and I just felt, even though this is not
my stop, I had to jump off, to…to tell you how beautiful you are," she says.
Pause.
Too long
For comfort,
Embarrassingly long.
"Thank you," says Harry, eventually.
"Great. Well, I just wanted you to know. I'd better go and catch another train.
Goodbye," she says and walks off.

188

Didn't work out
As she thought
It would.
Doesn't know
What she was thinking.
What did she think
It would achieve?
A Hollywood movie?
Strangers meet,
Fall hopelessly in love
At first sight?
Live happily ever after?
Hopefully,
Made him feel good
About himself,
At the very least.
That can't be a bad thing.
She said it,
That's the important thing.
Won't ever have that gnawing feeling of
'What if?'
Plaguing her
For years to come.
Time to go home
Put her supper on
And have a quiet evening
By herself.
Back in Highgate station,
Again,

She puts her bags down.

Retrieves her card

From her handbag.

"Excuse me."

A voice,

A vaguely familiar voice.

She turns around.

It's him,

The man

With the dark brown hair and freckles,

The most beautiful man in the world.

"Hello again," she says.

"I just wanted to say I think you are very beautiful too," says the man. "Sorry I didn't say it earlier, but I was caught a little off guard. Thankfully, my friend Rajid over there gave me a nudge in the right direction," he adds, pointing to the tall man with black hair and black glasses hanging back.

"Nice to meet you," says Rajid.

"Nice to meet you too. I'm Roxy," she replies to Rajid,

Without taking her eyes

Off his friend.

"And my name is Harry," says the man with the dark brown hair and freckles on his face.

"Nice to meet you, Harry," she says.

"I was wondering if you would like to meet for a coffee sometime?" asks Harry.

"Yes, that would be great," she answers.

"I know a lovely café in Hampstead, on the high street. It's got a great name," he says.

"What's it called?" she asks.

"Harry's Café!" he answers.

"That is a great name," agrees Roxy.

"Are you free tomorrow evening, say around 7 pm?" he asks.

"Yes, I am," she replies.

"Super, see you there."

"See you there," says Roxy. "Now I am going to catch my train. Nice to meet you both," and with that she picks up her bags,

And walks through the ticket gate

To catch her train home.
Five minutes later,
She boards a train,
Glowing,
Knowing,
She has just met
Her future husband.

189

"Here it comes,"
Says a woman,
Wearing a red waterproof jacket
With the red hood up,
Out loud
To herself,
As she prepares herself
For the muddiest,
The steepest,
Section of Richmond Park,
As far as she knows,
At any rate.
Off the beaten track,
At any rate.
Came face to face
With a large stag here once.
Kept a close eye on him,
As she,
And her Jack Russell,
Willy,
Crept past.
Hardly ever
Sees anyone up here,
Except today.
Saw a runner
Just moments ago.
Or rather,
The back of him,
Wearing a mud splattered white singlet,

Mud splattered black shorts
And mud splattered trainers.
Amazed he managed to keep his feet
With all this slippery mud.
Struggling to keep her own feet,
At any rate
As she makes her way
Up the hill.
Head down,
Feet angled
At ten to two
On an imaginary clock
On the ground,
She looks for the best purchase,
As she makes her way,
Slowly,
Up to the top,
While Willy just scampers up
On all fours
With consummate ease.
Makes it to the gate,
Without slipping.
Always feels good
Making it to the gate
Without slipping.
Feels like something has been achieved.
Looks up.
He's there,
The runner,
Waiting,
For her?
Holding the gate open
For her?
"Slippery today, that section," says the tall man with black hair and wearing black glasses.
"Isn't it just?" she answers.

"This gate has a stiff spring on it, thought I'd wait and hold it open for you," he says.

"Thank you, you are kind," says the woman in the red coat, as she and Willy pass through.

190

"Bentley!"
A white-haired,
Pink-cheeked man,
Calls
After his dog,
In Richmond Park.
His white labradoodle
Saw a deer,
Saw a playmate.
Ran off after the deer,
Ran off after the playmate.
Fancied a game of chase,
No doubt.
Only no one told the deer
About the game.
Frightened,
Instinct
Kicked in
And the deer
Ran off.
Only no one told the deer
That that was precisely
The game
Bentley
Wanted to play.
Off they went
Round and round
At first
In ever increasing circles

On a wide open plain,
In plain sight
Of Bentley's owner.
Until that is
The deer headed off
Into a wooded area
And out of sight
Of Bentley's owner.
Doubly worried now,
The owner runs
Into the woods
After the dog
And the deer.
Can't see them anywhere.
Only the sound
Of rustling leaves
And crunching twigs
Gives the game of chase away.
Follows the sounds.
Realises they are headed
Towards the East Sheen Cricket Club.
Realises they are headed
Towards the road.
Starts running,
Faster and faster.
Clears the woods.
Enters the open space
That is the cricket pitch.
Spots the deer.
Spots Bentley,
Heading straight towards the road.
"Bentley!" he yells, out loud.
No effect,
Whatsoever.
Bentley keeps on running,
Oblivious to his master's voice.

Until suddenly,

He stops

Next to a woman

In a red waterproof coat

With the red hood up.

"How on earth did she do that?" he asks himself.

"Thank you so much," says the man, breathless, as he catches up with the woman.

"No problem at all," she says. "I think he was heading into the road."

"He was, though thankfully, I saw the deer double back," says the man. "Regardless, you saved me from a morning of running around trying to catch my dog. Can I ask how you managed to stop him?" he asks.

"Bag of dried fish," she replies, shaking a bag of treats. "It's the only thing my Jack Russell ever responds to. Never fails," she reveals,

As she brings one out,

Throws it in the air

For her dog

To catch and gobble up

In one quick gulp.

"Good boy, Willy," she says.

Bentley sits politely,

Hopeful,

"Good boy, you can have one too."

"Well, I must get myself a bag of those," Bentley's owner says, cheeks pinker than ever.

191

15-year-old girl
With long blonde hair
Neatly tied back into a ponytail,
Walking with her mother
Back to their home
In Richmond,
South West London.
Spots a dog
And its owner
On the pavement ahead.
A white dog,
A labradoodle,
She thinks,
But can't be sure.
Feels a mixture of
Excitement
And trepidation.
Loves dogs
Or at least the idea of dogs.
But also fears dogs.
A scary encounter with a terrier
When she was four
Has had a lasting effect.
Shied away from dogs,
Ever since.
Has to admit
With its white fluffy coat,
Pink tongue hanging out
And jolly spring in its step,

This dog
Looks more like a teddy bear
Than the monster
The terrier was
All those years ago.
"Is that a labradoodle?" asks the girl, as she and her mother approach the man and the dog.
"Yes, that's right," replies the dog's owner.
"What's his name?" she asks.
"Bentley. Do you have a dog?" asks the owner.
"No, too scared of them," she admits.
"No need to be scared of Bentley. He's a big softy," says the owner. "Reckon he could help you banish your fears. Do you want to give him a stroke?" he asks.
"Would he mind?" she asks back.
"Not at all. He loves the attention," answers the man. "I'll hold him if you want. Start with his back. Nice and gentle."
"Really?" she asks, anxiously, excitedly.
"Absolutely," he answers.
Nervously,
She touches the dog's back
Only for the briefest of moments,
Before quickly raising her arm
Out of the dog's reach.
Bentley meanwhile
Remains still,
Remains placid.
She moves to touch the dog again.
This time for a little longer.
Repeats the process,
Again and again
Each time
With a bigger and bigger smile on her face,
Until eventually

She finds herself
Stroking and cuddling Bentley,
As if she had never had a fear of dogs.

192

Woman
At home
Sitting
On her sofa,
Stroking
Her pet dog
Curled up on her lap,
A Blenheim King Charles Spaniel
That goes by the name of Charlie.
Her only companion,
In her two-bedroomed house
In Richmond.
Adores Charlie
So much.
But because of her love,
She is thinking of doing
The unthinkable,
Giving Charlie up.
Job keeps her away
From home
Far too much.
Unfair on Charlie.
Hardly gets a walk
During the day,
Apart from a quick stroll,
Down the high street
And back.
Other option
Give up her job,

As a cook
In the kitchen
Of No. 10
Downing Street.
Been cooking for UK prime ministers
In the great kitchen
In the basement
Of the great building
For years.
Feels honoured.
Feels privileged
That she has fed the country's premiers,
And their venerable guests.
Feels she has played a small part
In the nation's fortunes
These last few decades.
Hears a knock
On her front door.
Opens the door.
It's Saskia,
Her neighbour's daughter,
Beautiful girl
Beautiful long blonde hair
Usually tied into a ponytail.

"Sorry to disturb you, Mrs Bloomfield," says Saskia.

"Not at all. Is everything okay?" asks Mrs Bloomfield.

"My mother was telling me that you might have to give up Charlie because you are very busy, what with your important job and all that, and I was wondering if you would let me walk Charlie for you when I finish school for the day? Be more than happy to and that way, you wouldn't have to give him up," offers Saskia.

"But I thought you were scared of dogs, Saskia?" asks Mrs Bloomfield.

"I was. But that's all changed now after I met the most beautiful white labradoodle the other day and fell in love."

"Well, I don't know what to say! You would be getting me out of a right pickle. Are you really happy to do this?" asks Mrs Bloomfield.

"Yes, I really am, and Mum has said she will come and walk with me at least for the first few times, just in case I need a hand."

"If you do, you must let me pay you something."

"Not at all, Mrs Bloomfield. Wouldn't dream of taking your money. Spending time with Charlie is payment enough for me," she says.

"I am so grateful to you and your mother, Saskia," replies the cook, with a tear in her eye,

For a great burden

Has been lifted

From her shoulders.

193

Lawn mowed.
Plants watered.
Weeds,
The few there were,
Removed.
End of a long hard day
In the garden
Of No. 10
Downing Street.
Head gardener
On his final rounds
Checking
Everything is
As it should be,
Checking
Everything is
Where it should be,
Before calling it a day.
Stops,
Suddenly.
Spots
Not one,
Not two,
Not three,
But six
Swallows
Weaving this way and that
In and out of the garden.
Dancing in the sky.

Soaring high,
Diving low
Again and again.
Pure unadulterated joy,
Oozing out
From every movement,
From every dive,
From every climb.
Mouth wide open
In awe
Of the dancing birds,
Time stands still.
Could stand still
In the middle
Of the garden
For hours
And hours
Watching the birds.
Reluctantly,
He drags his gaze away
From the visitors.
Inspired,
He cuts three pink roses.
Enters the building.
Changes his shoes.
Goes downstairs
Into the basement
To the kitchen
For a well-earned glass of water.

"Hello, Nick. Did you have a good day in the garden? Lovely day for it," says the cook.

"It was and to top it all off, I just saw half a dozen or so swallows. They know how to have fun, don't they?" he says.

"How lucky you are to have an office in the great outdoors," she says.

"Yes, I am. So uplifting watching those birds dart this way and that. They look like they are so enjoying themselves, it is infectious," replies Nick.

"Lovely creatures," she says.

"Yes, they are."

"Do you fancy a biscuit? Just made a batch. Thought everyone could do with a bit of cheering up. Upstairs won't miss one. So go ahead and grab one," she says.

"Oh, thank you very much. Promise I won't tell anyone," he says with a big smile on his face,

His day keeps on getting better

And better.

194

The Cabinet Room,
No. 10
Downing Street,
Where momentous decisions
That have shaped the course of British history,
And in some cases
The world's,
Have been taken,
Time and time again,
By generations of
Prime Ministers
And their ministers
All seated around the long table
That runs along
The middle of the room.
Not today.
Cabinet nowhere to be seen today,
Or at least not yet.
Could change
At a moment's notice,
Especially,
With all the trouble that is going on
With The Vigour.
All the more reason
To ensure the room is clean
And all is in order
At all times,
In case the room needs to be used
At a moment's notice.

A cleaner stands

In front of the grand marble fireplace,

Armed

With a spray gun

And a duster.

Turns around.

Sees Nick

Standing in the doorway.

The head gardener

Beckons her

Over to him.

"Is everything okay, Nick?" asks the cleaner.

"Yes, everything is great, Angie. Just wanted to give you these."

Right hand appears

From behind his back.

Three freshly cut pink roses appear

From behind his back.

"Thought these might brighten up your day. I know you have had a tough time of it lately," he says.

"They are so very beautiful, thank you, Nick," says Angie, "and they smell lovely."

"Don't they just. Glad you like them," says Nick.

195

The Garden Room,
No. 10
Downing Street.
Home
To the pool of typists
Who,
Together,
Churn out speech
After speech,
And letter
After letter
On behalf of the Prime Minister
Of the United Kingdom
And his office.
Only one typist
In the room
When the cleaner enters,
A woman,
In her early thirties
Wearing large brown spectacles,
Typing up a document.
Typist's mind is elsewhere though.
Back in her living room
At home,
Last night
To be precise.
Reliving the argument
She had with her husband
About his mother

Staying at their house
Next week.
Feels very bad.
Mother-in-law
Is not that bad.
Just doesn't want her staying
For two whole weeks
That's all.
Feels guilty
About standing her ground,
Feels guilty
About putting her husband
In an awkward position.
Brings out a hanky
To blow her nose
And dry her eyes,
At the exact moment
The cleaner
Enters the room
With her trolley.

"You okay, Jessica?" asks the cleaner.

"Yes, all good. Thank you for asking, Angie," replies Jessica.

"Doesn't look like it to me. Why don't I get you a cup of tea and if you feel like it, you can tell me what's on your mind," says Angie.

Quickly,
Leaves the room.
Quickly,
Returns with a cup and saucer
In one hand
And a chocolate biscuit
In the other.
Places them in front of the typist.

"Thank you, Angie. You're very kind. Just had an argument with Peter last night. Feel bad about it, that's all," she explains.

"Have you spoken to him today?" asks Angie.

"No, not yet," she answers.

"Sounds like you need to call him now and tell him how you feel. Go on, get that cuppa down you and give him a call," suggests the cleaner before she leaves the room.

An hour later,

The cleaner returns

To check up on the typist.

"Did you call him?" she asks.

"Yes, I did and it was lovely speaking to him. You were absolutely right. I feel so much better now. Thank you, Angie."

196

A man
In his sixties
Sits
In his office
In front of
A well-used,
A well-loved
Mahogany correspondence desk
Alone.
Boxed
Into a corner.
That's how he feels.
How did he get to this point?
Decisions.
Bad,
Rash,
Decisions
Led him
To this point.
And it is all his fault.
Could blame the advice he received,
Could blame the people around him,
But in the end
It was he
Who took the decisions,
He alone.
No choice now
But to go through with his threat.
Not convinced

He is up to the job though,
Never thought
He had it in him to do the job
In the first place.
Persuaded by others
That he has
What it takes.
Believed them.
Wanted to believe them.
Who wouldn't?
Before he knew it
He was swept away
By a wave
Of seemingly unconnected events,
And lots of good fortune,
Until he ended up here
In this office,
Alone.
"Buck up. Back to the matter in hand. The country is relying on you."
He says,
Out loud,
To himself.
"Yes, it is a mess but you have got to make the best of it."
He says,
Out loud,
To himself.
From a small trade dispute
To the brink of war.
Should never have sent The Vigour
Halfway across the world
To protect that cargo vessel.
Played right into their hands.
Now The Vigour is trapped
And the General is threatening
To blow her out of the water.
Have to try to save her.

Have to send the task force.

What else is there to do?

Looks down

At the report

On his desk.

Looks down

At the clock

On his desk.

Deadline looming,

Everyone will be watching,

Everyone will be expecting

His next move,

The only move

Left open to him,

They will assume,

And they will be right.

Picks up the report.

All in order.

All waiting

For his order

To give the greenlight.

Knock on the door,

More a gentle tap

Than a knock.

"Come in," he orders.

Looks up.

Jessica,

One of the typists,

Enters.

"Sorry to disturb you, Prime Minister, but you asked me to deliver this to you as soon as I finished typing it up," she says.

"Thank you, Jessica," says the Prime Minister in a low, melancholy voice.

"Is everything alright, Sir?" Jessica asks.

"Depends on what you mean by everything. Depends on what you mean by alright," he replies.

"Awful spot of bother," says Jessica.

"Yes, it is," replies the Prime Minister.

"I was thinking all this business must be such a heavy burden on your shoulders, Prime Minister, so I thought I'd put this together for you," she says.

She hands over a folder.

"What's this?" asks the Prime Minister.

"Just a few stories I found on the Internet. About good things happening all over the world. I thought you could read them if you have a spare five minutes," reveals Jessica.

"Thank you, Jessica. That's very thoughtful. I could do with a boost," reveals the Prime Minister.

"Do you need anything else, Prime Minister?" she asks.

"No, thank you, Jessica."

Jessica leaves the room.

He watches her leave.

He looks

At the folder

In his hand.

He reads the title

Of the folder

In his hand,

'Uplifting Stories'.

He opens the folder.

He reads the first story,

About an old man in Portugal,

Teaching poor children

To play music,

Being inundated

With instruments

From all over the world.

Another story

About a couple from Malta

Tracked down

On social media

Just so that a picture

Of the moment

They got engaged

On top of the Eiffel Tower
Could be given to them.
Another story
About Jewish volunteers
Driving into Gaza
To bring sick Palestinian children
Back to Jerusalem
For treatment
In a state-of-the-art hospital.
He puts the folder down.
He puts his glasses down.
He looks out of the window.
Swallows.
He sees swallows
Half a dozen
Or so
Of the beautiful,
Graceful birds,
Dancing in the sky
Without a care in the world.
He watches them,
Mesmerised,
Until,
All too quickly
They fly off
Out of view.
He turns back to his desk.
He has an urge
To try another way,
To find another way.
He picks up the phone.
"Yes, Prime Minister?" asks a familiar voice.
"Can you get the General on the line for me?" he asks.

197

Swoosh!
Up they fly.
Down they swoop.
Banking to the left.
Banking to the right.
A game of dare?
Who can fly the lowest?
The fastest?
Undercarriages threaten
To skim the rough stone path.
Closer and closer.
Contact never made.
Wings threaten
To clip ancient hedgerows,
Made of stone
But smothered in grass.
Closer and closer.
Contact never made.
Eyes fixed
On the meandering run ahead.
Left.
Right.
Right.
Left.
One finishes.
Another begins.
Back and forth.
Forth and back.
Again and again.

Six of them
In all
Come from afar,
From another land,
Across an ocean,
Chasing the summer,
The endless summer.
Stakes raised.
Orders received:
"Squadron. New formation!"
A flap of the wings,
Then another,
And another.
Soaring
To the heavens.
Out of sight,
Not quite.
First the climb,
Then the dive.
Dive.
Dive.
Dive.
Wings tucked in.
Faster.
Faster.
Faster.
Head first,
Like an arrow
Loosed
By the invisible bowman of the sky.
Back down
Towards the track.
Faster.
Faster.
Faster.
Bullseye?

No.
Perfect timing?
Yes.
Head up.
Wings spread.
Loop the loop.
Over to the next,
Then the next,
And the next.
No hunt.
No ritual.
No predator.
A celebration.
Nothing more.
Of what?
Of life.
Of love.
Of companionship.
Of course.
Who knows?
The swallows.
A rest?
No chance,
Too much fun.